# *Eyes of* JUSTICE

## Jake & Luke Thoene

Publishers Since 1798

THOMAS NELSON PUBLISHERS®
Nashville

Published in association with the literary agency of Alive Communications, 1465 Kelly Johnson Blvd., Suite #320, Colorado Springs, CO 80920.

Published in Nashville, Tennessee, by Thomas Nelson, Inc.

**Library of Congress Cataloging-in-Publication Data**

Thoene, Jake.
   Eyes of justice / Jake and Luke Thoene.
     p. cm. — (Portraits of destiny ; bk. 2)
   ISBN 0-7852-7146-5
   I. Thoene, Luke. II. Title. III. Series: Thoene, Jake.
   Portraits of destiny ; bk. 2.
   PS3570.H465E9 1999
   813'.54—dc21                        98-50087
                                     CIP

# PROLOGUE

---

Dawn light fell on a London shrouded in fog. From the top of Hampstead Heath, itself an island peeking out of the swirling mist, Christopher Wren's masterpiece, St. Paul's Cathedral, could be seen. Though miles away in the heart of the great city, its dome protruded above the vapors like a massive stone bell floating on a sea of silver wool.

The view was dramatic, and the warm sun that touched Hampstead very pleasant, but the minister of British Naval Intelligence, Anthony Pollard, noticed nothing except the placement of his men around the commonplace block of houses.

Intent on the business at hand, Pollard shook his curly red locks in frustration at the delay. He despised all mornings, pleasant or not, and was anxious to get the matter settled and return to hearth and breakfast.

"Blasted Frogs," he remarked to Sea Lord Malcolm. "Can't go to church decently, once a week at Sunday midday. Why must they practice their pagan rituals so near dawn?"

Malcolm reminded Pollard that the Church of England also had early morning services, but Pollard only grunted. Besides mornings, Pollard also despised all Frenchmen and all Catholics.

Hampstead High Street, three blocks away from where Pollard and Malcolm kept watch, was empty except for a man walking a horse-drawn hay cart. The road passed the Bull Bush Bakery, where the appetizing smell of fresh-baked bread lent its appeal to the morning air.

A short, dark-complected man, his form wrapped in a cloak and his features shadowed by a wide-brimmed hat, nodded to the carter and stopped in front of the bakery as if captivated by the enticing aromas. The swarthy-skinned man waited until the hay wagon had moved off down the hill and then looked around the street to see if he was being observed.

Satisfied at last that he was unnoticed, he entered the shop.

The baker was just removing the final row of fragrantly spicy rye loaves from his brick oven. Glancing up at the new arrival, he added the last of the bread to a neat stack, deposited a long, wooden paddle on the rack, then dusted flour from his hands. "Yes," he said, addressing his lone customer, "can I help you?"

"Do you have any baguettes?" the dark man inquired. "I am in need of a French baguette. Do you understand me?"

Though there was a heap of baguettes in plain sight, the baker reached below the counter and retrieved a single, long loaf, already wrapped in smooth, white paper.

"I think this is what you are after," the baker said.

"May I trouble you for a knife?" asked the customer. "I have to make certain it is satisfactory." Upon being handed a dull, short-bladed knife, the dark-skinned man tore back a portion of the paper wrapping, exposing a crusty length of baguette. Holding the blunt knife point downward, he plunged the blade into the bread, as if performing a ritual sacrifice. The crisp, golden crust crackled musically, then both men heard the distinct sound of rustling paper coming from inside the loaf. "Ah, this appears to be correct."

Coins changed hands, and the swart figure retreated out of the bakery, slamming the door behind him. He walked on toward Church Row, turning the corner toward the building being watched by Pollard and his men.

Tapping twice at a door midway up the block, he

was met by a gaunt form whose deathly pallor was even more pronounced than the short figure's dusky complexion. Once inside the house with the door again shut, the dark man thrust the paper-wrapped bread into the other's waiting hands.

"There's the signal," Pollard said with exasperation. "Our agent is finally in place. Wait here, Lord Malcolm. We'll soon have this affair wrapped up."

At a sign from Pollard, four burly men in dark-blue uniforms hurled themselves at the row house door, bursting in on a group of worshippers kneeling beneath a crucifix. A thin priest, coming from the altar with annoyance on his face, was shoved aside and held against a wall by one of Pollard's henchmen.

"Keep out of it, Father Moreau," Pollard hissed. "We have nothing against you . . . this time." Then facing the small congregation, Pollard pointed out two men, one extremely tall and light-complected, the other short and dark. "Sabean Sidon and Luc Nestor," he intoned. "I arrest you in the name of the Crown. You are charged with spying for Imperial France with whom we are at war."

Both men burst into elaborate denials. "I have done nothing!" Nestor vowed. "I am a refugee from the cursed Bonaparte! In fact, I hate Napoleon. I spit on him!"

"Very convincing, I'm sure," Pollard said dryly. "I know the firing squad will be impressed." He grabbed the bread from Sabean's hands and tore it in half, exposing a roll of paper on which were inscribed the names of British ships and their dates of sailing. "What do we have here?"

"I don't know what that is," Nestor protested. "It has nothing to do with me."

"Really?" Pollard commented, snapping his fingers over his shoulder.

Another blue-uniformed guard yanked a third captive figure into view—the proprietor from the Bull Bush Bakery.

Sabean Sidon smashed a fist into the face of the guard holding his arm and sprinted toward the entry of the church.

"Stop him!" Pollard roared.

Momentarily amazed that Sidon would try to escape despite such overwhelming odds, Nestor hesitated, then kicked his captor in the knee and ran toward the altar.

Sidon, his white skin even paler than before, was captured again at once. Flung to the ground, his arms were pinned behind his back, and a guard's booted foot planted atop his neck.

Nestor dodged past one guard who tried to tackle him, racing around the altar toward a narrow doorway.

Then a shot rang out, shattering a smoking censer over his head. Fragrant clouds of incense obscured the air as if on a battlefield, and flying ashes landed in the face and eyes of the guard closest behind Nestor, blinding him and making him abandon the pursuit.

Over the parishioners' screams and Father Moreau's protests, another shot was fired, clipping the arm off a statue of St. Joseph.

Finding the exit barred and locked, Nestor surprised his pursuers by reversing his direction and running at full speed toward the soldier who had last fired his weapon. Lowering his shoulder, Nestor crashed head-long into the startled guard, spinning him into a bench.

With three guards now out of action, and the others busy holding Sidon and the priest, only Pollard was between Nestor and the front door, and the red-haired Pollard was out of position to stop him. The light of a successful escape broke across Nestor's face, and he redoubled his speed, launching himself at the front step—straight into the barrel of a pistol in the hands of Sea Lord Malcolm. The muzzle stopped only inches from his left eye.

"One step farther," Malcolm said, "and no firing squad will be needed."

Outside again later, Minister Pollard said to the

portly, balding Lord Malcolm, "Thank you for your timely assistance. That went rather smoothly, I think."

Malcolm concurred, but added, "Small fish, Pollard. Small fish. We will not get on with our real task at this rate."

"Never fear," Pollard reassured his friend. "We have many nets in the water . . . and taking the biggest fish is merely a matter of finding the right-sized net."

# CHAPTER 1

*January 9, 1806*

**B**efore the dim, yellow eye of the early morning sun had even blinked a single, warm ray over the cobblestone streets of London, already the drummers of the volunteer corps beat out the slow, heavy funeral march. Steam rose from the mouths of the myriads of hushfaced mourners lining the streets between Whitehall and St. Paul's cathedral. Their collective breath hovered in one gray cloud that seemed to convey the unity of their gloomy thoughts. Not a window was without a face, not a face was without a tear or pinch-eyed expression that all was lost.

The deep-voiced bell of the cathedral's southwest tower tolled, echoing heavy and empty as the procession began. From the vantage point of Ludgate Hill the thousands of expectant mourners looking westward saw a perfectly straight line of cocked hats appear, then another and another. The precise ranks of headgear appeared to grow taller with each deliberate stride as if mechanical soldiers were climbing steps. The minute guns on Tower Hill boomed in the distance. Lancing through, the sun finally illuminated the marching troops. Labored sighs washed through the crowd like the waves of the sea, when the funeral car, fashioned to look like Nelson's heroic ship, *H.M.S. Victory*, halted. Like a host of black-shelled creatures flipping over and burying themselves in the sand, the men of the crowd simultaneously removed their hats. Several sailors, crewmen from the *Victory*, carried the ship's ensign. At the cathedral's west door, six admirals adorned with gold braid escorted the coffin inside.

William Sutton, his right arm bound tightly across his chest, joined the ranks of *Victory*'s crewmen.

A woman broke into sobs. "What benefit sees the country, if Nelson is lost!" she moaned.

It sent a shiver through William. Never in his life had he seen so many mourners for one man; it was as if they had *known* Lord Nelson. It had been three months since Nelson's death. William's mind flashed back, remembering the battle and Lord Nelson writhing in pain, bleeding on the deck of his ship. *Yes, it was overwhelming,*

William thought, shaking away the images. *But none of these people were there when it happened.*

Following the procession inside, William marched past the thousands assembled in the nave till he stood at last beneath the great dome towering hundreds and more feet above it. It was so quiet inside the church he could hear each winter sniffle, every cough and groan.

The choir sang anthems. Lessons were read from the Holy Scripture about a man laying down his life for his friends, and all the stages of a proper state funeral were meticulously undertaken. Three hours into the service, as the chill made William's injured arm ache, his mind began to wander from the subject. His eyes searched the high walls of the cathedral, up the vast reaching arches to the Whispering Gallery, where other grief-stricken Londoners leaned over to watch the proceedings.

William swayed from the stillness of the land, or rather from lack of the sea. The damp, cold air knotted the muscles around his broken collarbone, and he grew more restless. Letting out a sigh, he silently began to criticize the event. Perhaps the service was intentionally ponderous in order to make you sick of mourning; to make you tired of crying and ready to be done. It was like a gluttonous meal where you were forced to eat for hours and hours so that you may never desire to come back.

3

Dropping his eyes from the painted dome, past the center of the crossing and the space where a chandelier made of hundreds of burning lanterns smoked and sputtered, William's gaze fell on a young naval officer, his near equal in age and stature, who was intently following the service.

To William's complete surprise and pleasure, he discovered it was Thomas Burton, his best mate from childhood, one of the people who helped spark his recovery from a life-threatening bout of alcoholism and depression. "Thomas . . . ," he whispered aloud, grinning boyishly. Too late did he realize his murmur had cut through the thick silence like a sixteen-pound shot penetrating the side of a French sloop. Sour, disapproving glances flew from all directions. Composing himself, William took on the grumbling face of the others and scowled around for the senseless idiot who had uttered the name.

Whether William had meant to attract his friend's attention or not, his disturbance had achieved it. Pairs of wandering, accusatory eyes sent Thomas's searching for the cause of the disruption and by this he found William. Thomas lit up like a small boy with a new toy. William mouthed the name of his friend, and was unable to hold back his smile. Thomas looked the same as ever . . . a bit heavier perhaps in the face, but still the same easy cheerfulness and frank good nature. It had been months since they had seen each other.

When Thomas caught a hostile glance from an old woman veiled in black, he frowned down at the pavement. As soon as she turned away, his gaze went back toward William, not smiling outwardly this time, but deeply, within his eyes.

They stared at one another, almost ignoring the last hour of the service, in soundless interrogation. What had each experienced since they parted? William had been a royal marine, assigned duty aboard Nelson's flagship. Thomas, as a young marine officer, was aboard another vessel. Each had been fearful for the other's life.

Soon the coffin was lowered into a marble sarcophagus, and the service was concluded. The comrades could hardly wait for the procession to leave so they could talk. When the sailors from the *Victory* turned in a giant sweeping motion and marched down the center aisle, William followed, motioning to Thomas to meet him outside.

William was hardly through the doors when he broke free of the procession and made his way over to the north side of the steps. Moments later, He spotted Thomas's short brown hair above the crowd. "Thomas," he called, drawing the attention of many still in the grip of the solemnity of the occasion.

Thomas ducked his head at William's exuberant wave, weaving in a roundabout spiral that admitted no connection with the noisemaker until he sidled up alongside. He peered nervously around and warned with mock alarm: "Have you no control, man? There is a funeral here, in case you haven't heard, and you are liable to get us both thrown in Clink Prison. I wouldn't be surprised if Nelson himself came down and broadsided us with lightning bolts."

William laughed, negligently shrugging off his friend's concerns. "Let the others mourn. Sainthood is what Nelson wanted, and he's achieved that! But I'm sure he wouldn't object to *our* having a good time."

Thomas steered William around the north side of the building and into Paternoster Row, away from the teaming throng milling about on Fleet Street. At last he allowed himself to speak in a more normal tone. "When did you arrive?"

William yawned and squinted up at the clock face in the tower. "Only five hours ago."

"Five hours ago? Then you've not been in England for months? Since Trafalgar?"

"That's right. I'm off a merchant ship docked in the Pool of London. She was used as a personnel transport to get as many as possible of the Trafalgar wounded back for Nelson's funeral."

Thomas motioned toward the sling that enfolded William's arm. "When did this happen?"

"At Trafalgar," William said proudly, "when I dived into the water to avoid being hit by the mizzenmast."

"And where have you been since?"

William closed his eyes in remembrance. "I broke my collarbone when I hit a drifting longboat. And Thomas," he added in a tone that mingled wonder and disbelief, "the most amazing thing happened while I was in the water."

"Yes? Go on."

"While thrashing around, trying to find my way up, I felt an arm grab me. When I opened my eyes, I thought I was dead and staring at my own face. The soldier who rescued me was identical to me in every way."

"Maybe you were indeed near death," Thomas murmured sympathetically. "I've heard of this sort of thing happening to men who are close to the end and snatched back from the brink somehow. A fearsome delusion."

But William shook his head. "He was wearing a French uniform."

Thomas showed his confusion. "Did you talk to this apparition?"

"I told him about my brother, Charles. You know, my twin who was lost at sea when we were infants. He listened . . . and Thomas, every part of me is convinced it *was* him—Charles, I mean."

"But how?"

William's voice trailed off. Even he wondered if the vision were not some hallucination brought on in his feverish dreams. Perhaps the recollection, no matter how vivid, had never actually occurred. "Anyway, afterward I was so ill with fever and infection that they thought I might die if I were sent to sea. So I spent ages in the hospital at Gibraltar."

"I'm glad you're here, old chap," Thomas said, patting William on the uninjured shoulder. "And being wounded aboard *Victory* makes you a national hero."

William made a face and changed the subject. "And what about you? Are those lieutenant's stripes I see on your sleeve? And how does it happen that you were placed in the front rank of official mourners?"

"I commanded marines on the schooner that shot straight back to England with the news that Boney's fleet had lost and . . . the bad news that we had lost Nelson. The Admiralty seems to think highly of me for no more reason than that we made good time with the report. Even gave me a Navy commission."

"A pity I could not have sailed back with you," William said, "and supplemented your summation. After all, I was there when Nelson went down."

"You were?" Thomas asked excitedly. "What happened?"

"I attended to him when he fell."

Horror filled Thomas's expression. "Terrible. All England is mourning him so deeply it is as though life has stopped."

"Yes, but I can't help but wonder if he marked himself for destruction," William said. "He wore his medals out in plain sight, despite the warnings of his officers. I guess each man gets what he justly deserves."

"Even if you're right," Thomas said nervously, "I would be careful to whom I say that around here!"

"Only because it is you did I speak my mind," William answered. "Besides, I've got more important things to be concerned with."

"Such as?"

"Well, as I said I've only just arrived and . . ."

"Your family!"

"I've not seen them for many months. I don't know of my mother's health, if she still lives, nor of my grandfather's feelings toward me."

"Surely he felt nothing but pride in you," Thomas insisted, knowing even as he spoke that William and his grandfather had not parted on good terms. "You must go at once," Thomas insisted. "And certainly your grandfather would have written you if . . ." His words faded away as he recalled the perilous condition of William's mother's health, a semiconscious state for which William himself was partly to blame.

"But how could he have found me?" William worried. "In any case, I must learn the truth."

"Have faith, William. We must talk soon and catch up on the rest of life."

"Yes."

"When and where?"

"If I am welcomed home, then call upon me there tomorrow. If I am not, then you may find me sleeping in a sea of pint glasses at one of the local pubs."

Thomas shook his head ruefully at this reference to William's previous problem with drink. "I'll be there tomorrow," Thomas said, then replaced his cocked hat and made his way down the alley, hailing a cab at the corner of Newgate Street.

William watched as Thomas disappeared into the throng of sable-clad bodies. Shivering, he realized something more fearful than a sea battle lay directly ahead of him—going home.

Far away from the teeming masses of mourners in London, life was still in Branson Fen. A knobby flint wall stretched long, like a black-and-white speckled snake, across the marshy fields and rolling hills. Fog shrouded the thick folds of withered, hibernating grass. Beneath the stark, imploring branches of an oak tree knelt a black-cloaked figure, leaning forward with her fingers in the soil of a freshly piled grave. She was alone.

"Dear Father," she called in a trembling voice. With eyes closed, her head swayed forward. Soft, blond curls swung over her winter-flushed face. "Father, I'm waiting for you to wake me from this terrible nightmare." Her breathing was labored. "I'm waiting for you to lift me up and tell me everything is fine, lay my head on your shoulder and stroke my hair . . . Father!" she cried desperately, throwing herself over the mound. Her fingers dug into the soil, and she began to shake uncontrollably. "Please hear me and answer me!"

She lay trembling that way for a while, then turned her face slowly up from the ground. Moist dirt fell from her smooth skin. Some clung to her cheek. "You can't," she gasped helplessly, rocking to an upright position. She looked out at the blank wall of gray fog that surrounded her. It seemed to hold her there, hold her heart captive, even as she remembered she was going away. Her brown eyes dulled to match the color of the sodden earth.

Staring sadly at the rickety wooden cross perched near the head of the grave, Dora Donspy whispered, "I'm sorry neither Mother nor I will be here to take care of your grave. I won't even be here to see your headstone when it's finished . . . I hope the new vicar will care for it. I hope he will care for our house . . . walk softly through it and be gentle with the memories we had together there . . . but he won't. He shall be making his own memories there, oblivious to the sweet times we had."

Longing to do something nice, something memorable, she gazed around at the fields and nearby trees. "There aren't even any flowers to bring. No daffodils to leave. How you used to love them! You said they were such cheerful little yellow flowers—and that the world could always use cheering up."

She wished by some miracle she would find one, just one, growing in the midst of winter, that she could pick it and place it on her father's grave.

"I have much I want to say. I wonder why I never said these before, things that I felt so strongly. You were good to this family. You took care of this village, tending them like they were your own children. Father, you were the twine that bound us together in one beautiful bundle of flowers."

Her mind jumped over a million thoughts, as if each one were a piano string, plucked and discordantly jangling. She recalled pleasant times with her family, the people from the village she regarded as home, and William Sutton.

She remembered falling in love with William and, then, how he left for the war. She had never lost hope that he would come back. Then came the crushing day her father read the notice that William was lost at sea. She thought the world had ended. Getting through that time was the hardest thing she had ever done. She could not have done it without her father. Now what would she do? The fingers in her thoughts played on, pounding out some grim melody like hammers hitting strings, sending notes of loss vibrating through every bright recollection.

Though only a few days ago she had been speaking with her father, Dora could not bring back what he had said, or even the exact sound of his voice. She tried to picture his face and the loving way he used to look at her, but could not. She could see nothing but gray, like a sheet of dim, frosted glass in front of her. It was everywhere she looked.

Her search for help, for relief, was interrupted by the sound of boots on the gravel path. Since the carriage was waiting, she did not have to turn to know it was the driver of her carriage come to fetch her. Realizing her time at her father's grave was at an end, suddenly her symphony of grief stopped.

"I will come back often and visit you, Father," she vowed, though she knew it would be almost impossible.

"I have to go now, but I will keep your memory close to my heart. Even when the pain recedes, I will think of you. Every time I see a yellow flower, I will remember . . ."

Dora closed her eyes, pausing before she lifted her head, and stood. "Good-bye." Her voice sighed softly as she ventured up the path to a future as yet unknown.

Albert Penfeld wished he were somewhere else. Being summoned to the Paris offices of the French headquarters of the Grand Armée scared him, as it meant he would soon be leaving home. He had left his pregnant wife, Angelique, that morning with nothing but a kiss and a whisper that he would be back soon, knowing only too well he might have been lying.

Now as he stood at attention in the large reception hall of Joseph Fouche, the minister of the gendarmerie, the military constabulary, and overseer of the dreaded secret police, he hoped that would not be the case. Nothing was ever as it seemed with Minister Fouche's schemes, and this was especially true in the case of Albert's immediate superior, a man known as *Monsieur Maitre*. Maitre, whose real name no one knew, was a master spy. He had infiltrated the enemy Austrian headquarters under the name *Herr Schulmeister* and actually convinced the Austrian general that Schulmeister was spying for *them*. It was not surprising that Napoleon had known the details of the Austrian order of battle better than the Austrians ... and had punished them for their lack of security at the horrific Battle of Austerlitz.

The man known as *the schoolmaster* was back in Paris, training other spies. It was to this cadre that Albert had been moved from his position as cavalry trooper with the First Hussars.

Albert did not miss his duty as a horse soldier. Indeed, he wondered at the changes he had undergone since joining the Hussars. Since donning the light-blue uniform, he had acquired a hatred for what it represented. Every time he had ridden in battle, every time he had fired a rifle, it felt to Albert that the uniform's color had faded slightly, until at last it was as indistinguishable a blue as a battlefield sky filled with smoke.

Were it not for his growing disgust with the emperor's war, Albert had every reason to be deliriously happy. He and Angelique were expecting their first child soon, and for the past month he had been in special training that brought in more pay than was necessary to live comfortably, even in wartime. Hailed as a hero since his miraculous escape at the Battle of Trafalgar, his subsequent treatment in Napoleon's service seemed to be preferential, if not luxurious, and, Albert admitted to himself, suspiciously disproportionate to his deeds.

*But that,* thought Albert, *must be why I'm here. What did all my training mean?*

The walnut doors opened in front of him, and he was summoned into a waiting chamber outside Monsieur Maitre's door. He stopped short of the portal, expecting to wait more as had been the case when he was called here before, but the junior officer there told him to go straight in.

Before he walked on Albert smoothed his coat and ran his fingers through his dark-brown hair. Filling his lungs and setting his jaw, he strode through the inner door to Maitre's office. With a click of his heels, he saluted the frumpy man who sat behind the gigantic desk. "Albert Penfeld reporting as ordered, sir."

"Oh, please, Albert," Maitre urged in the tongue of France's English foes. English was one of the many things Albert had been learning for the last two months. Maitre motioned casually to a seat. "You're not here as a soldier today. Today, you are my guest."

Albert tried not to show his confusion. He recalled his previous visit to the little man and that when he last stood before him, he was harshly interrogated about his actions during the Battle of Trafalgar. He seated himself cautiously.

Reading Albert's expression, Maitre made an effort

to explain. "Penfeld, I know it did not seem a very friendly visit last time, but, you see, we had to be sure."

Again Albert's face betrayed his apprehension, and the schoolmaster guffawed heartily.

"Monsieur Penfeld, you remember your most remarkable story about the mad Englishman who claimed to be your brother?"

Albert nodded.

"After your return from the battle, word reached us of those unusual events also. That is why we called you here. You see, among my other duties, I am partially responsible for organizing a network of intelligence-gathering in England. As of late, information from my particular contacts has been scarce.

Maitre removed a crumpled piece of paper from a drawer in his desk, unfolded a pair of spectacles, and began reading in French. "'Arrests made, unable to send further word at this time' . . . And that, Albert," he resumed in English, "is the last communication we have had."

As Albert took in this news, his stomach began to tighten. *Please God, let this not be what it sounds.*

"That is why I have called you here today. As the story of the lunatic Englishman reached our ears, I began to see a way I could use you. Sutton is the name given you by your opponent? *Mon Dieu*, Sutton is a name the French government knows well! According to our earlier contacts in England, the Sutton family frequently transports goods for the military, goods we would rather not see arrive at their destinations. We've reviewed your past and know how ridiculous is this man's story. Many people have sworn to us they knew your grandmother for years, God rest her soul. But if this man, William Sutton, grandson to the British shipping magnate Lord Sutton, would take you in as his own and include you in their business, that might be valuable to us."

Albert sat mutely at the end of Maitre's explanation, though his color had blanched somewhat. He cleared his throat and responded in English, "Are you asking me to spy for you . . . in England?"

"No, Albert," Maitre declared bluntly, "I'm ordering you."

*There he is,* thought Albert, *there's the man to whom I first spoke. There is the grasp of duty to the emperor within the glove of privilege.*

"Oh, I know what you're thinking, Albert. You're worried about leaving your wife and child here alone for God knows how long. But trust me, they will be taken care of. And they will ensure," Monsieur Maitre quipped, "that you make a prodigious effort on your emperor's behalf and that you come back to us eventually."

Albert gritted his teeth. "Then tell me, sir, what it is I'm to do."

The schoolmaster extracted a wax-sealed envelope from another drawer and slid it across the desk to Albert. "Here you will find the name of your initial contact. He may be found in Holland at a city designated in your orders. Once there, you will shed your uniform and burn it. Your contact will arrange a revised appearance for you, one appropriate to your status. He will also help you find safe passage from Holland to England. Once there, you will seek out Lord Sutton. As you begin collecting your information, you will deliver it back to your first contact at a place designated by you. Your second goal will be to reestablish the connection with our agent in London. You will find only his false name there; that is all you know him by. Find him if you can, and send word to us of his status. Of course, you may say nothing to anyone of your duties, not even your wife. You leave tomorrow." As Albert snapped to attention, Maitre added dryly, "Good luck."

Albert wandered back from the offices in a daze. His world was once again unsteady, like the day his grandmother had told him he *was* an orphan, the foundling of a shipwreck. It was helpful, Albert reflected, that he had told no one of his grandmother's revelation except for Angelique and his closest friends in the army. None were any threat to talk. Angelique would not; her own father was imprisoned by the regime for being careless with his words. His comrades could not; they had all been killed in the war.

As Albert walked across Pont Neuf and onto the Left Bank of Paris, thoughts churned as to what he might tell Angelique about his departure. It would be difficult to lie to her since they had grown so accustomed to being together every day after his daily training was complete. Until now, His Majesty's government had made no restrictions on what he could and could not tell her. He would arrive home nightly and relate his progress in English studies, and they would wonder together why it might be he was asked to learn it. But if Albert had ever suspected what it meant, he never told her.

Now he was going away and wondered if he could bring himself to lie about his destination or purpose.

He turned into the street where they made their home. The courtyard off Rue St. Jacques was dilapidated and dirty, scarcely more than a dead-end alleyway. The cobbles of the street were missing in places, reminding Albert of the teeth of many of his grandmother's aged friends, some of whom still visited him in the ancient house. Garbage collected in the corners of the court-yard, and rats, sturdy black ones from the river Seine, came there to eat, often in daylight. The two-room home was close to the Seine, and sometimes, on hot days, waves of stench would linger there as if taking a rest from accompanying the dirty water on to the sea.

Even for these things, the Left Bank was his home. He had lived and played there for as long as he could remember. In those streets, he had shared his first kiss with Angelique and now made his life with her in the same house he had known since his youth.

In that house, his grandmother, Heloise, had instructed him as he matured to manhood, and then had almost destroyed him with a final revelation. In the room's curtained bedroom, as she lay minutes from death, she had told him that he was not her own, nor France's, most likely; that the ethereal figure Heloise had lovingly described as his mother was drawn from imagination alone.

At that moment, Albert had lost his hold on his life and everything he had considered certain. Even the Left Bank became foreign and suspect, and yet it was in this quarter of Paris that Albert and Angelique Penfeld conceived their child for whom they vowed a lifetime of the same love they shared for each other. Angelique was his reality now. As he stopped in front of the doorway of

21

their home, he smiled. Memories flashed through his mind and warmed his heart.

Leaning his shoulder against the ill-fitting door, Albert shunted it open and moved toward the rich aromas inside. Angelique, as if taking a lesson from Albert's grandmother, kept the hearth fire burning constantly, a pot of food always above it. Today it was the earthy aroma of her potato stew that touched Albert's nose, and his stomach began to clamor at the contact.

As his eyes adjusted to the dim interior, he saw Angelique in her usual chair near the hearth. She was knitting—her daily routine since the baby was close to arrival. She smiled up at him, and he walked near and leaned to kiss her flushed cheek.

"My love." He spoke softly and knelt beside her chair, gently caressing the rounded bulge of her stomach. "You are so beautiful today, as every day."

She lowered her gaze to his hand. "If I am, it is not until you arrive."

He stood again, walked to the iron pot bubbling over the fire and sloshed the stew with a ladle. "And *vichyssoise!* My favorite!" he said lightheartedly. But there was a tension in the room that had arrived on Albert's shoulder.

It was a long time before Angelique broke the spell. "I should know eventually, so it may as well be at once."

Albert gave the ladle another circuit before he responded. "I must leave again. They have told me I mustn't say where."

She raised a hand to stop him. "Then you mustn't say, but we both know I can imagine."

"Oh, Angelique," Albert called, falling to her side again and laying his head on her knee. "I can't help but think if I'd kept silent about the Englishman, I would never . . ."

She shushed him, running her fingers through his hair. "Albert, you cannot think this way. After all, we have needed the extra money . . . for the baby. And besides, you have been uneasy since you returned. You may deny it, but I see a restlessness in your eyes when you speak of England. What if that man *is* your brother? You know it is possible."

Albert lifted his head and kissed her. "It is possible," he said, "but what do I want with England when everything I love in the world is here in France?"

Neither spoke for a time, only gazing into each other's eyes, in the quest for an answer to the unanswerable.

"When do you leave?" She held his broad chin in her delicate hands.

"Tomorrow. Arrangements have been made to move you from this place to a nicer one, a home on a street in which you'll be safe and more comfortable. Neither will you have to be alone when the time comes to have our baby. They have promised me a midwife who'll attend your every need. I'm sorry." He buried his head in her lap again. "I wish I could be there."

"Enough of this," she said to comfort him. "If you must leave tomorrow, we'll have nothing but pleasantness until then. Get yourself some stew and sit with me while I finish these clothes for our child. Then you must rest. I'm sure you have a long journey ahead of you."

# CHAPTER 2

illiam Sutton stood, left fist raised before the front door of his grandfather's house for several minutes, carrying on a conversation with himself. "Should I knock? Of course I should knock, but what should I say when Samuel answers?"

It had been months since William had seen or heard of any from this household. "Too many months," he thought aloud. "If Mother has died, Grandfather will never forgive me."

Turning away from the door, William was near retreating when he heard a click of the latch. He swung around, expecting the aged steward, Samuel, but was shocked when the sour face of an unknown younger man appeared. "Who are you?"

The servant frowned at William. "My name is

Popham, and I am the steward of this establishment. Can I help you?" he asked in a feminine, bossy tone.

William, caught off guard, removed his hat. "I, uh, yes," he stuttered. "I have come to see my grandfather." He paused, waiting for some sort of reply. Seeing the suspicion in the servant's eyes, William thought at first to explain, then decided it could only sound defensive, so he waited.

Popham had obviously made up his mind to let the pause continue until it was toweringly awkward. Finally he replied, "And who might that be?"

"Lord Sutton! This is his house, is it not? He is your employer, yes?"

"Of course." The servant sneered, curling back his lip and revealing a most crooked set of lower teeth. "And you are?" he demanded in a tone that was flatly rude.

William's temper flared. *This was my house, too, my home,* he thought. *I should knock this scoundrel down.* The fist of his uninjured left arm clenched at the image, and William saw the steward's eyes widen with fear. Then a chilling notion struck him: What if the man had been instructed to treat him this way? Maybe he was not welcome, and the entire household, down to the lowliest scullery maid, had been told as much. That must be the answer.

William determined not to show his injury to this

ill-mannered lout. "I am William Sutton, grandson of Randolph Sutton and son of Lady Julia."

The chubby man pursed his lips so that his jowls clenched, exposing several wrinkles under his chin. "Oh yes, I've heard about you."

William cut in bluntly, "Good! Then you must know my mother. How is she?" He might be shunted away, but he would at least know if his mother lived.

Blinking rapidly three times before looking up, the pop-eyed Popham replied blandly, "You know, I really couldn't say. It is not my place to speak of Her Ladyship to . . . outsiders."

A huge knot tensing up in his stomach, William felt a hot blanket of worry wrap around him, drawing sweat from all over his body. *She* is *dead*, he decided. He was lost for words while his examiner stared him down and could barely pant the words, "Then ask if Lord Sutton will see me."

William had hardly finished his sentence when the man instructed him to wait there and shut the door in his face.

Suddenly dizzy, William sat down on the steps—the same steps where he had collapsed with dreadful burns and his appearance had destroyed his mother's fragile health. Better if he had died in the shipboard fire. "But my mother is dead instead of me." His head swooned in his hands. "That is why I'm not welcome."

William could hardly hold himself up. He replayed over and over again his falling down on the steps and his mother's anguish. The shock of seeing him in such a bad way and her already frail condition had brought her near to death.

Then Grandfather Sutton, out of anger at him for his foolish gambling, drinking, and thieving, had been pushed over the top. William felt the guilt once more of that morning he was bedridden and his grandfather had thrown him out. It had started him on a downhill slide. If not for Thomas, he would have died out in a tumble-down cottage, alone and in a drunken stupor. If not for Thomas, he never would have met Dora. Suddenly his mind leaped, grasping eagerly at a happier thought, and he whispered the name aloud. "*Dora.* I wonder how . . ."

The front door flew open again and Popham stood boldly in the entrance. "Yes, Lord Sutton says he remembers you. He will have a word with you in the parlor."

William staggered to his feet, following the surly steward into the grand entrance hall and through an open double door to the right. William seated himself stiffly on an uncomfortably firm sofa. Popham sniffed once and frowned around the room as if memorizing the contents, should William attempt to steal anything. "You will wait here," Popham said, smirking. Then the servant departed, shutting the doors behind him with a crash akin to the closing of a prison cell.

Feeling awkward, William held his Royal Marine uniform hat by the inside band. He twisted it around and around, as if it were an anchor line he could draw up from the bottom of the ocean before it pulled him in.

*Perhaps Grandfather wants to condemn me once again . . . speak his mind about what I have done . . . to give himself the satisfaction of throwing me out again.* William shrugged and sighed, hoping to find a reserve of courage.

He thought again of the words he had offered Thomas only that morning: "Each man gets what he justly deserves." William realized he would have to face his punishment, no matter how severe. He would have to face his grandfather, even if he would not be accepted back. It would be the only way he could ever live with himself.

As the doors slid apart, William jumped to his feet. Lord Randolph Sutton stood tall, quietly serious, with head held high and snow-white hair combed back. He had a slight hint of merriment in his eyes and at the corners of his mouth, which William judged to be enjoyment of punishment that was to come.

He strode across the carpet and came close to William. In fear of being struck, William backed slightly away. Then Lord Sutton spoke hoarsely. "William! How long has it been?"

"Half a year, sir," William answered solemnly, fixing his eyes on the ground.

"You were wounded at Trafalgar, I heard." His grandfather examined the sling on William's arm.

"When I had to jump overboard, yes, sir."

Lord Sutton went on as if he did not hear William's reply. "'Tis a long time to be away for you to come back now."

William stared at his hat, uncertain of what to do with it. "Yes, sir. I have come to pay my condolences about my mother, sir."

"Your condolences?"

"Yes, sir. I have been away at sea and in hospital and have only arrived for Lord Nelson's funeral this morning."

"I saw you there this morning." Lord Sutton studied William's uniform, the second-lieutenant's collar tab, and the Trafalgar medal that adorned his red marine officer's coat. He sniffed. "You have gone away and made something of yourself."

William detected the unexpected in his grandfather's tone. Looking up cautiously, he replied, "Yes, sir."

Grandfather Sutton grabbed William's shoulders in a viselike grasp. "I am so proud. Your mother will be too."

"My mother! Is she not dead?"

"No," Lord Sutton replied. "She is still gravely ill but has not gone a day since you left . . . since I asked you to leave . . . without calling for you, asking about you."

William breathed deeply with relief. His chest hurt, as if he had just swum a great distance underwater.

His grandfather continued, "And not a day has passed that I have not experienced shame for hastily doing what I did. To think that Bristol Sims burned the ship and not you, and yet I drove you out when you were nearly killed yourself. And here you are safely home. What a cause for thankfulness is mine!"

The two men clung to each other in quiet embrace. Then William asked, "Please, sir. May I see Mother right away?"

"She is bedridden and sleeping. I will agree, though I must warn you that I am doubtful she will respond."

"I will see her briefly then, and when she is better, I will talk to her."

Lord Sutton hugged him again. William wrapped his good arm tightly around his grandfather's bony back. He was like a child again, remembering how he used to embrace his grandfather—the only father he'd ever known.

William knew everything would be all right when his grandfather said, "Welcome home, my boy! I've missed you."

The room smelled heavy with the breath of someone very ill. The curtains were drawn, and it was dark. The only light in the room was that cast on the bed from the open door. Julia Howard Sutton's face was ghostly white and her eyes sunken back in their sockets. It frightened William to see her this way.

The chambermaid left the room, closing the door behind her. William sat in a chair beside his mother. He held her hand, willing her to wake up for what must have been hours before he got up the courage to chance waking her with speech.

"Mother. Mother, it's me." He waited for her to respond.

The chambermaid returned. Julia stirred in her sleep as the chambermaid placed a fresh, damp cloth on the patient's forehead. "The doctors say she has a recurring fever. She has been down with it for three days this time. She's hardly spoken a word."

William nodded, taking more courage to speak again. "Mother, it's William, your son."

Julia groaned within her trance.

The chambermaid touched Lady Julia's wrist before turning to William. "I think it best to let her rest. We don't want her to get stirred up. It might make her more ill."

"When will she be better, do you think?"

"It's hard to say, Master Sutton. Her sickness comes and goes. It could be tomorrow; it may not be until next week. But she is no worse this time than before."

"All right then," he agreed, casting a loving gaze upon his mother. "I shall look in on her again tomorrow." William kissed his mother's diminutive, blue-veined hand before standing up.

After William had bathed, he rejoined his grandfather. The two talked for a time, catching up. Each soon felt so comfortable it was as if the falling-out never happened. William told how he had come near death himself before Thomas's intervention and how meeting Father Donspy had almost certainly stopped him from committing suicide. He recounted training the Branson Fen militia and falling in love with Father Donspy's daughter, Dora, before being convicted of the need to serve in the Royal Marines. And he told of encountering a twin in the midst of battle.

"After we captured a French ship, Darlington, one of

my fellows, came to me astounded that I would have time to change into a French uniform and back from it after he had pointed the gun at me and I dived over the side. He was grateful he hadn't pulled the trigger. He could see I was perfectly dry."

"And you believe this was the same chap who saved you from drowning in the water at Trafalgar?"

"He looked exactly like me," William asserted. "It must be so. The uniform of a Hussar, as I said. It matches too perfectly to be coincidence."

Skeptical, Grandfather Sutton asked, "Are you sure it wasn't the heat of battle that made you see things?"

"We spoke, I swear. I said he must be my brother, Charles."

"And what did he say? Did he believe you? Was he convinced as well?"

"No, he denied it. And yet, part of me thinks he was not as certain as he hoped to sound."

Lord Sutton rocked in silent thought. "William . . . It is an amazing story, but I just don't know how it can be. All these years, with no word. Maybe you did see a man who looked much like you. And maybe, so did your friend. But to suppose he was your brother, who was only a tiny baby when he was lost at sea . . . How would he survive?"

"I don't know," William admitted. There was his

own wound and the fever that followed, of course, yet he searched for a way to believe. "I want to know what Mother thinks," he said stubbornly.

"No, William. Think this through carefully. Telling your mother such a thing would only upset her at a time when she has the joy of your return to cling to. And heaven forbid she might believe it; she may worry even more. I think it best not to speak of this to her."

Inside, William was burning to speak of Charles to his mother, to hear her respond to the astonishing news. But he acknowledged the warning given by his grandfather and reluctantly consented to keep the story from her for the time.

"Donspy Manor, my dear," the driver informed Dora, opening the dark leather coach door.

It had been a long and bumpy ride—almost one hundred miles through the marshy Fen lands, past Ely and Cambridge, crossing the river Ouse three times before leaving it finally at Bedford and dropping at last into the valley of the Thames just beyond Oxford. Sometimes the coach bowled along dusty roads, but the season being what it was, several times Dora alighted from the carriage while the driver heaved at a rear wheel bogged axle-deep in mud. After twelve and a half hours it was a relief for Dora to arrive at last at the home of her aunt, the widow of her father's brother. Dora climbed stiffly down without speaking a word.

"We've made good time," the coachman said, a trifle defensively. "Only half midnight. Judging by the way the horses pulled, you couldn't weigh more than eight, eight and a half stones. I suppose you stay away from the sweets."

Dora was always polite. It did not matter if it were midday or midnight. She managed to smile, though her pretty, heart-shaped face was almost lifeless in her exhaustion and sorrow. "Thank you, Mr. Radcliffe. You are kind to bring me all this way without stopping."

Radcliffe unloaded a carpetbag containing everything in the world that Dora owned. "I'll carry this for you. Welcome to Donspy Manor."

Dora squinted up at the rectangular shadow of the manor house. It was such a dark night, and after riding the last half hour with the compartment lamp lit, her vision needed a moment to adjust. Hardly a star in the sky, she noticed, as if a shadow lay over everything. Nor was there any light showing at the shapeless hulk of Cotswold stone that was to be her new home.

*Oh, come now, Dora,* she chided herself inwardly. *Be positive, be positive. This will be fine.* But the words of her thoughts did not have the same uplifting effect on her as when her father used to say them.

"Up the steps, Miss Dora," Radcliffe urged. "Mind your footing; it's a bit uneven-like."

She could see square limestone columns on each side of her. Dora rested her hand on one, leaning over to take off her muddy shoes.

The door opened and out stepped a rotund woman holding a lantern. She wore a light-gray dress and a white apron. Her hair was silver, parted down the middle and pulled back. "Dora, darlin', you're here!" she exclaimed joyfully in a rich, Scottish burr. "Ye may not call me to mind, but I have known ye from the time when ye were but a wee bairn, and I went along with the master to call on your father, God rest his soul."

Dora nodded girlishly as she recalled the cheerful woman, at a slimmer age, who pinched her cheeks and made much of her. "Oh, yes! I know you, Missus Honeywell!"

"But here now," Mrs. Honeywell fretted. "I've left you standin' outside. Quick, quick, come in." The housekeeper fanned her plump hands to hurry Dora and Radcliffe along. "I'll take that," she said, motioning for the bag.

"Goodnight, Miss Dora." Radcliffe tipped his hat before retreating toward the barn.

Dora tilted her head to one side. "Thank you again,

Mister Radcliffe. I shall come and see the stables tomorrow, if I may."

"Yes, do that." He waved his hat and beamed in bucktoothed delight.

Ahead of Dora a wide, red-carpeted staircase rose to a landing where it split into flights that reversed their direction in climbing to the upper level. There was hardly light enough to see—just the shine of the housekeeper's lantern reflecting off the wood flooring. A shadowed room off to Dora's left contained low objects appearing to be chairs, in what looked to be a parlor. Over her right shoulder she caught the glimmer of the unlit grand crystal chandeliers in what must be a dining salon. Dora was leaning in for a closer inspection when the orange glow of a light on the staircase caught her attention.

Dora was so startled by the appearance of a bodiless, leaden mask descending from the landing that she squeaked like a mouse. It was a woman, clothed in black, who carried a single flickering candle. Her hair was iron gray and severely drawn back from her angular jaw. Brooding eyes regarded Dora down a long, pointed nose.

The thin-lipped smile on the newcomer's face was not reassuring, but the housekeeper remarked blithely enough, "Madam Etheldreda. Look who's arrived."

"So I gathered," the specter on the stairs replied coldly. "Dora Donspy. My dear niece, how are you?"

Dora leaned to kiss her aunt on the cheek. The skin her lips brushed felt dry and caked with face powder. "I'm fine, Aunt Etheldreda, though it was quite a long—"

Aunt Etheldreda cut her off. "You're terribly dirty!"

A hot flush mounted to Dora's cheeks. Embarrassed, she gazed down over her mud-spattered travel dress. "I'm sorry. I must look a sight. It was such a long journey, and I had been mourning my father at his grave."

Unconcerned with voicing any sympathy, Aunt Etheldreda continued, "And your nails . . ." She held up Dora's hand to the light. "Have you been digging in the dirt?"

"Yes, I . . ." Dora pulled her hand away. "I was sitting on the ground."

Waving Dora to silence, Aunt Etheldreda concluded, "Never mind. Missus Honeywell will take you up right away and scrub you for bed. Breakfast is at seven sharp. Wear something nice. There will be guests tomorrow shortly after." Without awaiting Dora's response, Aunt Etheldreda reascended the stairs, taking with her half the light in the gloomy entryway.

Dora felt a lump in her throat. Longing for her home in Branson Fen, she blinked back tears. Still, she sought to express the gratitude she believed she should be experiencing, even if her emotions betrayed her. She called, "Aunt Etheldreda?"

The sinewy woman stopped without pivoting around. "Yes, child?"

"I shall be forever grateful to you for letting me stay here."

"Thank you for saying so. Your father's in heaven with his brother, my dead husband, and your mother in that . . . home. I don't think there was much choice in the matter, do you? But you are welcome." With that she continued on out of sight.

Seeing tears streak Dora's cheeks, Mrs. Honeywell wrapped her arm around the distraught girl's back and said, "There, there. It will be all right. Let me show ye to your room, then I shall bring up hot water for a good wash." She leaned close and whispered, "Don't ye fret. I'll take care of ye."

Just before the reverse of the staircase on the landing, Dora spied the brief flare of a match in the parlor. It dimmed twice as if being sucked into the top of a pipe. She peered uncertainly back into the gloom, but was tugged on by Mrs. Honeywell, who did not seem to notice anything amiss. Dora wanted to inquire who had been listening to their entire conversation while she was being humiliated, but did not for fear of the unknown listener hearing her.

At the top landing, Dora was led down a hallway on the right. Mrs. Honeywell lit a green glass lamp on a stand by a grand bed and then bustled away to fetch the promised wash water. Dora made her way over to a high-back chair by a window. The top of a full moon was rising above the forest. It cast a shimmer over the grounds and teased shadows out from under the beech trees.

Contemplating the last month's events, Dora could hardly believe how much her life had changed. Yesterday she had been in her own bed. "Oh Father, if only I could tell you my worries, and you could let me know it *would* be all right."

She tried to remember the things her father had told her: *Dora, you take the good with the bad, and you deal with whatever you receive. Remember that the eyes of the Lord are on the righteous in all their circumstances, and for such folk, all things work together for the good. The Lord says so.*

Dora blinked out of the spell of her father's memory. The moon was brighter, cresting up full above the tree line. Shortly after Mrs. Honeywell returned with the water and a glass of warm milk on a tray. The wash was refreshing, and the milk made Dora sleepy. She slipped on her nightgown and climbed into bed. Mrs. Honeywell tucked her under a down-filled duvet.

Glancing over to the nightstand, Dora noticed something else lying on the tray. "What is that?"

"Oh this," Mrs. Honeywell said, reaching for the fragment of color. "From the greenhouse. I thought a wee bit of cheer would be nice."

It was a small yellow flower. Dora smiled as she thought of her father. "He really *can* hear me," she whispered.

Mrs. Honeywell gazed lovingly at her. "Yes, I imagine he can. Get some rest," she said, twisting down the wick of the lamp and blowing it out.

The burgundy satin curtains were like a corset, squeezing out the morning sun. Dora could have slept forever.

*When will it become light?* she wondered, as she rolled over, half awake for the fifth time. The question she asked forced an unwanted consciousness, requiring her to consider her circumstances.

She realized anew where she was. "Aunt Etheldreda's . . ." Thinking she heard a noise, Dora lay motionless and focused on the clamor within the walls of the house.

It sounded like people being received at the front door, and yet, it could not be. No one was meant to arrive until . . . Dora shot up and looked at the clock on the mantel above the fireplace. She strained to see the hands, then exclaimed, "Ten-thirty!"

She flew from the bed to the long cherry-wood dresser, where a basin and pitcher sat next to her carpetbag. Dora squinted, patting her cheeks with cool water. It was refreshing, though not enough to shake the dreadful feeling of rising late. Her meager belongings did even less to comfort her: in her things were nothing but plain clothes, ordinary clothes for ordinary days in an ordinary village.

In wondering what sort of people might be attending the gathering today, Dora hurried to the window. Twitching aside the curtain, the sun was blinding. She shaded her eyes to see through the glare, and her gaze locked with that of a handsome young gentleman who stared right back up at her. Dora was frozen, blinking in the light and shy about being seen in her nightdress. The stranger tipped his hat, and her heart dropped as she yanked the curtains back together.

Dora held her breath. With hands to cheeks, she spun round to look at herself in the mirror: no makeup, hair sticking up, her swollen eyes looking as if she had pressed bread dough around them. Her heart skipped another beat. "Oh, no! I look dreadful!"

There came a peremptory knock at the door, followed by a cheerless voice. "Dora? It's Aunt Etheldreda."

"Yes?" Dora answered in a quaking voice.

"Dora! You must come down at once! My guests have already arrived."

"At once, Aunt Etheldreda." Dora picked up her traveling costume from the day before as being the nicest dress she owned and had almost put it on before realizing it was covered in dust and mud from the long journey. Back on the floor it landed, as Dora gave a wail of dismay.

From her carpetbag flew a cascade of clothing until the dresser and bed were festooned with apparel, none of which suited the quality of the attire on the young man in his tight trousers, top hat, and crisply wrapped stock tied high under his chin. In a panic, Dora retrieved the travel dress and sponged frantically at the worst stains, but only succeeded in smearing the mud onto previously unblemished places.

Then there was another knock at the door. This time it was softer. "Yes, Aunt Etheldreda. I'm coming," Dora promised.

"It's Missus Honeywell, dear. I've come to help ye ready yourself."

"Oh, Missus Honeywell!" Dora was filled with gratitude as she opened the door and found the housekeeper standing with a yellow silk gown draped over her arm.

"I thought ye might need this."

"Yes," Dora concurred, spinning around in helpless desperation as she gestured at the explosion of attire. "My nice clothes are dirty, and I have nothing else that will do."

"Here now, turn around." Mrs. Honeywell laced Dora into the dress. The young woman's dainty hands stroked the smooth folds of the shiny fabric, woven with a flowered pattern.

"It's *lovely!*" Dora exclaimed, admiring the elaborate lacework in the mirror. "I've never worn anything like it."

Mrs. Honeywell gently patted her face. "Hurry along."

Dressed and having lightly powdered her face, Dora tiptoed delicately down the stairs. From the parlor on the right she could hear women's chatter and laughter, along with a piano being played.

It would be her first time to attend anything as formal as this, she thought. A women's society luncheon— what would her girlfriends back in the Fen say? How should she act?

An older gentleman dressed in a coat and tails and black bow tie motioned for Dora to enter. The room was bursting with women in fancy lace, silk, and satin dresses, all cheerful colors with high waists and low necklines in the latest empire style. Seated around a wide oak table, which must have been twenty feet long, the ladies were being served tea and cakes. Others rested in parlor chairs beside leaded-glass windows that rose almost from the floor to the high ceiling.

Several of the guests turned when Dora entered. Dora nodded and smiled politely, though she received sour, questioning looks in return.

Aunt Etheldreda was surrounded by buoyant, chattering acquaintances when she caught sight of her niece.

"Good of you to finally join us, Dora," Aunt Etheldreda said loudly enough for all to hear. The room grew quiet as heads again turned her way. "I'm glad to see you've made use of my old dress."

Dora grew hot from the attention. The room became even quieter as she answered softly, "Thank you, Aunt Etheldreda. It is extremely beautiful."

"Oh, don't be silly. It's quite out of date. I haven't worn it since the year zero, before your uncle died." Etheldreda turned to the ladies and introduced Dora: "This is my niece, daughter of my late brother-in-law."

One woman near Dora spoke to Etheldreda as if the young woman were not even present. "She is beautiful. I thought you said she was a girl of the country."

Dora's aunt retorted, "Yes, I suppose she does look pretty in that dress, in a country sort of way."

"Do come sit down with us, Dora," a pinch-cheeked woman invited from a round table at the side of the room.

Dora felt hugely awkward; she had never been around ladies such as these. Her mother was warm and easygoing. Everyone back in Branson Fen was plain and uncultured. There had been no preparation for this.

A woman with curly red hair introduced herself. "I'm Cynthia Harding. This is Florence Russell and Mary Alderman."

"I'm pleased to meet you," Dora responded politely.

"Tea for you?" Mary queried, offering a silver pot.

"Yes, please." Dora melted in the center of their attention, struggling for anything to say.

Finally one of her inspectors broke the silence. "You should feel lucky to be here, Dora," Florence Russell said, patting her on the leg. "What a change in your circumstance to go from an unknown village to the heart of Oxfordshire society. Where did your aunt say you were from? Something or other Bog?"

Lost for words, Dora felt so small, so unimportant, so anything *but* lucky. "I . . . Yes, I know I am lucky to be here in this house with Aunt Etheldreda."

Mary smacked her red lips on the china cup. "We are dying to know how it was you came to be here. Do tell us."

Dora thought they must have known already. Maybe they were only asking to make conversation, or maybe to make fun of her, but she answered anyway. "When my father passed away, my mother and I were forced to move out with the arrival of the succeeding vicar. Mother has gone to Salisbury. My father served a church there for several years before they met and married. He earned the right for Mother to retire to the Clergymen's Widows Home there, but of course they cannot take families, so I came here. Aunt Etheldreda was kind enough to take me in."

"Oh dear," Cynthia Harding said, fanning herself. "I can't imagine living in a widows' dormitory. And village parsons never take any thought for tomorrow. Always poor as church mice. Careless and imprudent."

Dora allowed insults to herself to roll off, but she bristled at the slight to her father. Before she could frame a suitable reply, Aunt Etheldreda returned to the table. "Dora, there's someone I'd like you to meet."

"Yes, Aunt Etheldreda," Dora said, patting her mouth as she stood.

She spun round, expecting to face another overbearing, self-important woman but instead found herself face-to-face with a handsome young man.

"Niece Dora, this is my cousin, Nicholas Parry."

It was the same man who had seen her in disarray at

the window that morning. Dora was flustered but managed to return evenly, "Very nice to meet you, sir," as she extended her hand.

Grasping it eagerly, Nicholas Parry tipped his hat. "The pleasure is all mine. How nice to learn your name," he added slyly. Then he commented to Aunt Etheldreda, "We saw each other briefly earlier this morning."

Dora tried to yank her hand away, but Nicholas squeezed it even tighter. Aunt Etheldreda remarked, "Nicholas is a student at Oxford and a guest of the house."

"How wonderful," Dora began to say as her head spun.

Parry regarded her with concern. "Are you feeling well? You look pale."

"Actually, no," Dora admitted. "I think it must be from the long journey I took yesterday."

"Should I escort you up the stairs to your room?"

"No, no, I'll be fine."

"Go then," Aunt Etheldreda gave a disparaging wave and returned immediately to Nicholas and the women at the table.

"How inconsiderate," Dora heard them agree as she hurried out of the room. "She didn't even make a proper good-bye."

# CHAPTER 3

———— ✦ ————

At the end of the Rhine River's snakelike course through the Netherlands, it empties into a large delta known as the *Zuider Zee*. On top of the peninsula, which is Holland, lies a city called *Helder-Niewediep*. The city is at the most extreme north and west point before the country is broken up into a series of islands. Albert's orders sent him there, to a place where he might find passage to England through the North Sea.

Some days earlier he had set out from Paris. Traveling almost constantly, he finally neared his destination with only hours to spare before the designated meeting time. At last his mount had refused to carry him farther, and he led it by the reins. By the time he and the weary horse marched into town, the sun was dipping into a horizon of fire on the water.

It was like no other city he had ever seen. Formerly

a fishing village, it had spread almost overnight at the onslaught of Napoleon's occupation there. Its position on the point of land made it ideal for guarding the delta from potential invaders.

However, soon after the installation of forces there, French tacticians decided the resources were better used elsewhere, and the city once again grew silent. But former residents were seldom met with, preferring to keep to their shoreside camps, should a strong military force return.

From what Albert knew of the city, only a minute garrison of the gendarmerie remained, keeping a slack hold of ventures there, and profiting, no doubt, from the black market.

The locals who remained after their properties were commandeered were a rough crowd, dealing primarily in smuggling while masquerading as honest fishermen. Among such loyal sons of the empire, Albert was to seek his contact.

The uniform he wore was soiled and stained, and he felt less a soldier than merely a tired and hungry man, but the Dutchmen Albert met shied from him.

*Perhaps,* Albert pondered, *they've had their fill of French interrogation.*

For a long time he wandered around the waterfront, hoping his contact would be drawn to the remaining powder-blue of his uniform where it showed through the mud. However, when the sun set and night fell, Albert had seen no one fitting the description he had or answering to the name he called. As he stood in a daze, keeping a loose grip on his horse's lead, a light mist began to fall, tugging dust from his brow and cascading it into tiny slides of mud that came to rest near his nose and on his cheeks.

He watched as fishermen bounded for their upturned dories and took shelter underneath. Some clutched rolled-up cloaks for comfort, while others embraced bottles.

From beneath one of those boats came a burst of raucous merriment, and at the peak of it, a French accent.

*Or at least,* thought Albert, *it is different from the other voices I hear.*

Albert led the horse into the thick mud alongside the boat, and promptly the noise within ceased. A moment of silence followed before a voice called out something he could not understand.

"*Bon soir,*" Albert returned, hoping it was his man. "I am looking for Monsieur Heinzen."

"*Oui?*" the voice called back.

"Perhaps, sir, we could talk face-to-face?" Albert disliked the idea of a man staring at his feet as he spoke.

More hushed whispers rose from beneath the improvised shelter before a man popped up on the opposite side of the boat from Albert.

He was of medium height with close-cropped light hair. His brows appeared fixed in a state of constant surprise, which Albert decided went well with the barrage of queries that followed.

"Who wants to know?" the figure demanded, and before Albert could respond, asserted, "I have done nothing wrong. All the drink I have, I paid for. Why have you come here?"

At some point during the barrage of protests and questions, Heinzen noticed that Albert's uniform was not the dark blue of the military police. "Sir," he saluted groggily, "I apologize. I did not see you there at first."

Albert chuckled because he was too tired to do more, and he was invited to join the others under cover.

"Monsieur . . . ," Heinzen began as Albert removed his shako, ducked under the lip of the boat, and sat down on the planks arranged there, jarring a lantern that rested near the inverted bow. "I am sorry, I do not know your name."

"Albert Penfeld," he responded, scanning the faces of the other two guests of the dory.

"Monsieur Penfeld, these are my good friends,

Wilhelm Roomsburg and his first mate . . . pardon, monsieur, what is your name again?"

Roomsburg translated the French into Dutch for the man who responded simply, "Lange," then returned to his silence again.

"So," began Roomsburg, "you are the deserter, yes?"

Albert was taken aback by the candor with which Roomsburg mentioned the supposedly highly secretive business, and the young man's anxious expression betrayed him.

Heinzen spoke up. "Monsieur Penfeld, have no fear. We are friends here. Roomsburg is your captain for the voyage to England. I have arranged for you to travel on his steady ship, the *Kruier*."

At the mention of the ship's name, Lange grinned, showing a mouthful of brown-stained teeth. He gave a slight, wheezing laugh.

Albert was about to inquire the cause of the merriment when Heinzen began again, "So, monsieur, I have your new suit here. I understand you are to destroy the other."

Albert nodded and traced the outline of his shako badge with the insignia of the First Hussars. He would be sorry to see it go after all.

"Then," said Heinzen, "when this drizzle stops, we

shall light a fire. In the meantime, have a drink, and change into these fine clothes."

From behind his back, Heinzen produced a clear green bottle of suspect liquid and a set of rags, which Albert knew he would learn to hate even more than his dirty uniform.

As if in disbelief of the trade he was making, the three men watched as Albert began to unbutton his coat. When he paused and glanced up, Heinzen was the first to speak. "Gentlemen, let us give the man privacy."

The order was delayed briefly as Roomsburg translated it into Dutch for Lange, but soon the three were out from under the boat. Only Heinzen's hand reappeared momentarily to retrieve the bottle.

In the gentle glow of the lantern, Albert could see their feet outside scuffling about as they picked up bits of wood, forming a pyre nearby on which his uniform would be cremated.

When he was dressed again in the rags provided for him, he neatly folded his uniform the way he had always done at night when finished with a hard day of training. Trousers twice over, with the pleat . . . coat in half, then quartered . . . shako on top of the rest.

Albert looked at the bundle of blue material lying on the planks, then gathered it up. He moved to slide from beneath the boat but caught himself. Resting the pile back on the planks, he took the brass badge from his shako and shoved it deep into his pocket.

The fire outside was already crackling by the time it was covered with the pale blue wool. The flames choked and sputtered but soon caught hold and sent the entire honorable uniform of the First Regiment of Napoleon's Hussars spiraling upward as ash. Albert borrowed a knife from Heinzen and with it sliced off the distinctive braided earlocks that also identified a cavalry trooper and added them to the flames.

"Come," said Heinzen. "We will show you the *Kruier.*"

A carriage in front of the alleyway opening onto Rue St. Jacques was loaded with almost all of Albert and Angelique Penfeld's meager possessions. The soldiers sent to help Angelique with her moving were bringing the last of the cookware she kept and placing it in the bed of the horse-drawn cart. Angelique already sat on the seat of the wagon, delicately tapping on her stomach in response to a rhythm she sensed her child drumming within her.

*Most likely,* she thought, *he is protesting this move.*

Angelique herself was sorry to go. As the guards made the trips bearing her clothes, blankets, and furniture, she stared longingly through the open doorway into the gloom beyond and wondered whether she would ever cross that threshold again.

She could still smell the smoke of that morning's fire drifting lazily into the open air. She knew it had never been a magnificent home, being tiny and windowless, but memories lingered there as no other she had lived in. She wondered if Albert felt the same or was happy she would be moved.

He had been gone six days, and she missed him badly. She missed the way his whiskers would tickle her belly as he talked to their child. She missed feeding him, taking care of him, loving him. How long, she wondered, until he would return safely and permanently.

The clatter of her soup pot landing on the rest of her things brought her out of her daydream.

"Finished," said a gruff, one-armed soldier as the other shut the stubborn door. "I suppose we'll be on our way."

The one-armed man walked to the other side of the cart and pulled himself up, taking the reins in his remaining brawny fist. He waited for the other man to step onto the back, then clucked his tongue to start the swaybacked horse moving forward. As they began rolling along the shoddy cobbles, a woman came jogging after.

"Angelique!" the latecomer shouted, "Angelique, wait, dear, wait!"

"Madame Mendl," Angelique called as the wagon lurched into a crevice in the road, the draft animal perfectly willing to stop again. "What is the matter?"

"Nothing dear, not with me. What is the matter with you? Where are they taking you?"

Angelique knew the cause of Madame Mendl's interest. A neighbor in Angelique's courtyard, she was always gossiping about another resident or friend. Madame Mendl's stature was that of a small barrel, her mouth as big as the opening. She often enjoyed coming to Angelique, especially as the last few months made her a captive audience, with outlandish stories of the evil-doings of the other inhabitants.

If there was one thing on this street Angelique would not miss, it was the tales carried by Madame Mendl. Abruptly, Angelique turned from her perch on the carriage and said, "I have been asked to a special appointment with Emperor Napoleon this evening regarding the bright future my husband, Albert, has in his Imperial army."

As she pivoted away from the aged gossip, trying not to smile, the two soldiers shared a glance of amusement. With a regal nod, the one-armed soldier clucked again to the horse. They drove on, leaving Madame Mendl standing in the street, her mouth agape and, for once, empty of words.

Angelique was amazed at her new home. Seized many years back from an aristocrat during the revolution, it had been maintained simply as an emergency residence for anyone of importance to the emperor who might be passing through Paris. It was located far from the river in Buttes Chaumont near an open space of grass and trees. The air was different, lighter somehow, and Angelique breathed in deeply and slowly. The three-story home had windows and spacious open rooms in which she could foresee many happy times to come with Albert and their child.

As if in response to her joyful pondering, the baby began to kick again, and she rested herself on a chair near the drawing-room window to caress and hold the child through her expanded middle.

The walls of the house were whitewashed and decorated with beautiful oil paintings of flowers, angels, and many important-looking people she did not recognize.

There was a knock at the door. "Come in," she called, as if she had been there for years. From the doorway stepped a pair of uniformed servants, a man and a woman.

"*Bonjour*, Madame Penfeld," the man said. "My name

is Phillippe, and this is my wife, Claudette." The woman curtsied. "We maintain this property for guests of the emperor and serve those guests during their stay. Your things have been put in your bedroom, at the top of the stairs there," he said, gesturing behind him, "and we will be serving dinner in one hour, in the formal dining room downstairs. Perhaps you would like a rest before then."

Angelique was speechless. She had never had such attention to her needs in all her life and, it occurred to her, it would not do.

"*S'il vous plaît,*" she said, when at last she could speak, "I am perfectly capable of doing many things myself, and I would be grateful if you would call me Angelique. You do not have to wear those uniforms if you do not wish to, and I would enjoy it if you would dine with me and allow me to help with the cooking."

The couple were speechless, exchanging a look of bewilderment at their guest's kindness. The man was the first to speak.

"Madame, we are not allowed to dine with our visitors, and we would not hear of your lifting a finger, though it is kind of you to offer. Now, perhaps you would like to rest?"

Only mildly put off by their formality, Angelique

declined. "No, thank you. I would like a stroll around the gardens though."

The woman shook her head. "No, I'm sorry. We have orders to not allow you to leave the house. It is for your own protection."

Angelique masked her dismay and decided instead to take their advice and rest before dinner was served.

*Very strange,* she thought as she climbed the stairs to her boudoir. *What do I need protection from?*

"*Bon voyage,* monsieur," Heinzen called to Albert from the hatch above *Kruier*'s hold, "and *bon chance . . .* you will need it!" The hatch cover banged shut and was ratcheted down.

Examining the cramped hold, now his temporary prison, Albert realized how little Heinzen was joking. From the starboard came a spurting leak of water, from port the screech of rats. Before he could object to his accommodations however, the ship was under way. Albert was an indifferent sailor at the best of times, so he set about trying to make himself comfortable. Aft was a pile of cargo covered with a tarpaulin.

*There is my blanket,* Albert thought.

As he unknotted the first of the ropes holding down the cargo's cover, the ship began to bounce. They were exiting the harbor and moving into open ocean. Already

Albert could tell the vessel would not ride well, even on the calmest of seas, and the motion and combination of odors in the hold made him queasy.

On the deck above his head, he could hear Captain Roomsburg and his crew laughing heartily. Albert knew they likely bought a sizable amount of liquor with the money he had paid them and were consuming it quickly to make their journey more passable.

"What will I do?" he questioned a passing rat. The rodent made no reply, which was well since Albert's query mixed up equal parts of mal de mer with uncertainty about his orders.

Continuing to untie the ropes, he felt a suspiciously familiar shape beneath the cover. The corner loosened, he folded it back to reveal an open box of French musketoons. Albert did not need to uncover the lot to know what they were. These men were no mere smugglers of Calvados brandy or traders in stolen French property; they were gunrunners.

He had no time to think further before the hatch above him opened to reveal the face of Captain Roomsburg, slightly masked behind a cocked pistol.

Roomsburg spoke in broken French. "Friend, if you have so much money to come aboard, much more you have to go to England. From you it will be taken."

The mate, Lange, let a rope ladder down into the hold and descended on it.

"And have you money not," Roomsburg resumed, "I will kill you."

Albert was enraged. "Then kill me you should now," he mimicked, "for money I have not."

From somewhere else above him, Albert heard a cry of alarm, though he did not understand the language. Lange quickly remounted the swaying steps and disappeared, pulling the ladder up after. Roomsburg vanished in turn, leaving the hatch cover open wide.

Albert tried to discern what was happening by the sounds alone. Twice he could make out the corner of a sail being hoisted into view, and twice the *Kruier* shifted before the wind as she came about on the opposing tacks. The stays creaked and groaned, as did the timbers, and the leak increased to a spurting jet. Frantic Dutch voices yelled at one another until finally a cannon's report was heard. A strange, deep rumble struck the ship's hull as a shot landed in the water somewhere nearby. Albert knew his navy was near. He could only hope the Dutchmen were not fool enough to run. The French fleet may not have been the equal of the British at Trafalgar, but its warships were formidable to the coastal waters. More shouting followed and the sounds of voices in shrill argument. It took no special skill to surmise that part of the crew favored flight, even in the face of superior force.

*As well they might,* Albert thought anxiously. *Gun-running means swift and sure execution.*

A crash high in the rigging overhead was followed by more panicked shouts, the report of the cannon, and then the noise of yards and timbers smashing to the deck.

Albert saw crewmen scrambling past the hold to loosen lines, and an instant later the *Kruier's* sails flapped loosely. It was the signal of surrender.

Motionless in the water, the *Kruier* waited to be boarded by the French. As soon as he heard shouted orders in French alongside, Albert began to cry for help. Roomsburg looked over the hatch with such a grimace that Albert thought he might still be shot before he was rescued, but continued to call out anyway.

The boarding party was shortly standing over him and lowering a ladder for his ascent. As he reached the deck, he came face-to-face with a stout gendarme whose expression rivaled Roomsburg's in hatred for him.

"I am Colonel Dahlen," the policeman announced gruffly. "What have you to say for yourself?"

"Sir." Albert saluted the gendarme. "These men are

thieves and enemies of France. My name is Albert Penfeld. I am on a special mission for the emperor himself."

Dahlen snorted out a rude guffaw that was to Albert like a slap in the face. "You swine, you cargo rat, you expect me to believe that you are *the* Albert Penfeld who fired the shot that killed Admiral Nelson at Trafalgar?"

Roomsburg, who was following the conversation intently, chimed in, "He is a man who would desert from the French empire. He has paid me much to take him to England. But we, of course, were only waiting the opportunity to surrender him to you."

"But of course! And we know what an ally *you* are to the emperor," Dahlen scoffed, then laughed again.

"But what I say is true, sir," Albert protested. "I *am* here on special business. These men are smuggling stolen arms, which I only just discovered moments ago."

"If you are Penfeld, where is your uniform? What business would the emperor have for one of his soldiers that would require wearing no uniform at all?"

In his mind, Albert pleaded for the man to think it through.

"If these Dutch pirates were headed for England," Dahlen proceeded, "and you were in their hold, then you were headed for England as well. That is treason, punishable by death."

Roomsburg once again spoke. "Sir, yes, he is much a traitor. There is perhaps a reward for his capture?"

Cocking his dragoon pistol, Dahlen shot the Dutchman in the stomach. Roomsburg's body, flung backward against the rail, slid downward. "There is your reward," he said to the corpse. "The next to speak out of turn will have the same."

His complexion ashen, Albert remained deathly silent. From the corner of his vision he saw Lange shy away from the proceedings toward the railing, and Albert wondered if he would try to jump overboard.

"Well?" the gendarme demanded. "What is the truth?"

Afraid to say again who he was, Albert stood mute for a time. Then he felt something in his pocket. *Of course*, he thought.

Producing the insignia he had retrieved from his shako, Albert said, "There. You see, sir, I *am* a member of the hussars. And I am on special business for the emperor—business I can discuss with only a few people."

"I don't know who you stole this from," Dahlen said, snatching the brass plate from Albert's upturned palm, "but you will accompany me to Paris where you will be made an example of for your perfidy."

Albert was shackled and transferred to the French

vessel. His last view before being marched into the brig was of French soldiers heaving Roomsburg's body over-board.

# CHAPTER 4

———— ❧ ————

**I**'m glad you could make it, William." Thomas hailed his friend from the curb outside the Covent Garden Theater. The naval officer was clad in a formal dress uniform, resplendent with gold braid and sporting a fancy silver-headed cane.

William stepped from the hansom cab, replaced his top hat, and paid the driver. "Hello, old man!" His hand met Thomas's shoulder with a firm grasp. "What is this surprise for which you demanded my attendance?"

"Oh, no!" Thomas grinned. "Closely guarded secret. Not until the end of the performance."

William cocked his head to read the sign overhead. "*Taming of the Shrew.* And why on earth this performance? I've seen this bit of the Bard a hundred times and seldom noticed anything new. Come on now, just a hint."

"Wild horses could not drag it from me before the time. Follow me and be patient." Thomas led the way up the steps, past the high marble columns and brass-fitted doors.

The doorman stopped him. "Tickets, please. Oh, it's you, Captain Burton. I'm sorry I didn't recognize you." The slight, gray-haired man apologized, brushing a piece of lint off Thomas's shoulder.

William's eyes twinkled. So Thomas had achieved enough notoriety that doormen knew his name. Was that the surprise?

"Fine evening, Mr. Winifred. It's good to see you."

"It's nice to see you too. Please go in. Your box is ready for you. And I shall have a barman up for any drinks you may wish to order."

"Thank you," Thomas returned, handing over a tip that glinted like a gold sovereign.

"Do not forget your playbills." Winifred handed them two sheets of paper, folded lengthwise.

Thomas thanked him again as they entered the theater.

William grabbed the back of his friend's elbow. "Shall we, *Captain* Burton? Are you certain it isn't *Admiral*?"

Thomas stopped the charm and spoke more seriously as they headed up red carpeted steps guided by a

**69**

gleaming brass handrail. "Please don't joke like that! I have a position to maintain."

"And you are captain of what vessel?"

Narrowing his eyes, Thomas retorted, "You know enough about naval matters to understand that I have not made post. My appointment is honorary until a command becomes available. But the Admiralty has promised . . ."

William's nod was accompanied by raised eyebrows. "I see. And how long will that be? You see, I'm wondering how long you will continue to play Lord Bountiful. Officers ashore awaiting assignments are on half-pay, are they not?"

Thomas ignored this last thrust and opened the door to the balcony terrace. "Down the steps there." He motioned to a private box, one level above and near the stage.

"Well done for a thief and a liar," William quipped. "If I had known the benefits were so good, I'd have made myself an admiral."

Thomas leaned near him nervously. "Quiet down," he hissed. "You may ruin everything if someone hears you."

William sat back, crossing his legs. "So there's more to this, is there?"

"And something for you if you're good." Thomas

removed a silver case from his jacket pocket and removed a short, thin cigar. To William's surprise, he lit it and began smoking.

A woman opened the door to their box. "What can I get for you gentlemen?"

"For myself, a brandy. And for my good man, William . . ."

"Nothing, thanks," William declined.

"Nothing, are you sure?"

"I've had my fill for a while, but tell me, when did you start taking tobacco? And drinking brandy?"

Thomas flicked his ash confidently. "Since it became the gentlemanly thing to do."

Numerous men carrying long, forked sticks walked around turning down the jets of the house lights. A lamp made of thirty bright lanterns was hoisted above the stage as the curtains were drawn open.

The performance began. While Thomas watched, absorbed in the comedy, William thought to himself how different Thomas had become, just in the short period they were apart. Thomas, drinking and smoking, and passing himself off as wealthy? What on earth had the navy done to him? There must be some other as yet unknown factors motivating him. William decided he could not let it go without comment, and so he whispered, "Thomas, Thomas, have you inherited a fortune?"

With a pointed shushing noise, Thomas instructed, "Look! There she is." An enchanting young actress playing the part of Katherine the shrew entered the stage for the first time. "Isn't she stunning?"

William flipped open his playbill. "Fanny McReady," he read. He studied the buxom, blond woman with the upturned nose and flashing eyes. "She is a stunner," he concurred.

"Yes, she is," Thomas murmured, without taking his eyes from the stage. "And afterward, you shall meet her and see how genuinely wonderful she is, and Jane, one of her friends." He waited for another woman to enter the stage. "There Jane is now. Playing Bianca."

William thought shy and bumbling Thomas was having him on when he spoke of meeting the actresses, but after the rest of the changes decided it was better to watch and see what followed. Thomas's drink came and later, the interval. During the break several well-dressed gentlemen seated below in the stalls hailed "Captain Burton" greetings, which Thomas acknowledged with a lordly wave of his cane.

The second half began, and for a while, William was absorbed in the work. Then the shrew did something that reminded him of Dora. Was it the way she spoke so softly after her onstage conversion? Maybe it was the gentle way she looked or how she acted humble and adoring. Dora was all of those things. At that moment, William wondered why she had not written him back. Certainly she should have gotten the letter and had time to write. Maybe the mail carrier was slow, maybe the letter was lost. Perhaps her missive was still trying to follow him from Gibraltar. He would have written her again except for his injured arm, plus each day he had expected to be shipped home and so delayed asking for help with it.

Before William realized he was dreaming the night away, the performance was over. The actors returned onstage for the applause that followed. Miss Fanny McReady bowed when it was her turn, then turned to the balcony where the two men sat and, raising both slender arms to her lips, blew a long kiss to Thomas.

William could hardly believe it. Thomas smacked his hands together fast and loud. His cheeks were red and his eyes big and wide as a pair of eggs.

Before the curtain had even hit the stage the final time, Thomas was clamoring to get out of the box and down to the stage door.

"Why didn't you tell me you already knew her?" William demanded.

"You wouldn't have believed me anyway! Hurry! Jane Doorty, Bianca, is anxious to meet you."

"What do you mean?"

"She knows you're heir to the entire Sutton shipping estate. She could hardly believe it. Her father works in the Sutton shipyards."

"Why did you tell her that? How will I ever know her real motives if she appears interested in me?"

"Use any means possible to get what you want, William. I learned that from you."

"Listen, Thomas," William argued. "I'm not like that anymore. It got me nothing but trouble. I want a woman who will like me for who I am, not what she will get when she has me."

They made their way down a long corridor leading backstage. Thomas renewed his charm when Mr. Winifred greeted them there and let them pass. As they approached the dressing-room doors, Thomas stopped. "William, I understand what you're telling me. I remember Judy and the fire and the bad things that happened to you. But I want this one thing more than any other. This woman is the brightest star in the heavens to me."

"Speaking of stars," William interrupted. "Whatever happened to your old true love? Abigail? The one who played the piano, and whom you had picnics with and talked to while looking at the stars and planets? She always acted sweet and good-humored."

"We had an argument. A nasty, terrible argument."

"Over what? What could have made you give up such a girl?"

Thomas looked dumbfounded. "Fanny," he answered, swallowing hard.

William burst into amused snorts. "This Fanny? What happened?"

"We were here, and I was dressed up in uniform. Abigail wanted to meet the cast, so I ventured with her to see them. Anyway, Fanny took an interest in me, and Abby got extremely jealous. Of course, I told her she had no reason to be, but we left unhappy. I came back later to apologize to Fanny for Abby's behavior and . . . I never spoke to Abby again. I really don't want to talk about it."

William could hardly believe his ears. He bellowed with laughter. This was not the Thomas he knew. "Thomas," he said, as he struggled to catch his breath, "I guess I taught you too well."

"What? Don't mock, William," Thomas ordered helplessly. "I'm serious about this girl! I've never courted an actress, and anyway, I did nothing wrong. Abby was plain and . . . controlling . . . and Fanny is beautiful and likes me for who I am."

William roared even louder. "Whatever you say, my Lord Admiral!"

"I should have known you'd do this," Thomas

remarked with bitterness. "Please, William, don't muck this one up."

William simmered down, examining his friend's worried eyes and seeing he was sincere. "All right, Thomas. I'll be careful."

"Really! You must promise me."

"I promise."

Thomas nodded sharply and knocked briskly on a red door bearing the brass numeral one.

A woman's voice, muted and seductive, asked who it was.

"It is I, Fanny. Thomas Burton."

"Come in, Captain Burton."

The room was lavishly decorated with gilt paint, and several tapestries. But William noted that the room's columns were from a stage set and the wall hangings were cheap imitations.

"Hello, Thomas," a breathy voice called from behind a screen painted with peacocks. "Are you alone?"

Thomas spoke clumsily, "No, Fanny. I didn't think . . . I have brought my friend, William, along."

"I thought I saw another man up in the box with you." From behind the dressing screen the actress appeared in a long, cream-colored silk robe.

She was even more desirable than she appeared on stage. Thomas leaned to kiss her, stumbling on the edge of a thick, woolen rug. He tripped again, this time over his words. "You were marvelous, I mean *marvelous!* What delivery, what passion!"

"Thank you, Thomas. I love the flowers," Fanny added, gesturing to a huge, colorful bundle on the dressing table. "They smell wonderful. And you must be William, the man I've been hearing so much about. It's lovely to meet you."

While William was impressed with Fanny's looks and manners, she reminded him of Judy, his former barmaid girlfriend, a woman who deserved to be called a tart. *It must be the way she flaunts herself,* he thought. "Thomas has hardly stopped talking about you," he said truthfully.

"How charming." She batted her eyes at Thomas, drawing from him a childish grin. "And do you recognize the robe?" she asked, lounging back onto a low fainting couch and kicking up her painted toes.

He sat down beside her on the sofa. "Of course," he answered, running his hand over the smooth, cool material covering her leg. "It's from the Orient. The finest silk in the world."

"Yes, and I love it."

Standing, William watched the scene from a mental distance while the others carried on. *Silk from the Orient,* he thought. *This can't last long. Thomas will be penniless.* The more he watched, the farther he withdrew. *After my past experiences, Thomas should know a woman's beauty will only go so far. Besides, a woman like Fanny will drop a man as fast as she takes him up, sending him falling to the ground a broken man.*

His mind drifted to a happier day and place, to a woman who made him feel like a man without exploiting herself, someone as pure as a dove. *Dora, what are you doing tonight? I must see you.*

"William!" Thomas snapped. "Where are you, man?"

William resolved his thoughts in a restless instant. "I'm sorry, I must go."

Shocked, Thomas demanded, "Go where?"

Fanny chimed in, using her actress charm. "You mustn't go. Jane will be over any minute, and she will be sad if you don't stay." She made a puppy-dog face at him.

"No, I'm sorry. I shall have to meet her another time," William said, opening the door. "I've just remembered there is something important I must do tonight. Thomas, I'll speak to you in several days." William hardly waited for Thomas to acknowledge the good-bye before shutting the door.

In hurrying back up the corridor, William ran into the shorter brunette actress who had played Bianca.

"Please excuse me," he offered abruptly as he almost

sprinted toward the exit. His thoughts of Dora would allow him to wait no longer. He must find her that very night.

William's carriage transported him rapidly up Hampstead Heath. Soon he was home and had his horse saddled before he even realized what he was doing. It was crazy to ride all the way to Branson Fen that night. The weather was growing bitterly cold. He realized he could fall off and break his leg in a ditch, and no one would know where to find him.

But his desire to see Dora at once, without another instant's delay, overpowered every reasonable argument to the contrary. Even the postponement of a few minutes threatened that Dora would forget him and fall in love with someone else. Suddenly the lack of a letter from her overwhelmed William with anxiety.

He determined to show up at her home first thing in the morning and surprise her. "Besides," he reminded the bay gelding, "I'm a grown man and can do as I please."

Almost as if a starting pistol had been fired, his contrary thoughts were stilled, and the race began.

He headed north to Cambridge and beyond. For the first hours, William's thoughts continuously jumped between Dora and the ludicrousness of undertaking such a trip. Would she be there? But where else could she be? Would she want to see him? He concluded that even if she was angry at him for leaving, Dora Donspy would still be happy to see him. He was confident she was the woman for him—and he was the man for her.

Should he ask her to marry him? That thought crashed through the others. He had not seen her in months, but the journey was so long that he might not have time to make it again. If any of his commanding officers found he was sound enough to ride, they would ship him off again.

The drifting spell of being awake at early morning set in heavily, and his collarbone began to ache intensely. Heedless of the danger, he whipped the horse into a run again, if only to break the boredom. The bay snorted and tossed its head in protest.

Within several hours, William's again empty mind was like a machine with one purpose, and he had no ability to question it. Even the pain in his chest and shoulder had gone numb. The sun was beginning to rise, and he was already several miles past Cambridge with only five more miles to go to the northeast. The gelding stumbled, and William reined it in.

Just when he thought the horse could go no farther, they came over a hill and there, laid out below him, was the marshy valley of Branson Fen. It was like waking up from a solid sleep as William took in the richly moist smells of peat moss and dormant barley fields. The aromas were like doors to his memories of afternoon picnics and drilling with the Branson Fen militia, of Dora and Father Donspy.

On the last hill, with the high road pointing like an arrow toward the square tower of the church of St. Thomas à Becket, William spotted a fresh grave. It was just beyond a stone wall, in the shade of a venerable oak. William spared a moment's reflection for the occupant: likely one of the elderly militiamen.

William was overjoyed when he climbed down from the saddle in front of the Donspys' two-story vicarage. He knocked on the solidly built plank door as the bay, released from his saddle girth, lay down and rolled on the dirt and winter-bleached grass.

A second later a man with light-brown hair and olive skin, dressed in a black vicar's coat with a stiff white collar, answered and greeted him. "Good morning to you," William bubbled happily. "You must be a new vicar for Father Donspy." He meant *assistant* vicar, but his tired brain omitted the word.

"That is correct. I'm Steven Vickers," the young man of about thirty years answered. "Can I help you?"

"You were born for the job, Vicar Vickers," William said, laughing.

Vickers chuckled at the far-from-original joke, then waited patiently for William to come to the point of his early morning visit.

"I have ridden all the way from London last night to see Dora. Will she marry me . . . I . . . that is . . . will she see me?"

Concerned, Steven Vickers clasped his strong hands together. "I am unsure of how to tell you this, though I suppose straightaway is always best. Dora is not here."

William's heart hit the ground. He noticed the energy leave his body in that fragment of time. "Where has she gone? Have the Donspys moved away?" William nodded, as if replying to his own query. "Father Donspy has taken another church elsewhere, yes?"

Father Vickers seemed surprised and even more troubled since it was obvious William was unaware of Donspy's death. "Yes, the family has moved on, so to speak. Will you come in?"

Confused over what could be the matter in such a straightforward-sounding alteration, William agreed.

Slumped down on a pine chair in the kitchen, William kept still while Father Vickers poured cups of steaming coffee. "Cream and sugar, William?"

Screwing up his courage, William inquired, "So tell me the bad news, Father Vickers."

Vickers sighed heavily as he passed a chipped mug.

"I'm sorry to be the one . . . ," he began, seating himself across from William. "Father Donspy passed on recently."

Staring into Father Vickers's hazel eyes, William's mind flashed to the fresh grave on the hillside, under the tree. "When did this happen?"

"Several weeks ago, I'm afraid. I am the replacement vicar sent by the diocese at Ely."

"Where is Dora? Where is her mother, Emily?"

"Emily is in the Clergymen's Widows Home in Salisbury. Dora has gone to live with an aunt near Oxford."

"Oxford?" Shocked by the unexpected news, William asked, "What happened? How did he die?"

Father Vickers reached out and placed his hand on William's. "His heart, they think. I'm sorry, I don't know any more. I hardly got to know Emily and Dora in the short time I was here before they left."

"She must feel so alone," William said, wincing. "How was she?"

"Both mother and daughter were hit hard by his death."

William clutched his cup. It warmed his hands, but not his thoughts. He grew quiet, recalling the day he first came to Branson Fen. "I met Father Donspy on a road. I had been out of my mind with drink and near to jumping off a cliff. When his carriage almost went over the side, I helped him. He asked me if I would come back here, to Branson Fen, with him. My whole being was turned around, and soon I enlisted with the Royal Marines. He saved my life . . ." William's voice faded.

Father Vickers patted his shoulder. "There are few words I can offer to comfort you, but I do know that God has given every man on earth a purpose in life. Some are to live so that others can live and change the world, William. Father Donspy was saved that day," Vickers continued, "that you might live to fulfill a purpose yet unknown. I know little of the circumstances, but I do know it is part of God's plan. Not even a sparrow falls that He doesn't see."

An energy surged through William. It was the power of the Spirit, a force that roused him and made him aware of the cosmic scale to which his life might grow. A sense of responsibility filled him, and hard on the heels of the emotion, he thought of Dora again. "I am in love with her—Dora, that is."

The vicar nodded.

"I haven't seen her since I left, but I feel so strongly for her. There was an audible voice in my head that said, 'Go to her, find her.' I rode all night, all the way out here, to ask her hand in marriage. And now that Father Donspy is gone, I know that is what I must do." He recollected the letter he had sent to Dora. "Did you receive a letter here for her? I posted it some time ago."

Father Vickers tilted his head. "Oh, yes. I sent it on to the house in Oxfordshire where Dora is staying. Have you received a response from her yet?"

"No. That's why I rode out to talk." William stood up. "I must go to Father Donspy's graveside and ask his permission to marry his daughter."

"That would be a proper thing," Father Vickers replied. "It will help you come to terms with his death, too, I think. Can I offer you food, a bed?"

Tired enough to stare vacantly, William merely answered, "No, thank you. I must go visit Father Donspy's grave, and then I must away back to London."

"One minute while I write down Widow Donspy's and Dora's addresses for you." He scrawled something on a piece of paper. "Here."

William examined it briefly, folded it, and placed it inside his jacket pocket.

"May I pray with you before you go?"

"Yes, please, Father."

Vickers rested his hands on William's shoulders as they knelt down. "Dear Lord, I ask that You be with this man, William, as he deals with these obstacles. I ask that You send Your angels to guard him on the road. I pray Your hand will guide him and Dora, and may You watch over the Donspy family in this time of grief. Fill William with Your Holy Spirit and keep him safe, as much may depend on his future. Amen."

"Thank you, Father," William said as he hugged Vickers. "I can't tell you how much I appreciate seeing you here today."

William walked to the graveside, leading the horse. There he prayed while the horse grazed. He expressed his regrets, but most of all his thanks to Father Donspy. He asked for Donspy's permission to marry Dora, regretting anew that he could receive no answer.

Then something fell from the ancient oak. It skimmed down William's bad shoulder and fell into his jacket pocket. William hurried to remove it. "An acorn!" he exclaimed.

William mounted his horse with renewed confidence and resolution. With the nut tucked in his pocket, he spurred off for London.

There was a loud creak from the trophy room door and a shaft of light arced across the room, illuminating a prone and unmoving form on the leather couch.

As the beam of sunshine illuminated his eyelids, William cringed away from it, tugging a tiger hide across his back. He rolled away from the flash to face the sofa.

"William, what are you doing in the trophy room?"

Lord Sutton demanded while examining the closed wooden shutters. "Where have you been?"

William groaned. "What time is it?"

"It's four o'clock in the afternoon! You were missed at services today!"

Squinting up at his grandfather's ominous silhouette, William inquired groggily, "How can it be four? I only lay down at three-thirty, and I'm sure I must have slept longer . . . Did you say services *today?*" He realized he had slept an entire twenty-four-hour day. Suddenly he was wide awake.

"Yes! Where have you been? Out on another drinking binge for two days!?" Lord Sutton exploded, fearing his grandson had returned to his former behavior.

"No, Grandfather, I . . ." William's thoughts were jumbled, and he had to question himself before recounting his actions to another. Had he really ridden the whole way to the Fen lands and back? "The night I went out with Thomas I began to miss Dora so much that I decided to ride to her house . . . it's north, past Cambridge . . . to see her."

"Who in the world is Dora? Let me smell your breath."

Lord Sutton's insistent behavior and accusations wore down William's patience, and he snapped, "Grandfather! Dora is the one I told you of. Her father is dead, and she has moved away! No, I haven't been drinking. I am a grown man, and I will thank you to stop treating me as a child."

Lord Sutton was speechless. William had never talked to him that way before. "I . . . I'm sorry. I was worried. You've not been out drinking, then?" he questioned in a cautious, more considerate tone.

Sitting up, William scratched his head in the light. "No, sir, not even a drink with Thomas the other night. And my dear friend, Father Donspy, is dead."

With a clenched lip, Lord Sutton expressed his remorse. "I'm sorry, William. I'm sorry for treating you like a child, and I understand because I know how much he meant to you."

William could hardly believe his ears. Was this the same man he grew up knowing? A lot of things had changed in William's life. "Thank you, sir. I'm sorry also."

"William, I've been concerned. Yesterday, while you were gone, your orders came. A new assignment."

"When must I depart?"

Lord Sutton was gloomy when he reported, "Ten days. You leave from Portsmouth to the Mediterranean to join the blockade." He waved a scrap of paper in his gnarled, veined left hand. "To Second Lieutenant William Sutton," he read. "We trust you have made a full recovery and are ready to resume serving the king on His Majesty's ship, *Dorchester*. You will present yourself in order to depart from Portsmouth Harbor . . . and so forth."

"Blockade duty!" William moaned. "I can't think of a more dulling experience than that."

"There is time to amend this," Lord Sutton proposed calmly.

"Time for what? I have only ten days left," William said, sliding down the couch.

"I would like to present you an option."

"What sort of option?"

"This is why I was anxious that you not be out throwing your life away, William. I need a man I can trust."

"What sort of option, sir?" William repeated.

Lord Sutton sat down beside him. Rubbing his snowy whiskers in thought, he answered, "I have in hand a new agreement with the army to transport supplies from England to parts of Spain, around the Mediterranean and elsewhere, as needed. I require someone with military experience like yourself—someone who has had experience on seafaring vessels."

William mopped his eyes. "You want me to do what?"

"See that things are secure on the ships and organize

defense against piracy. A bad captain could sell us out to the French. Even our best ships' masters run foul of French privateers. The losses would hurt our business, our men, and our country. I need someone able to organize and train others."

"But what about the Royal Marines? I'm enlisted, and my term is not yet up."

"Since the navy is committed to escort duty to protect merchantmen, they can scarcely object if I take steps to see to my own protection," Lord Sutton insisted. "I do not ask this lightly. It could be extremely dangerous for you. Much more so than blockading any harbor. Granted, our ships will have military support most of the time, but even with it, they will be targets for the French and their allies."

"But why me? Certainly there must be other men out there with more experience than me."

Lord Sutton placed a hand on William's back. Patting it, he asserted, "But none I can trust as much as you. You are family, and I want you to be a part of this family's business." He stood up. "You'll have several days to think about it. Shall we say one week at the longest, so there still will be time to change plans?"

William nodded slowly, making brief eye contact with his grandfather.

"Let me know, my boy," Lord Sutton said before leaving the room.

William was left in true indecision. He felt honored that his grandfather trusted him. It made him feel respected and loved. But the other side of William was disappointed that his grandfather was not proud enough of his accomplishments with the Royal Marines that he would wish for William to stay in the military. William was pleased with what he had accomplished on his own. Should he give it up?

*What would make me leave the Marines?* he questioned himself. It would not be the money, he decided. Perhaps he would accept in order to have more freedom to do as he wished, without being ordered when and where to go. And it would mean more responsibility. What would make him choose his grandfather's way over the way he had made for himself? He considered it, but could come up with only one answer: *Dora. If there is a chance I can see her, possibly marry her, I'll stay out of the blockade. But first I must contact her to see if there is even a chance.* He would go upstairs and write her at once.

# CHAPTER 5

**F**lanked by a pair of guards, Albert was led into a cramped room. Once inside, they seated him on a low stool before the raised desk of the officers of the court. There in front of him was Colonel Steen, who had been present at Albert's installation in the prison cells beneath the Palais de Justice. To the right and left of Steen were two other officers Albert did not recognize. The guards took their posts beside the door behind him to ensure he would not try to escape.

*As if I might,* Albert thought, *with twenty pounds of shackles on my legs and arms.*

"Monsieur Penfeld?" Colonel Steen addressed him coldly.

"*Oui,* I am Albert Penfeld." He rose when his name was called. For the past twenty-four hours, another soldier who was imprisoned in the same cell with Albert had instructed him on proper behavior at the tribunal hearings. His fellow captive had been through three of them.

"Monsieur Penfeld, we call this tribunal to order in the matter of your desertion from Napoleon's army and your treason to the French empire." Gesturing to his left and right Steen said, "These are Captains Larochette and Meuse. They will be considering testimony in this matter and helping me arrive at a judgment. How do you plead?"

"I am not guilty," Albert asserted firmly. "You may contact Monsieur Maitre."

"Silence!" the colonel barked. He was built as stoutly as a bull mastiff, though his wide, down-turned mouth reminded Albert more of a bullfrog. "You will have time to speak in your defense, in answer to our questions."

Albert noted the contradiction in the colonel's statement and thought he saw the twitch of a smile in the frog's mouth.

"Tell us," Colonel Steen began again, "why were you on board that black marketeer's vessel? One that was carrying weapons to England? Stolen French army weapons, I might add."

The questioning was biased and unfair to Albert, but he tried to respond. "I was on board under special orders from Monsieur Maitre. I was unaware of the rifles being carried until I was locked on board. Shortly after we sailed, the captain of that vessel threatened to kill me if I did not give him the rest of my money. I—"

The officer who had been introduced to Albert as Larochette interrupted him. His uniform was obscured to Albert because of the way he sat in his chair and crossed his arms over his chest. "Do you intend to say, Monsieur Penfeld, that you had already given the man money?"

"I had," Albert responded, frustrated by his inability to speak more frankly in light of the secrecy required by the schoolmaster. "But it was merely for transportation."

Colonel Steen's face contorted into the image of a frog about to leap at a fly. "A vessel carrying stolen French weapons was obviously headed for England or allies of that country. Yet you openly admit you paid the captain of that vessel for transportation to wherever he was bound. You stand convicted by your own words."

Albert tried to reason with him. "Colonel Steen, please, if you will only contact Monsieur Maitre, he will confirm my orders."

"Ah, yes," Steen said, licking his lips. "Let us speak of this 'schoolmaster.' As discussed before the commencement of this tribunal, not a single panel member has ever heard of this man. Even if he does exist and is a part of the French army, he has no authority to save a deserter from execution." Albert's expression tumbled, and his color faded. "That is correct, Penfeld, execution! That is what Emperor Napoleon does with those who break faith with the brave soldiers of the Grand Armée; especially those who are trying to assist his enemies—which, as far as I am concerned, you are."

At the end of this barrage Albert remained mute. His throat was dry, and he could only croak the words, "Please, sir, contact Maitre . . ."

"Gentlemen of this panel," Steen said, rising from his chair, "I suggest we decide this case immediately, so he may promptly be made an example."

Slowly the other officers rose. All removed black hats from the table before them and added these grim articles to their already foreboding visages.

"Gentlemen of this panel, in the case of deserter, defector Albert Penfeld, how do you find?"

"Guilty." The others spoke simultaneously. Albert's jaw was agape.

"Gentlemen of this panel, in the matter of smuggler, black marketeer Albert Penfeld, how do you find?"

Again the guilty verdict came, and Albert's mind spun.

Colonel Steen spoke directly to Albert. "Then, Monsieur Penfeld, as you are stripped of your rank in our emperor's army and considered an enemy of the emperor himself, the mandatory penalty is execution by firing squad. Sentence is to be carried out within seventy-two hours from this date. This hearing is adjourned."

Albert slumped back on his stool, heedlessly staring as the officers rose from their seats and filed through a door behind them. He was heaved up by the guards and led back the way he had come.

The cell door thudded closed behind Albert as he walked to his flimsy cot and sat down. A trivial shaft of light shone through a miserable window set too high in the wall for him to reach. Though it was open, the window brought no air to the confined cell, and Albert imagined the lingering odor of nervous sweat; the apprehension of hundreds of other prisoners waiting to be executed, just like him.

Graffiti of all kinds in all languages was scratched into the stone walls. How, and with what, Albert could only guess. Some were merely names and dates, others elaborate poems to lost loves, and still more were cryptic diagrams, possibly intended as magic spells by which locks would unlock themselves and freedom would be obtained. The most poignant were those that contained rudely scribed crosses together with names and self-composed epitaphs.

"They had much more time than me," he mumbled. How unfair it was that he had not even enough time to scratch his name, or Angelique's, or to talk with her one last time, or to ever hold his baby.

With those morose thoughts piling up like ocean waves above a drowning man, Albert flopped over on the hard bed and allowed a few tears to build their size and trickle from his eyes.

He was near sleep as his thoughts drifted, being mostly of Angelique. But from somewhere came the haunting idea that he was adrift. After his service to France, France no longer wanted him. Albert was more and more a man without a country, though he had always done as his country asked him to do, even as far as pretending he was not loyal to France. How ironic that France asked him to do so, yet he would be punished for it.

Albert tumbled into a restless sleep where his mind continued to ponder the questions.

Elsewhere in the prison, among the maze of stone hallways and cells, Colonel Steen was reviewing Albert's preposterous story.

At last he decided to investigate rather than execute an innocent man at the cost, perhaps, of his own position.

Calling a courier wearing the uniform of the Twenty-ninth Dragoon regiment, Steen sent a letter to Marshall Berthier of the Imperial General Staff, referring to the name Maitre, which Albert had mentioned. Steen asked Berthier to either verify or disclaim Albert's secretive work for the emperor.

Aunt Etheldreda watched through the parlor windows with scheming eyes as Nicholas Parry helped Dora Donspy down from a dapple-gray mare. "Such a pity she's no more than a country girl," she complained to herself through a pinch-faced sneer. "Nicholas appears to enjoy toying with her though."

The young people made their way from the gravel path up the steps, entering the house. Aunt Etheldreda was there to meet them at the entrance to the parlor.

Dora was flushed from the chilly air and joyful from the excitement of the ride. "Good afternoon, Aunt," she called.

Projecting charm with everything but her eyes, Aunt Etheldreda remarked, "And a good afternoon to you both. Dora, I trust you have been well cared for by Mister Parry?"

Nicholas shut the door. Smiling, he returned, "The pleasure was mine. I've been out showing Dora the chapel ruins on the property."

"Yes," Dora added, "they were grand. And he showed me the hole leading to the secret passageway where Catholics in the time of Henry the Eighth were smuggled underground to the secret place of meeting!"

"Dreadful place! I should have it demolished," Aunt Etheldreda vowed.

"On no, Aunt," Dora responded. "I think it's lovely, and the romantic story about the young lady and lord from different houses and different religions who used to meet there in the passageway in the middle of the night reminded me of Romeo and Juliet."

Shooting Nicholas a surly look, Aunt Etheldreda rebuked him. "You've been telling the child stories?"

"Guilty as charged," Nicholas joked back, ignoring the scorn in Aunt Etheldreda's tone.

Dora chimed in again. "It was fascinating. I'd love to climb down and see it sometime."

"Don't talk foolish nonsense," Etheldreda scolded. "A dirty hole like that is no place for a lady! The dirt and spiders! Probably rodents as well." Etheldreda studied Dora up and down. "But by the look of you, it seems as though you have."

"Yes, look at me," Dora replied, reviewing the state of her clothing, but otherwise ignoring the comment. "I do look a fright."

"You must go up at once and change for dinner," Dora's aunt commanded.

"Yes, Aunt Etheldreda," Dora said, heading briskly up the stairs.

"Dora!" Nicholas called, waving his brown felt riding bowler. She paused on the steps. "I had a wonderful time today."

"I did too," Dora replied innocently, thinking how nice it was to have companionship and activity back in her life. "Thank you, Nicholas." With that, she hurried upstairs.

There was a knock at the front door and then another. From the cellar entry beneath the staircase, Mrs. Honeywell hurried out to greet the caller. Through the glass panels beside the portal could be seen a chestnut postman's horse with leather saddlebags. Nicholas Parry stood beside the housekeeper as she opened the door.

"Are you the master of the house, sir?" the courier questioned. "I have letters for a Dora Donspy; postpaid, from an Emily Donspy and another from a William . . ."

"Quite," Nicholas replied, but before he had time to take the letters, Aunt Etheldreda snatched them out of the man's hand.

Etheldreda scowled. "I am the master of this house, thank you!"

The postman said fearfully, "Yes, madam. I thank you very much."

"Good day," she concluded, shutting the door in his face.

Mrs. Honeywell reached for the letters. "I'll take those up to her, madam."

Dora's aunt ignored the comment, while examining the envelopes with a hard glint in her eyes. "No, that will not be necessary," Aunt Etheldreda replied in a flat voice. "Return to your duties. I shall deliver them myself."

"Are ye sure, madam? I am goin' upstairs to change the linens right this minute, and it would be no trouble to—"

"No, thank you!" Etheldreda's voice boomed, startling the housemaid. "If you are finished in the cellar I think the flowers need changing in the dining room, Missus Honeywell. See to it at once."

Mrs. Honeywell lowered her head the way a scolded dog would. "Yes, madam," she said meekly, before hurrying off.

Nicholas waited anxiously for her to leave. Then, almost jealously, he asked, "Who the devil would be writing her? Has she got another man?"

"Come with me," Aunt Etheldreda instructed, leading him into the parlor and shutting the leaded doors behind her. When they were seated by the fireplace, she noted, "He has written her before."

"He has?!" Nicholas inquired. "And what do you make of him?"

"A long-lost friend who, up until now, has remained lost."

"What do you mean?"

Etheldreda let the letters, along with her hands, fall into her lap as she explained. "When I saw you had taken a liking to Dora and the first letter came, addressed from this William character, I thought it better to hold on to it. He is some desperate chap who has a history with her, apparently when he was a guest of the Donspys in Branson Fen."

Nicholas made a face of disgust. "And does he have a claim on her? Could any prior commitment be argued?"

Etheldreda did nothing to soothe his concerns. "Perhaps. You know what a simple girl she is."

Nicholas slid to the edge of his seat, reaching for the letter. "Then we must read it."

"Not yet," Etheldreda snapped, unwilling to give up control. "This letter from her mother has come with it, and since they appeared together, I find the coincidence suspiciously convenient. Let us read Emily's first."

Etheldreda opened the letter from Emily with nimble fingers and began to read.

*Dear Dora, I hope these notes find you in good health and spirits. I was overjoyed when I received the letter from William, proving him to be alive. I know how hard you took it when he was listed as dead, and you must be thrilled to hear otherwise. You must write him back immediately, as he is near to leaving aboard a ship for the blockading that is taking place in the Mediterranean. In case his letter did not arrive with this one, here is his address. Also, I have written to inform him of Aunt Etheldreda's address, so he may contact you directly. Praise God, my dear, for it is a wonderful thing in our time of mourning that William Sutton is alive. My warmest regards to you, Mother.*

Nicholas sat without speaking for a time. Etheldreda made a disparaging statement to test Nicholas's resolve. "She *is* beneath you, Nicholas."

Visibly chafed by the thought of losing out to another man and fidgeting in his chair, Nicholas declared, "But she is lovely . . . and I'll not wish to see her with someone else."

In scheming contemplation, Etheldreda waited for him to go on.

"Things are going smoothly, and I don't want them upset with this trite message of a long-lost love, thought to be dead and miraculously returning gloriously from the grave. Something must be done!"

"There is one simple thing we could do," Etheldreda counseled, pressing her bony fingers to her lips.

"Go on."

"If something were to happen to these letters, say . . . they could become mysteriously lost. Then this William chap could remain deceased and buried."

"Yes, yes, yes!" Nicholas exulted. "If that were to happen to these letters, I would remain undisputedly the man in charge. But what of Missus Honeywell? She knows."

"Leave that to me. Missus Honeywell is only an employee and, besides, she did not see the letters." Aunt Etheldreda paced about the parlor, slapping her palm with the letters. She stopped and did an about-face, reaching out a hand. "I trust you know what to do with these."

Nicholas took the pages and removed a match from his pocket. He lit the match but hesitated before igniting the letters. "But first, madam, tell me why you should allow me to do this?"

Hiding her true intentions, she answered sweetly, "You, my dear, are family, and I would like nothing better than to see you happy."

Nicholas Parry smirked as if he had the supreme power in the world. Holding the letters above the half-burned match, he watched them become engulfed in flames before pitching them into the fireplace. He exhaled as if pressure equal to a man's weight had been lifted off his chest. "It's quite liberating, that."

"You have done the right thing," Aunt Etheldreda said with an evil grin, as they watched the embers die. "Now we are partners besides being devoted cousins."

The air reminded William of a blacksmith's furnace that was so unbelievably hot the flames were more than fiery red, they were a wave of white heat. Only this morning was white *cold*. The whole heath, and as far as the eye could see, was covered in ice. Bushes, wet from an evening rain, were ablaze with flames of ice. Light reflected from the surfaces until every view glistened like a crackling fire. Drawing an unguarded breath meant receiving the scorching thrust of an icy dagger in the lungs.

His bay horse with sable face, mane, tail, and stockings cantered powerfully up the hill beyond Hampstead early on the frozen morning. When in doubt, stuck with indecision, or faced with a serious conflict, there was nothing better to clarify William's thinking than thundering up the heath, stitching the hillside with half-moon-shaped chunks of dirt, grass, and ice thrown up by the hooves of his horse. He called the animal *powder* because gunpowder was what he was, firing off like a bullet at the spark of a touch.

Not useful for much else but the dawn rides, William kept him around for just that. It maintained his mind awake and free from entangling thoughts when there were more immediate things to be dealt with such as fallen logs, low branches, and any noise that might cause the horse to jet off in an unexpected flash like a misfired musket.

At the top of the hill of Hampstead, William dismounted and loosened the cinch, allowing the horse to breathe better. He then walked the last yards to White Stone Pond to water the beast. The slower pace allowed his concerns to catch up with him again.

Dora was at the top of his pondering, though he knew directly beneath her image were other unresolved decisions.

Hearing from Dora would be the best thing to help him decide what to do, but what if he did not? What if she never wrote back, and the time came that he would have to choose whether to stay or go?

William began again to question the value of his service to his country. Certainly he would be useful aboard the blockading ships, maintaining discipline and drilling troops. But should he agree to his grandfather's wishes, might his role in protecting important supplies for those same troops be of more value? He juggled the opposing choices.

The watering pond, used in the summer for cooling carriage brakes and animals after the long journey up from London, was frozen. Not a soul was in sight. Powder had to paw at the ice before it cracked and a hole opened.

William watched the spirals of steam rising from the body of the sweating animal. It reminded him of the war, of the smoke of a gun that had recently been fired. Like the day, the war also appeared whitened to William, though it was hard to tell if Britain was in hot victory or cold defeat.

He rattled off the recent battles. In October of the previous year, Britain had beaten the French armada at Trafalgar. But on November fourteenth, Napoleon had captured Vienna, and two days later had defeated the Russians at Oberhollabrunn. Then came December second and the French Emperor's masterful triumph at Austerlitz when he decimated the combined forces of Austria and Russia. Before year's end the Austrians had sued for peace. They'd had enough and would be beaten no further.

White . . . hot or cold. There was no question France was a powerful force. With the exception of the Russians and a few petty German states, England was the only force left standing against France in the entire world. William was astonished at the thought. Britain controlled the sea after Trafalgar, but Napoleon controlled everything else, from the tip of Spain almost to the Russian border.

It was scary for William to reflect on what things would be like had England lost at Trafalgar. He remembered a conversation with Thomas. "We'd all be speaking French."

Thinking out loud, William said, "Napoleon is like a ghost—scary to the small, childlike states."

William's thoughtful gaze passed over a shadowed form standing at the tree line. Cloaked and hooded in black, it seemed to be watching him. The figure matched so well with the semblance of the French emperor that at first it looked like only an overflow of his own imaginings. Then when the form's physical presence registered more fully and he glanced again, it was gone.

He wondered if he had in fact dreamed the shape.

Was it real? Was it evil, another example of Napoleon's spectral presence?

He searched the trees. The cloaked being was nowhere in sight.

Suddenly Powder spooked and slipped violently on the ice. The horse clattered its feet in a flurry to regain its balance. The ice broke wide, and the horse sank, only to find traction on the shallow stone bottom. In a single convulsive effort to escape the grip of wet winter, Powder reared back, kicking his hooves in the air.

"Whoa!" William screamed, trying to hold on to the reins as the beast started to run. He slid sideways, and the horse almost dragged him under the pounding hooves. Refusing to let go, William bounded alongside for a stride, then catapulted himself up. Simultaneously yanking the reins and using his momentum to project him forward, William was flung into the saddle. He pawed to hang on, his inadequate grip allowing him to be nearly pitched off headlong on the far side of the animal. William swayed from side to side, clinging to the saddle for his life, as Powder launched into a full run toward home. There was no stopping and no looking back for another glimpse of the ghostly presence.

# CHAPTER 6

Etienne Traimer was a foot messenger in Napoleon's army. He had begun as a courier three years before when his father enlisted in the army, but Etienne was too young to follow. Refusing to let that stop him from serving, he made himself available to the junior officer serving the Imperial General Staff as an unpaid volunteer dispatch rider.

When Etienne held the first message in his hand with orders that it be delivered with haste, he was proud to be an integral part of his country's forces. Later he was inducted into a regular unit and allowed to wear the dark-green surtout of the dragoons, though he was still never given a horse to ride.

As time dragged on, he carried hundreds of messages marked *urgent* and *confidential*. He began to realize the truly important dispatches were written in code, carried on horseback, and accompanied by an entire division of cavalry for safety. Traimer came to know that he was no more than a postal service for the army, and as he arrived that day, promptly at six o'clock in the morning, he was given another urgent message marked *confidential*. To Traimer it was no more than another meaningless letter, which no one would notice if it went missing.

"Deliver this to the Palais de Justice at once," his sergeant commanded. "And see that you do not dally."

Traimer mouthed the words *do not dally* behind his superior's back and trudged from the office. The officer had said that same phrase regarding every message he had ever carried.

The sun was still below the horizon, though the sky was lightening. Traimer watched as street vendors moved their carts into position along the Rue St. Jacques and began setting up for the day.

Peddlers of prepared foods, fruits, and vegetables lined the street on his way to the Quai St. Michelle.

As he walked past one brightly colored cart, an enticing aroma caught his nose. He jingled the bit of money he had in his pocket and purchased a freshly baked baguette. With the bread tucked under one arm, he slowed his pace as he neared the river.

*Soon,* he thought, *I shall arrive at the Palais de Justice;*

*then they will send me back with another urgently nonsensical note.*

He crossed the Petit Pont, and instead of turning left toward the prison as his duty should have demanded, he walked on toward the Quai de la Corse. Traimer had decided to walk around the prison, instead of directly to it. As he neared it again, this time from the north, he walked on again, deciding to go and view the clock set in one tower of the Palais de Justice. The timepiece had always fascinated him, and he reasoned that an important Imperial messenger should know the correct time.

The sun gilded the corner of the mammoth prison when Etienne Traimer sat down to rest, taking in the sight of the river and the buildings around him in the comfortable glow of dawn. He broke the baguette in half and stuffed chunks of fluffy dough into his mouth.

The crisp morning air normally would have been a welcome to Albert as it touched and stung his cheeks. But its arrival that day meant the end of his life.

As he was led in shackles from the depths of the stone prison into the center courtyard, he blinked away the light and peered desperately around for anyone to save him. Only a few soldiers stood nearby, leaning groggily on their rifles. Beyond these, seated at a table strewn with papers, was a colonel whom Albert imagined to be in charge of the day's proceedings. Standing behind him was Colonel Dahlen, the gendarme who had arrested Albert as a deserter.

The sky was a cobalt blue, brightening as the sun lifted from its horizon and tinting the air around them. The scent of the well-kept grass that formed the central square of the courtyard became nauseating, instead of the pleasing outdoor aroma Albert usually enjoyed.

His knees were weak, and he shuffled his feet to keep from falling down. His slowed pace earned him the press of a bayonet point in his back, and he struggled to keep from falling against it. A leafless tree, visible over the wall of the courtyard, appeared to hold a thousand blackbirds, waiting silently for his demise. One for each of the questions that scrolled endlessly through his weary brain.

*If I am to be an example,* Albert wondered, *why is there no one here to see me die?*

The wall toward which he was being prodded was chipped and pocked from the executions of countless traitors, dissidents, and other enemies of the emperor. Albert found himself strangely guessing how many flattened ounces of lead might be recovered from that stone.

*So many enemies,* he thought.

While yet in the shadow of the building from which

he was being moved, he saw, across the courtyard, another prisoner marching toward the same wall. The man's skin was almost transparent, detailing with ease the network of veins that ran beneath it. Albert temporarily forgot his own ordeal, watching the man squinting uncontrollably in the rising sun. As they neared each other, Albert could see the prisoner was aged. His hair was long and dirty yellow, his bones sagging with the weight of his atrophied muscles and ragged clothing.

Albert's mouth fell open. How long had this poor man been here, underground in this rotten prison, only to be executed now in the daylight? He looked at the other soldiers for expressions of horror equal to the one he was sure he wore. None took notice, preferring to inspect their documents or examine their rifles until the moment came to fire.

Most shocking to Albert was the expression on the old man's face. He wore a look of tired relief and near joy as he dragged his twisted and broken body toward the place where he would die.

Albert was so taken with the scene in front of him that he continued to walk forward, unaided, in the same direction until, at a barked order, he was seized by the arms and forced to stop. He continued to watch as the elderly prisoner was led into position in front of the wall

and the riflemen loaded their weapons, each as method-
ical in their moves as if they were once again in training,
preparing to fire at targets.

The decrepit man, standing before the firing squad,
blinked into the sun, which shone behind them. His
hands shook slightly, jingling out a delicate rhythm from
the shackles that weighed them down. Slowly the
expression that contorted his face in the harsh light
eased. Somewhere in the distance, Albert heard the
colonel call the ready for the executioners.

*Insane,* thought Albert. *Where is the drummer, the
blindfold, the last request?*

But the marked man seemed at ease to Albert, his
face turning up toward the sun.

"Aim," cried the colonel.

*Won't you even rise from your seat?* Albert wanted to
scream. The tired prisoner now faced the sun directly, a
toothless smile on his pallid, emaciated face. The soldiers
cocked back the hammers on their weapons, sending
sharp clicks into Albert's ears.

*But he's had no time.* Albert formed the words on his
lips, though no sound came.

"Fire!"

The sound of a ricocheted ball and a sickening thud
came from the man's chest at the same time the triggers

were pulled. He fell into the wall, then collapsed, the ground already soaked with his blood.

Albert fell to his knees. "God, my God!" he cried over and again, trying to hide his eyes.

At the shot the blackbirds scattered into the air, screaming in violent voices about the murder done there.

The soldiers hefted Albert to his feet and began marching him toward the wall as other men dragged away the still-warm body of the dead man.

Albert continued to plead for deliverance in a brief prayer: "My God." And though he did not realize it, a disturbance in the courtyard behind him meant deliverance *had* come: Etienne Traimer had finished his baguette.

Albert felt strangely strengthened, though they had to help him back to his cell. The chains had been removed from his ankles and wrists, and the guards, once prodding Albert toward death, were now helping him to safety. Everything was beautiful to him; even the prison walls were welcomed by his eyes as a sign that he could still see, was still alive. His light steps echoed in ringing cacophony with those of the accompanying soldiers as they helped him down the endless passages. Corridors he thought he would never see again became expansive vistas as he was led along them.

*Could it be?* Albert thought. *Was it only minutes ago?* Time had ceased, then both sped and crawled by, as Albert witnessed the other execution and visualized his own end against that disfigured wall.

Eased onto his cot, he was unaware of the reasons behind his escape from that violent death.

*Perhaps,* he reasoned, *it will still come.*

For the time, however, he felt a joy. The release of coming close to death and surviving filled him with a kind of glow, and he looked around the cell with wonder. For Albert, the act of looking meant living.

He reread the graffiti-marred walls and gazed raptly at the narrow square of light above him. There, dividing the window were two perpendicular metal bars, sectioning the opening further still and eliminating hope of escape. But to Albert, as the bars divided the light that streamed in and materialized in the dusty air, they formed a crucifix, silhouetted by golden rays. He was reminded again to give thanks, as he had done every moment since he was led away from the courtyard; as he would do for every moment of life he was allowed, from then on.

Only then did he realize how exhausted he was. He lay back on the bed and gazed out the open cell doorway.

The fact that it was open meant nothing to Albert, until it was filled moments later with Monsieur Maitre holding a brown, paper-wrapped package. This Maitre dropped onto the bed before leaning against the wall nearby.

"You were nearly dead, Albert."

Albert nodded solemnly.

"And yet you did not proclaim your business aloud. That is a true mark of your character."

"Many times I tried to tell them," Albert protested, "but they would not hear me."

"Indeed? Colonel Steen has sworn he knew nothing of your true status, or he would not have dared to execute you."

The men shared a look of comprehension.

"In fact," Maitre continued, "the colonel is waiting outside to deliver his apologies."

"I do not wish to see him." Albert spoke firmly, his heartbeat quickening. In truth, he thought, *I might hurt him if I did.*

"Very well," said the schoolmaster as he gestured casually toward the package. "There are some new clothes for you. Quite a shame what happened to your other ones."

With that, he turned and paused in the doorway. "As soon as you are ready, they will escort you safely out of here. No, Monsieur Penfeld, you will not be executed . . . today." He smiled and walked away.

Angered by the dispassionate way in which the schoolmaster spoke of his life, Albert's fingers shook as he tore the paper away from the clothing. It appeared to be an Imperial Guardsman's uniform, not the pale-blue color of the First Hussars, but a royal-blue instead. He quickly shed the ordinary garments, tossing them to the floor.

As he donned the Guardsman's coat, he noticed a folded square in the pocket below the left breast. The letter he retrieved contained his orders. Informing him simply of his post at the prisoner-of-war facility at Ouessant, the writing was followed by three words: "Proceed as before."

He did not want to believe he would be asked to perform such dangerous tasks so soon after his brush with death. Reading the orders again, a piece of Scripture crept unbidden among his thoughts: *A man's enemies are the men of his own household.*

Crumpling the paper, Albert shoved it back into his pocket. "Therefore I will look to the Lord."

At the gates of the prison, he was handed the reins of a stout gray horse, and Albert set out for the coast and the Isle of Ouessant.

"Just tell her no, Thomas."

"Come now," Thomas pleaded with William as they sat together at the Ruffled Hen Pub around the corner from the Admiralty offices in Whitehall.

William wiped a blot of mustard from his mouth with his napkin and tossed it on the plate in front of him. "I had enough of actresses the other night, thank you very much." He shook his head insistently. "I'm not going."

Defensive, Thomas said, "And what's wrong with Fanny? She's the most glorious, funniest, sweet creature a man has ever seen!"

"Gently now," William said in a calming tone. "I've been with women like those, Thomas. Beautiful, sweet, and kind *acting* they may be, but in my experience they amount to a lot of trouble. They're never fully yours."

Disappointed, Thomas replied, "Not my Fanny. She really cares for me. The way she looks at me . . . I suppose you're saying that's acting?"

"That she looks at you, no," William corrected. "I bet that her eyes are her own and directed at you when she appears to be looking at you." He raised his hand palm outward to shut off another objection. "Her smile, yes, that too. When she smiles, it is at you, no doubt, but *whom* is she thinking of when she's holding you?"

"Oh, that's enough! If you're saying she's thinking of another. . . ." Thomas hung his head in petulant misery.

Glancing around at how silent the pub had become, William continued. "Now don't misunderstand me. It's not that she thinks of another—or that she doesn't. It's more accurate to say she thinks of herself."

Thomas could not disagree but had to defend his love. "A girl like Fanny has a right to be concerned with herself and her future. Otherwise every bloke off the street pretending to be a captain would be with her."

William winked and added in a droll tone, "Precisely! And every bloke doesn't have the money of a real captain either."

Thomas frowned when William mentioned money again. William could tell it was a sore subject. He leaned forward and whispered to Thomas, "Friend to friend, how *are* your funds holding out?"

Thomas pointed at a passing horse-drawn omnibus bearing an advertisement for *Taming of the Shrew* as if trying to divert William's attention. Finally he admitted, "Nearly gone."

William practically choked. "Gone!" he blurted out. Thomas was embarrassed, hushing him with his hand. William resumed in a softer tone. "Nearly gone? All of your prize money and earnings from the navy? How?"

"What else is there to say? Fanny. She's an expensive

lady to keep. Dining out, having flowers delivered every night. Special clothing . . . I don't know. And this intolerable delay over my ship. No positions available on any ships for me. How can that be? I have haunted the Admiralty offices every day. Sea Lord Malcolm promised me the first opening. Now he refuses to see me. A man has to have some means of making some cash."

"Look, Thomas, you've got to do something. You can't go on spending admiral's earnings on less than lieutenant's wages. It won't last, and she'll find out soon enough anyway. Then where will you be?"

Thomas scratched his short, brown, already-mussed hair. "What do you suggest?"

William leaned back confidently with the expression of one well-versed in affairs of the heart. "Don't call on her for a while. Stop sending flowers so much. Become extremely busy, or . . . I know: Say your ship has come in and that you must go away on a voyage. A secret mission about which you can give no details. It will be perfect!"

Excited, Thomas said, "Yes, I will take her out the way a proper gentleman would tomorrow night and pledge my devotion to her, and so she will commit hers to me."

"There you are."

"I already have tickets to a chamber music concert . . .

very dignified. Once there I shall tell her I must away on my ship, but I will think only of her and will long for her until the day I return! Then I shall disappear and hoard my money until I can afford to return and see her again."

"That's the idea!" William congratulated Thomas with a shake of his hand.

"Thank you, William," Thomas said gratefully. "You are the master of these things."

Smiling ruefully, William confessed, "I wrote the book, you know, but the research cost me dearly. Don't repeat my mistakes."

"I won't," Thomas said. "And since it's the last time I shall be able to be seen in public, will you not join us tomorrow night? Fanny and Jane and me."

William considered the event but could think only of Dora. "I don't think so . . ."

"What is it!? It's the question of this Miss Dora Donspy still, isn't it?"

William was hesitant to give in. After what he had done to convince Thomas, he was doubtful about admitting he had problems of his own. "If you must know, yes, I've been waiting for her to write back, and . . . I don't know, it's not like Dora."

"And how do you know, William? Don't be caught by the same trap you are trying to free me from. And what are you going to do about sailing? What about your decision either to sail with the Royal Marines or take up work for your grandfather? Will you be waiting for her until the day of departure? Don't be a fool. There are plenty more women."

William interrupted testily, "Ladies. Dora's a lady."

"There are plenty more ladies like Dora out there. You can't wait your whole life for one to return a letter."

It occurred to William that he and Thomas had switched places. He did not know where either would be without the other. "You're right. I suppose I mustn't wait for her. She obviously has not waited for me."

"Don't be altogether down. It may not be that bad."

"No, you're right. And I'm going to do something about it." William paused. Thomas hung on his words, curious as to what this solution might be. "I'm going out with you tomorrow night."

"You are!" Thomas exclaimed, as if he'd personally won the war. "That's the spirit! The only way to forget a woman is to find another."

"Lady," William scolded.

Thomas covered his grin. "Yes, sorry—*lady*."

# CHAPTER 7

It was a blustery morn when Albert arrived at the westernmost tip of France that was Brittany. There a military outpost regulated transportation to and from the Isle of Ouessant. He was supposed to contact the commanding officer when he arrived and found him squatting near a campfire, sloppily devouring his breakfast.

The figure pointed out as the commandant was obnoxiously huge, not merely fat, though he was grossly overweight. Most notable about him were the eight extra inches of height he would have over Albert when he rose, and the booming voice that accompanied them. His name was Colonel Patrick Ney, half brother to Napoleon's famous Marshall Michel Ney and consequently referred to as *Frere*—meaning "brother"—Ney whenever his back was turned.

He greeted Albert with foul breath and an ability to fire crumbs from his mouth with every word he spoke. "You are the new guard?" he queried, without ceasing to chew.

"Yes, sir, I am Albert Penfeld."

Ney turned to his compatriots around the meager fire. "I cannot understand why they continue to send me such useless amounts of men. Men who eat our supplies and do nothing but drown prisoners." He bellowed a guffaw, and Albert noticed one of the nearby soldiers lower his head in embarrassment.

Albert thought he could now understand how someone with so famous a brother could be stuck in a backwater post like this.

"So then," said Ney, rising from the log, ground into the damp earth with his weight, "come along, and I shall show you your duties."

Albert followed as Ney pushed his girth between the well-ordered tents of the garrison camp. In between each of the tents were piles of rifles, tangled up by the bayonets so they stood upright in triangular clumps.

"Here is yours." Ney gestured to a tent set at the top of the wagon tracks that ran the length of the camp. "Hated because it is on the slope, and rainwater will course right through it. Additionally hated for Maurice, the other occupant that resides within. I'm sure you will likewise tire of him quickly. Your posting here will include mounting one night of guard duty per week, most likely tonight if I know my other soldiers correctly. Your orders also specify you as a special attendant on every prisoner exchange to take place instead of the normal rotation men usually make." He stopped midstride. "You have made someone angry, no?"

Continuing on toward the sand and waves, Albert could see a more permanent-seeming hut perched above the beach. This was Frere Ney's personal lodging, made at the cost of many an enlisted man's firewood. "Here below my residence," Ney continued, "is the launch we take out there."

Albert was surprised to see a ship he had not seen before anchored just offshore.

"That is *La Prevost*. On board is a garrison of twenty men who remain there for a fortnight at a time. We use the ship as a floating platform from which we can more easily perform the prisoner exchanges with the English."

Albert could not understand how he might make a defection from such a regulated and guarded situation.

"Your job, Penfeld, whenever the English vessel is near, is to come to this launch and wait for the other guards to escort the prisoners to you. You and another warder row out to *La Prevost* and wait for the English to return our men, then safely put their men in their launch and bid *adieu* to them for another day. Understand?"

Albert nodded, a vague plan forming as to how he would undertake his apparent desertion.

"Then get some sleep. You've traveled far, and the next consignment of prisoners to arrive will be early tomorrow."

Drizzle signed on the ground, freshening the air, giving it crispness and vibrancy. The sky was winter blue, brightly contrasting with the green creekside fields of Oxfordshire.

Mrs. Honeywell stood ankle-deep in long rows of rich soil, filling a wicker basket with the season's crop of root vegetables. In a pretty white hat adorned by a bow, Dora stepped from the kitchen. Standing on the stone landing, she took in the countryside and its evening beauty with a clear, deep breath. Her eyes were calm and warm, with an alert shine that gave evidence of her happy heart. She thought of Branson Fen and of home, though she did not miss it. "Oh what a place is this." A tingle of tranquility washed over her. "I could stay forever."

Dora was in such high spirits that she almost skipped over to the housekeeper, acting as if she were a schoolgirl again let out for Christmas holiday. "Missus Honey-well!" she called, holding her bonnet atop her head, while waving with her other hand.

Mrs. Honeywell placed her hand to the small of her back and arched upward, a beet in each hand. "Hello, child. How are ye this afternoon?"

Dora trotted to a stop beside the last row of leafy greens. "Wonderful," she said, closing her eyes and inhaling the grassy, after-rain fragrance. "The hills, the sky, the fields . . . everything is awake today, and so am I."

Stretching out a kink in her side, the housekeeper joked, "Well, if ye have so much a' that, maybe ye could share some with me."

"As much as you want, Missus Honeywell."

"And what is to blame for all of these terrible feelin's?"

Hands in pockets, Dora shrugged shyly. "Nicholas Parry has asked Aunt Etheldreda if I may accompany him to a concert . . . in London! And she has given her permission." She giggled happily.

"Oh gracious! That's lovely and excitin' news!"

Dora beamed.

Mrs. Honeywell looked her over. Stepping from the garden soil with basket in hand, she observed, "Well dear, if I didn't know any better, I would say you're in love."

Dora blushed, nodded quickly, and glanced away. Composing herself, she added, "He's taking me to hear my first real chamber music performance . . . a premiere of a Beethoven piece. Then I'm to stay with Aunt Etheldreda's sister, so all will be quite proper."

Delighted for the girl, Mrs. Honeywell whistled through pursed lips.

"And Nicholas says if I really enjoy it, he'll take me to London again, to hear Chopin played in Belgrave Square."

"Oh that's lovely, child!" Mrs. Honeywell hugged Dora, careful not to get the soil of the garden on her dress. "And how is your dear mother, then?"

"My mother?" Dora repeated, slightly surprised and curious. "I don't know. I suppose she's fine. I've written her every day, and I have been expecting to hear back. But perhaps she has much to occupy her time at the Widows Home. Then, too, perhaps the post does not run as regularly here as it did in Cambridgeshire."

"Oh, no, dear!" the housekeeper corrected. "A letter arrived from your mum the other day! In fact two letters for ye—one from a gentleman as well. Has Madam Etheldreda forgotten to give them to ye?"

"She must have. I've not heard a word on the matter." Then, after a thoughtful pause, Dora inquired, "But what was the gentleman's name?"

"It was . . . I believe his name was . . ." Mrs. Honeywell clasped thumbs and forefingers to temples, giving herself twin black marks in the process. "Oh, I can't remember, but we'll go see at once. Come child, help me with these baskets."

They lugged three wicker containers, loaded to the brims, up the lawn in search of Aunt Etheldreda. What they did not realize was that, spying from behind the curtains at an open second-story window, Aunt Etheldreda had already heard of their quest.

"Aunt Etheldreda," Dora called as she rounded the corner from the kitchen into the wood-paneled hallway.

"I'm here, my dear," a voice returned distantly from the abovestairs.

"Aunt Etheldreda, have you a letter for me from my mother?"

No answer came at first, then, "Did I ever tell you dear Dora, that I was named after St. Etheldreda who founded the monastery in Ely? Back in your own Fen country. Though why such a saintly woman would choose to live in such an ungodly place is quite beyond me."

"Excuse me for interrupting, Aunt Etheldreda," Dora apologized, ascending the steps two at a time. "*Have* you the letter that came for me?" She confronted her aunt in the sewing room.

"Letters for you. Let me think . . . Yes, the post did come."

"For me?"

Etheldreda acted annoyed. "No, one from your mother to me. The other one was for your mother, mistakenly sent here from Branson Fen."

Dora's mood wilted. "What did my mother say? Did she not ask about me? May I see the letter?"

"She hopes you are well. She has been ever so busy and is afraid she will not have time to write you as often as she hoped," Etheldreda finished. "Have you been in the garden in your pretty things? My goodness, girl, will you never stop acting like a farmer?"

Dora stood rock steady and unblinking in the face of this renewed criticism. "But Aunt Etheldreda, can I read it?"

"Oh, it's around somewhere, I'm sure. When I find it, I will give it to you."

Deeply disappointed not to hear from her mother and desperate to somehow find out more, Dora continued, "And the other. Can I inquire as to whom it was from?"

Facing away from her niece, Etheldreda clenched her jaw and answered, "My dear Dora, it wasn't addressed to you, nor me, and it would not be polite to involve ourselves in the affairs of others."

Tears welled up. "I'm sorry, Aunt Etheldreda." Dora managed to choke out the words, "Thank you," before fleeing back downstairs.

Mrs. Honeywell emerged from the kitchen, expecting to find Dora still in joyful spirits. "Did ye get your post?" Dora's beaten expression answered the inquiry faster than words.

Dora looked to Mrs. Honeywell for support, a smile—anything so that she would not break down and cry. Grieved for the girl, Mrs. Honeywell did not say a word, instead laying a plump finger across her lips to urge Dora to remain silent.

In the space that followed, Dora heard her aunt take several steps out of the sewing room and stop, as if listening for conversation from below. Then came the sound of Aunt Etheldreda's footsteps tapping rapidly up toward her own rooms on the upper floor.

The smell of dust, smothered on the roads by moisture, drifted in through the opening of the shabby tent where Albert lay. He knew it was beginning to rain. The first pat of a drop on the canvas above his head confirmed the theory, and he crept to the door to watch the increasing downpour.

The encampment at Ouessant was still, except for a few early laborers hauling supplies into various tents and the far-off sound of thunder. From Albert's vantage point, he could see the ocean, turbulent and shrouded with the storm that was moving inland. In that gray mist he saw the first flashes of lightning that divided the clouds briefly before disappearing.

As the patter of the drops became heavier on his tent roof, platter-sized pools collected in recessions there. The water soaked through the material slowly, forming a dark spot, then glistening drops that were reluctant to release their holds. In the sparse trees behind the camp, birds huddled together and chattered, protesting the damp that invaded their nests.

The sun was tardy in rising, leaving the sky the same shade it had been before dawn. Albert had been awake for a long time contemplating the dangerous activities that lay ahead of him. If he were not uneasy before, the storm had worked its way inside him and twisted his stomach into a queasy knot as the clouds rolled over each other heading for dry land.

"Why today?" he mused aloud. Maurice, the other guard who shared the tent, rolled in his bedding and mumbled incoherently.

In deliberate slowness Albert donned his uniform to walk to the beach. The rain intensified, becoming pelting musketshots as he stepped gingerly over puddles forming in the wagon tracks that partitioned the camp.

Albert came to Colonel Ney's shack at the edge of the beach. He, too, was awake, and watching the increasing strength of the storm.

"*Bonjour*, Penfeld." Ney's greeting was punctuated by a rumble in the sky.

"I would not say so," Albert returned. "Will the ship still come today?"

"Oh, yes, they would have left last evening before this began. With this wind behind them, they may even be here before time."

As Albert looked out to where their own ship, *La Prevost,* was anchored, it seemed the surf might swamp a rowboat before it could break free of the waves. Ney followed his gaze.

"Do not fret, Penfeld," he said. "It is shallow beneath the waves, even if the boat does sink." He chuckled and retreated inside to don his coat.

Albert continued to watch the froth of the waves turn brown as it churned the sand beneath them. As his stare drifted through the foam that blew from their crests he saw a hazy shape in the water.

At the same time, a bugle call sounded from the camp, and Frere Ney reemerged from his quarters, half shaven. "They *are* early!" he moaned. "Get to your post, Penfeld."

Albert walked down the hill to the rowboat and

waited there for Maurice to arrive. He came soon after, leading a pair of English prisoners in chains who were, in turn, followed by two more guards.

When they arrived at the boat, the prisoners' shackles were removed. Albert had just learned of other captives who had drowned when the rowboat capsized because the chains had been left on them. The roar of the surf was overwhelming as the men, including the prisoners, hefted the boat toward the water.

Maurice took his position at the oars, Albert at the tiller in the stern. They waited as the other soldiers helped the prisoners in, then pushed the boat into the water, wading in knee-deep.

The waves crashed over the bow as Maurice dipped and pulled the oars mightily, barely able to move outward as the waves rejected his efforts. Albert tasted the salt in the soaking spray. Ponderously they cleared the rolling combers and, though the incoming swells remained massive, they made progress toward the waiting vessels. With each stroke of the oars, Albert's anxiety increased, and he wondered if it would be visible to Maurice.

It was. "Penfeld," the other sentry said, grinning as he labored, "are you afraid of the ocean?"

But Albert had no time to answer before one of the English prisoners vomited overboard. The others turned away for fear the sight might make the sickness contagious. They were pitched up high onto the swells, and with each rise, Albert was able to see both ships, the English vessel appearing closer each time.

They neared *La Prevost* as it pitched and slammed down again, straining against the anchor line as a dog might pull against its lead when another is close. The soldiers on board rolled out a rope ladder for their ascent, but it was some time before it was safe to near the vessel for fear they might be crushed by its jouncing. Timing his leap to the swells, Albert grabbed for and swarmed up the ladder.

Albert was amazed how much steadier the prison craft felt to him when he was standing on its deck. Though at water level it crashed and bounced, all above seemed fairly calm. Maurice tied the rowboat to *La Prevost* and was soon standing on the deck next to Albert and the prisoners.

The rain hammered the deck, but the four arrivals were already drenched from the waves. The English ship was alongside, and Albert could read the name written across the bow.

*Legerdemain*'s deck was massed with soldiers who stared defiantly at the occupants of *La Prevost*. Albert wondered what sort of reception he might have when he was on board. It was the first time he had allowed a concrete thought about his defection to surface since he had awakened.

He watched with a pain in his stomach as the English let down a craft with three soldiers and one French prisoner. The English prisoners were ushered to the opposite rail and helped onto another rope ladder there.

Albert walked to the opposite side of the deck, away from the onlookers, and allowed himself one last gaze at the French coast before descending the ladder and dropping into the water next to the rowboat. The seawater was frigid, and he feared his gasp might have been heard from above as its chill penetrated his skin. He groped his way along the side of the ship by way of different lines that hung there. Once near the stern, he kicked away from the vessel and toward the *Legerdemain*. The distance between the ships was short, not more than twenty yards, but the swimming was difficult as he fought the roll of the waves and the soggy clothes that weighed him down.

A brief look to his left reassured him that no one had noticed him. The proceedings there were almost over, the English stepping into the boat and the Frenchmen safely out of it and, as yet, no one had seen him. He bumped into the stern of the *Legerdemain* without looking and was grateful to find a line dangling there to which he could hold and rest.

The English launch was tied up alongside the ship a short distance along the portside, and Albert forced himself to lower his head farther into the water to reduce the chance he might be seen by either party until the time was right. One by one the men mounted a ladder, and the launch was secured and hoisted into place on the deck. Soon after, Albert began to slide along the side of the vessel to make use of the same ladder. His limbs would not move for the cold, and he had difficulty making that last movement to safety.

As he grasped the bottom rung of the ladder, the English were beginning to unfurl their sails to return home. From behind him, Albert heard his name shouted by Maurice.

An English soldier, puzzled at the excitement, stepped to the rail and gasped at the sight of Albert dangling there. Unsure what to do, he made no move to help Albert, so Albert was forced to drag himself the remainder of the way.

Across the chasm that separated the ships, Albert heard the exclamations mounting. What must they think of his actions? The English were disturbed, several gathering above him with rifle muzzles centered on his head.

Then Albert heard a shot fired, and the Englishmen ducked as a chunk of railing disintegrated near his head.

Desperately Albert flung himself over the rail and lay flat on the deck of the English vessel.

He was face-to-face with another man taking shelter there. "Please," Albert pleaded in English, "I must speak with your captain."

A muscular, dark-haired man strode up, pushing the other sailors away and ordering them back to work. The anchor had already been raised, and they were drifting dangerously close to *La Prevost*.

"I am Captain Dorsey Richmond," he said, leaning close to Albert's face. "You are on my ship, and your presence is threatening these prisoner exchanges. Tell me why, or I shall throw you overboard."

They could both hear the French agitation across the narrow gap of water that separated the ships. "My name is Albert Penfeld, and I have an important message for Lord Sutton of England. I wish to leave France," Albert sputtered through a shivering voice.

"Hoist the main," Captain Richmond yelled, lifting Albert to his feet.

Immediately the ship began to move.

When it became apparent to the Frenchmen lining *La Prevost*'s rail that Albert was either being taken or leaving by choice on the English ship, they scurried chaotically around the deck. But to raise the anchors and make an attempt to sail after *Legerdemain* was not possible: *La Prevost* had been only a moored platform for too long and, besides, none of the men were sailors, only guards.

Scattered rifle reports were heard, but the *Legerdemain* was far ahead and making for open water, for England.

# CHAPTER 8

———— ❧ ————

Lively and playful, the sound of Beethoven's Piano Concerto no. 3 filled the vast hall, inflating the room with a tangible energy that tingled not only one's ears, but one's heart, mind, and spine.

So alive was the music that the air swirled from the musicians planted on glossy marble floors to dance with the ivory pillars and caress the lustrous chandeliers. Dimming during stately moments as if clouds were passing over, the music lulled the flames. The candles dwindled during each dying phrase, until the steadily building swell of a sunrise in the melody resurrected each flame, causing them to glow brighter than before.

With Thomas, Fanny, and Jane, William made his progress around the room, as if he had triumphed in the boarding of a triple-masted ship of the line. "This is absolutely exquisite," William noted, ignoring his restless feelings toward the women. Proudly wearing the crimson of an officer of the Royal Marines, he took in all the sights, sounds, and smells.

Thomas, dressed in full navy uniform from polished shoes to gold braid, smiled with unreserved delight. "It is all I hoped it would be."

But the expressions of the ladies, Jane Doherty and Fanny McReady, were in distinct contrast to their male companions. Distant and reserved, each surveyed the surroundings as intently as shipboard lookouts in enemy territory. Her blond locks wrapped elegantly in a loose bun, Fanny wore a gown of shimmering red satin. Jane's silky azure dress offered a similar, stunning effect. Both were blue-eyed, red-lipped, and dangerously enticing.

William suspected he knew what was inside their hearts: cracked mirrors reflecting nothing but bitter faces and an almost frantic need to hang on to the bloom of youth. Fear of aging and losing their attention-getting qualities lent a serious air to the evening; Fanny and Jane were scanning the room both for rivals and prospects.

William and Thomas had only delayed briefly to discuss London's finest musicians and the glittering exhibition of wealth before the ladies slipped away, leaving the men alone. As soon as they did, Thomas apologized. "I'm sorry, William. I didn't know this would happen."

Shrugging, William said, "The Doherty woman has no class. From the first time I heard of this Jane and her father's employment at the Sutton yards, I suspected what she'd be about."

"I must say, William, never would I have guessed she would bring up such a thing as a promotion . . . and in the carriage on the way here."

"Her father, of all people. I inquired about him. Nothing but a sloth. But never mind. I came here to enjoy the night with or without her."

A man decked with silver trays perched atop each hand offered the men bubbling glasses. "Champagne, gentlemen?"

"To tonight!" William said, grinning.

Thomas nodded excitedly. "Tonight it is. I shall declare my love with this." He extracted from his pocket a shimmering diamond ring that dwarfed the delicate gold band it was perched on.

"Great blooming moneybags!" William exclaimed, hunching over it. "Where did you find this?"

"Whitechapel. I purchased it today. Do you think it impressive enough? The shopkeeper swore it was the largest stone in the quarter."

"Have you gone mad?" William demanded as he reached for it. "This must have cost a year's wages!"

Thomas jerked the jewelry back with alarm at

William's response. "It *was* everything I had," he reported.

"Now, Thomas," William spoke sternly. "This was not what you planned. You were to pick up a *token* of your love for her. Just a trifle to remember you by until you return."

Thomas grew uneasy. "I don't know what came over me. I was looking at the plain gold bands and thought to myself, *I want to get her a present that complements her beauty; a gift that doesn't look out of place.*"

"Yes, but you didn't have to buy out the shop!"

"One thing led to another," Thomas explained regretfully. "You know how the jewelers line them up, smallest to greatest, each one costing a bit more. You look at one just above the one in your price range and then the one right next to it looks nicer. The man asks you about your lady, and you tell him what a wonderful treasure she is. Then he says, 'Is this quite special enough for such a lady?' And it gets you thinking, *Maybe just a little larger stone, or possibly the more elaborately worked gold band would be finer.* Then you say to yourself: *It's a once-in-a-lifetime purchase. I want it to last. I can afford more, just a little more, a tiny bit more*—until you've doubled, tripled your price, returned to your bank a second time and walked out of the jeweler's shop with an object almost too heavy to carry."

"Everything you had—unbelievable!" William commented with astonishment. "Is it too late to take it back?"

Thomas chuckled nervously, then shuffled his feet and stared at the ground. "I've already attempted to do so."

William slapped his forehead. "And the shopkeeper refused it."

Thomas nodded sadly.

"Then why don't you go to another shop and try to recover your money?"

"It's not worth it."

"Not worth it? Have you tried?"

Deflated, Thomas agreed again.

"By thunder, Thomas. What *will* they give for it?"

Thomas fidgeted with the ring in his pocket awhile before answering. "A third of what I paid."

Wincing, William covered his face. "Thomas, my dear fellow . . ." Realizing there was nothing to do then but be positive, he suggested, "Then I guess you will *have* to make this the night of her life and yours."

Thomas frowned. "I suppose so."

William attempted to cheer up his friend. "Look. There she is now."

The music stopped, and then the chamber orchestra began to play a waltz. Couples joined and thronged the arena where once spectators had stood. Thomas glanced at a long procession of linen-covered tables. Waiters had begun to load them with trays and bowls of food perched in ranks like the battlements of a silver fortress. Fanny stood near an older gentleman. He was balding and round-bellied, but distinguished in black tie and tails. The man laughed as Fanny talked to him.

"I can only imagine what they're talking about," William muttered.

"Don't jump to conclusions," Thomas warned sternly. "Fanny has explained this sort of thing to me. You see, it's business. She has a nose for two types of people: men with money who might potentially finance a theatrical production and those who know people in the arts world, who may be a valuable connection. Besides, that is none other than Lord Malcolm of the Admiralty. You know, the one who promised me my command."

Patting him hard on the back, William said, "Well, go talk to her then."

"Fanny?" Thomas questioned politely, clearing his throat to show that he knew he was interrupting.

She continued to talk to Lord Malcolm as if Thomas were not even present. "At the Covent Garden Theater, anytime."

Thomas waited beside her patiently. She glanced at

him to see what the disturbance was about. He held up a glass, motioning in question, would she like champagne? She shook her head and continued speaking. At one point Malcolm glared at Thomas but gave no acknowledgment he was even acquainted with Captain Burton.

After standing awkwardly around for several minutes, he and William retreated, then both returned, bearing fresh drinks.

Fanny was giggling coyly. "Oh, my favorite play in the whole world is 'How to Get Married.'"

"Yes, I know that one! By Thomas Morton, I believe," Lord Malcolm bubbled. "Quite a role for your talents, eh? I say, how droll. Quite a role for your talents, what? Quite a subject matter," he added, red-faced and winking.

Fanny acted as if she were charmed.

Thinking the laughter a reasonable time to interrupt, Thomas interjected, "I brought you some champagne, my dear."

Her expression was distant. "Oh, Thomas! I thought I told you I didn't want any." But since Malcolm was watching every move, she quickly changed her tone to, "Darling. Thank you, but I'm fine."

Sea Lord Malcolm smirked with a sense of confidence. Thomas asked if he could have a word with

Fanny. She hissed that she was busy, talking with an old friend, but he expressed how important it was. Fanny made a face, as if it were the worst timing in the world.

Swallowing hard, Thomas persisted. Sea Lord Malcolm was already pointedly ignoring him, which could not be good for Thomas's captaincy. Worse, he could not speak of a "secret assignment" in front of the man best able to expose the lie.

"Darling, please," Thomas pleaded with Fanny. "It is important that you be happy with me while I tell you my news."

With obvious reluctance, Fanny allowed herself to be led away, after giving elaborate promises to Sea Lord Malcolm that she would be back shortly and after an apologetic bow from Thomas. "Really, Thomas," she snapped. "That man is interested in financing a theatrical production."

Desperate, Thomas explained, "I know his importance. That is a high Admiralty official. I understand. I'm sorry. Maybe this isn't the right time, but I'm leaving in two days, and I . . ."

"You're leaving?" Fanny interrupted. "Have you received your posting?"

She was happy for him, and this was going to be easy, Thomas thought. Aloud, he said, "Fanny dear, my ship has come in. I'm a captain with a command of my own. And I am off at once on a secret mission."

William saw her eyes light up with the warmth and affection that would make a man trade his life for a kiss. "That's wonderful!" she exclaimed, then became sad. "But you will be leaving me?"

"That is why I have picked tonight to ask you something special."

Instantly Fanny began to distance herself from him, until he removed the ring from his pocket. "It's for you," Thomas said, his voice quivering.

She gasped at the blinding sparkle of the stone. "It's exquisite, Thomas!" She kissed him passionately.

Pulling away from him, she took the ring away as well, sliding it on her finger. "Dear Thomas," she gushed, "you got me something to show that you'll be faithful while you're away." She kissed him again. Then she dragged him over to the far side of the crowded auditorium to show Jane the wonderful going away gift he had given her.

William realized that pride would not let Thomas change his mind. Thomas apparently feared that if he did say that the token of the ring should mean more than just his love for her, she might reject the offer. The moment was over; for now, the opportunity lost.

While William reflected on his friend's bondage,

wishing there were a graceful way to intervene, he spotted a familiar face in the crowd. *It couldn't be,* William thought, imagining that a woman he saw dancing with a young, handsome cavalier was Dora Donspy. His heart lurched as the lissome form disappeared behind the rotating pairs of bodies.

Though arguing reasonably with himself that it could not be her, he could not shake the thought. What if it was? The haunting visage, however briefly glimpsed, reflected perfect contentment in the other man's arms. That would explain why Dora had not answered his letters.

He was frozen in place when the couple came twirling around again. As the song ended, the man kissed his partner affectionately on the cheek.

William's eyes met those of the young woman. His heart hit the floor, and she looked as if she were staring at the face of a ghost. "Dora!" William cried despairingly. "Dora!" he called again, running to her side to catch her arms.

Her gaze clouded. She slumped in Nicholas Parry's arms. "William," she gasped as her eyes rolled back in her head. "But you are dead!"

Dozens of guests huddled around them. Soon the music stopped. "Dead? What does she mean I am dead?"

Nicholas was hotly defensive. "She told me about you!" he said. "Keep back!"

William was baffled and overwhelmed by the sight of her with another man, another man who shouted things at him and belittled him in the middle of a crowded room.

"Did she not get my letters?" Why did she not hear him and explain? "Dora! Dora, wake up! Tell him it's not true!"

"Yes, she got your letters," Nicholas asserted over Dora's unconscious form. "They upset her greatly." Nicholas cradled the young woman in his arms. "Stay away from my fiancée, you madman." He appealed to the crowd. "Look what this chap has done. Someone help me! This man is drunk!"

More people gathered around. There was chatter and speculation about what William had done to the poor girl. He became sick to his stomach, weakened by the whole ordeal. When a pair of porters seized him, he could not even resist. "Please sir," one said politely but pointedly, "leave the young lady alone and come along without any trouble."

Finding himself on the sidewalk in the night air woke him from his spell. His ears were throbbing. The voices of those watching, the clatter of hooves on the street, even the sound of his breathing swirled together into confusion.

Attempting to go back up the steps, William was chased down by the porters. He staggered into the street, nearly getting run down by a hansom cab. "How did this happen?" he moaned. He did not see Nicholas Parry whisper to one of the porters and press money into the man's hand.

William wandered for several blocks. The champagne added to his confusion as he walked the street alone. He heard a noise behind him and stopped. Afraid to look back, he listened. When at last he spun around, he was startled at the sight of a figure cloaked and hooded in black.

"William," a woman called in a mysterious voice.

Chills shot through William's body as he wondered if this might be his time to die. Was this the messenger of death, come to call him to account?

The woman made her way along the street toward him, seemingly gliding above the ground. He saw dark lips move on a pallid face before he even heard the words.

"William, I have come to take you somewhere." She appeared to hover right up to him. "This concerns your life, your name, and your family."

William churned the possibilities over and over in his head. "Who are you, and what do you want?"

"You must come with me."

As she got closer, William could see that she was as scared of him, if not more so, as he was of her. She trembled as she spoke. "William, I have come with news of Judy."

"Judy?" William whispered. It was a name he had stopped thinking of months before. What could it mean?

Lord Sutton strode boldly to the cart of liquors and spirits set out for him by Hugh Popham and chose for himself a fine brandy. Dinner had long passed, and the drawing room of Sutton Manor was saturated with the smoke of ten expensive cigars, smoked by Lord Sutton's gentlemen guests.

The dinner company varied in prominence in the English government, but had been summoned by Sutton to discuss military contracts with his shipping company.

He paced the room, cigar in one hand, snifter in the other, speaking authoritatively on the matters at hand. His guests encircled him, seated meekly on the furniture as pupils being lectured by an intimidating schoolmaster.

"I do not mean to tell you your strategy, gentlemen," he pronounced, then proceeded to do so anyway. Lord Sutton trod the wooden planks of the dining room until they met the marble floor of the manor's entryway, then spun abruptly, each pass brimming with advice. "England has the monetary capability to dispatch other ships . . . my ships . . . in place of your military vessels, thereby freeing yours for the more important matter of winning this war. In other words, giving greater employment to Sutton ships will move your supplies more efficiently and cost-effectively."

He leaned heavily on the stone fireplace, pointing with his dying cigar at the captive audience. "We know that the sooner this matter is put to rest, the cheaper it will be for Mother England."

At last he hesitated long enough to swig the brandy and gave enough time for one man to speak. But the men looked at each other questioningly, wondering who would be first, and the delay was catastrophic.

Sutton continued, "I am not asking for more money . . . never. But if these contracts are not renewed or fail to be more extensive than before, I cannot be held responsible for the fate of our nation. You gentlemen . . ." He stabbed the air with his now lifeless cigar for effect. "Yours shall be the heads to roll."

The gentlemen were pummeled and weary as Sutton strode to refill his glass. Seated there were ten of the highest-ranking decision makers in England's government, including Admiral Cornwallis, Sea Lord Malcolm, and Minister Pollard. Yet none could find words to reply, except for Andrew Woodford.

Woodford was not big in comparison to Lord Sutton, but had known him longer than anyone else present. They had been schoolmates together, played and fought with each other, and continued fighting together during their mutual service in England's forces. In that service, Woodford had lost his eyes, the victim of a misfired weapon. Lord Sutton had been lucky that day, as it was Woodford who had been standing in Sutton's normal position.

Woodford's life was not without difficulties, but he was very independent, requiring help only when he traveled. Consequently, he had an attendant known only as Tim, who journeyed with him everywhere.

Sutton and Woodford had the gravest respect for one another, and though Sutton towered above him, Woodford drew himself up and spoke. "Randolph, you have noted time and again the benefit you can be to your country, but I don't believe these gentlemen will be impressed unless you openly admit what charms these contracts have to you."

"Well sir, I shall tell you." Lord Sutton corked his brandy, offering no refill to his patient listeners. "For my undying devotion to your transport needs, for my readiness to embark at a hound's cry, I shall be the foremost shipping magnate at the end of this conflict. When this is over, my willingness to work, even at substantial risk to my ships and property, will have been a venture worth the gamble. Business will have been steady, and I might even expand during the years to come, better suiting me to carry on normally after this mess is over."

His guests nodded and Woodford bobbed his head, proud at the frankness with which Lord Randolph Sutton could discuss his ambitions. Woodford turned toward the nine seated and spoke again. "You see, gentlemen, he is an honest businessman, capable of the utmost quality in service and value to us because it is proper business to do so. Please enjoy Randolph's hospitality as you continue your deliberations."

As low-voiced discussions occurred in pairs and trios around the group, Sutton inwardly fumed over not being able to hear all at once. Woodford reached out to him and clapped him on the back, drawing him away. Woodford could tell the general conversations were in favor of Sutton. "Fret not," he said, sensing Sutton's tension. "I know you have won their hearts, if not yet the money entrusted to them."

Woodford could not and Sutton did not notice the signal that passed between Sea Lord Malcolm and Pollard. These two drew apart from the rest to conduct their conference, but not so far as to cause remark.

Woodford and Lord Sutton prolonged their own side conversation, and the entire group helped themselves to another round of drinks and cigars each, to the unregarded displeasure of Lord Sutton. It was costing him what he would call "an excessive sum" for luxuries, but yet he experienced enormous gratitude for Woodford. The blind man had managed to bring the decision makers together at this important engagement.

Long after the crowd had dispersed, the old friends sat up and talked. Bachelors, one by death, one by choice, they spoke of bygone times and loves lost, well past respectable hours.

Even the servants had retired, with Sutton's reluctant permission and Woodford's cajoling, though Woodford's attendant, Tim, now sat alone in the great kitchen drinking coffee. They were indulging in the memory of the cause of one of their most violent rows, a girl named Dorothea whom Sutton had successfully wooed away from Woodford before their service in the navy. Sutton later lost her to the embrace of consumption.

During the recital of those fond memories came a bold, resonant knock at the stately front door.

Lord Sutton wrested it open with an expression of malice, intent on spurning the intruder for the late disruption to his respectable household. He was cut off by a uniformed messenger who spoke only these urgent words before dashing back to the carriage that awaited them both. "Please sir, you must attend. It is about your grandson."

Sutton sputtered until Woodford approached, feeling his way along the wall. "Go," he said, "I shall find my way home."

Lord Sutton alighted in the carriage and was gone.

Albert had been locked in the cell for some time, wondering if anyone believed his story enough to actually send for Lord Sutton. He had seen and marveled at the great city only briefly on the twilight ride in the prisoner carriage en route to the Tower of London. His clothes had never fully dried, and the damp chill of the stone walls was inescapable. He paced constantly to try to return warmth to his bones.

His steps reverberated strangely in the confined space, coming both from everywhere and nowhere at once. In the iron door before him was a tiny rectangular opening where trays of food could be slid in to the prisoners. Albert had asked for food, but the sergeant who placed him in the cell merely laughed, locking the substantial bolt behind him. "Hope someone confirms your story," he had said as he walked down the hall, "or we shall give you your fill of lead shot!"

Vaguely, Albert guessed at what Colonel Ney was thinking then, having lost a soldier after just acquiring him. "He would rather have me dead," Albert muttered, "than safe with the English." But Albert knew he was not secure yet. Not until someone found Lord Sutton, and even then it was a considerable gamble.

The block of holding cells had been silent except for Albert's pacing. The hour was nearing three in the morning. With each step, the exhaustion of his ordeal slowed him down, body and mind. His head began to hang, and his arms uncrossed from his chest, dangling at his sides and releasing the warmth they had captured. He shuffled ever slower, eyes closed, waiting for the familiar touch of the wall where he would revolve and travel the route again. His thoughts wandered, drifting to Angelique, and he wondered if she had had their child yet. He hoped she was in a protected place, sheltered and comfortable, and not too anxious for him.

As he stopped the pacing and stood instead, swaying, eyes shut and near sleep in the center of the cell, he heard a noise. A rusty groan echoed faintly down the corridor outside, followed by voices. One was quiet, which Albert recognized as the sergeant's; another was obnoxiously loud.

He forced his eyes open and turned to face the door as they neared his cell. The sergeant outside called for some guards to attend as he twisted the key in the lock. Albert stepped backward and leaned against the wall as he heard the second voice bellow, "What do you mean pulled on board? What is the meaning of this?"

The door swung open with another complaint of the corroded hinges, and Albert was confronted by four men: the guards who entered the cell, the sergeant, and another white-haired gentleman who remained outside.

"William," the old man cried, "just what is happening—" The man's query was cut short as his eyes widened at the sight of Albert. All present were silent as the elderly man scanned Albert from brow to toe. Flustered by his gaze, Albert looked at the floor.

"Do you know him, sir?" the sergeant asked the distinguished looking man.

"Of course I do," Lord Sutton replied. "That appears to be my grandson ... *Charles*."

Albert was relieved but unimpressed. He had thought that, after all the miles he had traveled, through all the dangers he had come, he would know at first sight whether this man, Lord Randolph Sutton, was truly his grandfather and William his brother. Instead he was as unsure as the sergeant, relying on Lord Sutton to tell him whether or not it was the case.

Even as he was led from the cell, he was of despondent heart. Wrenched away from the woman he regarded as his beloved grandmother, and now from Angelique, what had he received in return? He had never felt so unsure of his place in the world.

# CHAPTER 9

A sober William entered a hallway. The door creaked behind him. It was almost colder there than it had been outside. William wondered how he had ever been talked into coming with this unknown woman. For all he knew it could be a trap of some kind, though he sensed it was somehow much more serious.

"Let me turn up the lamp," the woman said.

William had not even asked her name. He had not even thought to ask. She acted as though she knew everything about him.

The entryway reeked of rotting wood. As the lantern warmed from orange to yellow, he could see the building was truly a slum. Moldy, water-streaked cracks stained the wall. Fallen plaster littered the corridor.

The hooded woman led him to another door at the back. It was narrow and swollen. As she yanked it free from the jam, it snapped open, revealing a steep, rickety set of bare, wooden steps. As William followed warily behind, he was reminded of a barn his family had demolished after taking over a property. That structure had been deemed unsuitable for animals.

The basement room was slightly warmer, just enough to make the dank odors even more profound. Ducking his head at the last step, his eyes were drawn to a candle by a bed, where a red-haired woman was sleeping. William walked cautiously to her.

"Judy." The hooded figure gently shook the woman in bed. "Judy, he's here."

This Judy was not like William remembered her. Her once fiery hair was matted and dull, and when she opened her eyes, they did not sparkle like green emeralds and lock his gaze upon them. Instead his stare was riveted upon her vacant expression as she searched languidly, without apparent interest.

"William?" she whispered, almost too softly for him to hear.

William hesitated, but there was no running, no denying that he was present. "Yes, Judy. I'm here."

She reached for him. "William, William, William," was all she could mutter.

He offered his hand, his words calm and sympathetic. "Yes, Judy. I'm here." He wondered what this news was that was so important. What was it she must tell him in the midst of such illness? "What is it?"

She wrestled to face him. "William." A single tear formed in her eye, hanging for a moment before trickling down her nose and cheek. "Sit down . . . I must tell you something that concerns you greatly . . ."

"I prefer to stand. Tell me, what is this important news?"

"I am very ill, William. I have childbed fever."

Her words hammered him. *Childbed fever,* he thought. *She has borne a baby.* He denied the fears that the baby could be his—that was what the entire visit was about. *But my name, my life, and my family,* he recalled. "Tell me, Judy."

Judy breathed laboriously. "I have had your child."

William said nothing in return. He rejected the notion, remembering the way she used to be—a liar and a tramp. "How could it be my child?" he questioned, thinking back to the date he had last seen her.

Sensing his refusal to believe, she became restless. "April, William. We were together last April. That day in the field. The field of flowers you took me to."

William remembered their picnic, the way she looked that day in a pretty, white dress. He saw her sitting in the tall grass, with the hills covered in purples, pinks, and yellows. He saw himself leaning close to her for a kiss that day. He quickly opened his eyes, shocked when he saw the reality there again.

"That was two months after I broke up with Bristol Sims," she insisted.

"But how do I know that you didn't see him again? How do I know the child is not his, or someone else's?"

She pulled his hand to her. "Look, William," she called desperately. "The child is there . . . there in his bed . . ."

Afraid at what he might find, William rotated slowly around. In the corner of the room near the stove sat the shadow of a young girl on a rocking chair by a wooden crate. Her scared eyes shone in the darkness. *Poor girl*, William thought. *How could anyone survive in these conditions?* As he looked more closely, he saw that the child's face was dirty and bony. Her clothes were in rags.

"Come here, Sallie," the hooded woman instructed. "Come, let the nice gentleman sit there." She brought the lantern over, setting it on a board shelf. "There in the bed, Master William." She motioned to the crate.

William crept to it, leaning over to peer in. Wrapped in tattered sheets and holey blankets, was a baby, fast asleep.

"He looks just like you," Judy said, smiling.

William recalled a portrait of himself as a child, of his brother, too, before he was swept away. This infant had his nose, straight and symmetrical, with a round knob on the end. The baby's cheeks were like his, and the chin was wide and would someday be very masculine. William cringed. The muscles in his neck and forehead tightened, and he struggled to breathe, doing so only in spastic gasps. Moisture overflowed his eyes as he saw what was undeniably his child.

Judy watched him, sinking back down as she relaxed. "He is so handsome, William. Won't you hold him?"

Angry and at the same time overwhelmed with the idea of an enormous responsibility, William searched the room. "Why does the child not have a proper bed?"

Judy's expression saddened, growing worried. "It was all I could find. He was born right here, and I have not left since."

"Why is it so cold in here? A child will die in these conditions."

"I'm sorry, William. I had nothing else to do. For a long time, Bristol thought it was his, until right before he went to jail. He beat me up so badly, I had to hide." Judy began to sob uncontrollably.

William collapsed into the feeble chair. He realized it was not only her fault. It was as much his. To do such a thing as he did to someone who had no other means, and without any kind of commitment. His head fell into his hands. Judy cried herself to sleep.

Time passed. Finally the woman in black took Sallie and started to leave the room. "I will leave you two alone," she said.

"No!" William exclaimed. "You mustn't go outside with your child. It is bitterly cold, and she is hardly clothed." He thought of the baby and then of Judy. Suddenly, concerned for Judy, he whispered, "How sick is she?"

The woman held her girl close and said to William, "She may die soon. Childbed fever is a bad thing, Master William. She has been sick for a long time."

William crossed his arms. "When will the doctor come see her again?"

"Doctor, sir? She has no money for a doctor."

"No doctor!" William raised his voice. "Who has been caring for her?"

"Myself, but there is nothing to be done."

"This is ludicrous. The child cannot survive without his mother. You must go at once to a doctor. Do you know where one is?"

"Yes, but Master William, he will not come without money, and of that I have none."

"Here," he said, taking a gold coin from his pocket.

"Leave your child with me and run and fetch the doctor. Tell him it is most urgent."

Setting the child down, the woman held the coin in her open hand. It was more money in one piece than she had ever seen in her life. "Yes, Master William, I will hurry." Turning to Sallie, she said, "Master William will stay with you. Do as he says."

The child barely muttered yes as the black-cloaked woman rushed off.

William sat a long time in the chair, watching Judy and his baby sleep. He wondered where Sallie's father was, so he asked her. She did not answer him, her expression showing plainly that the question carried no meaning to her at all. He thought of the tiny baby and what his life would be like if he had no father to care for him.

He wanted to run away. Dora was lost, and now this news in the same night. He thought about what would happen if Judy should die. There would be no one to care for the baby . . . his baby.

He sighed and stood to his feet, running his hands through his hair. This poor, poor child. He leaned close to the sleeping baby boy, realizing that he did not even know his name. *Oh God, I pray that this child will not end up in a workhouse somewhere, laboring and starving.* His heart ached for this innocent life, a life he knew he would feel responsible for, for the rest of his own.

Remembering how reassuring it felt to hug his mother or his grandfather when he was afraid or alone, William realized that with how sick Judy was, the child was probably rarely held. He slid his hands under the light bundle. It weighed almost nothing, he thought, cradling it close. The infant stirred, and William spoke kind words to him with loving eyes. "Are you hungry?" he asked. Thinking again of Judy's illness, he wondered how the child even ate.

"William," Judy's voice said faintly from behind him.

He faced her. "What is it?"

"William is his name." She looked longingly at him. "I named him after his father, so that one day he will grow up to be as good as you."

"I was terrible to you, Judy." William's voice trembled with pain. "Nothing like a good man."

"Oh, but William, I know what kind of man you will become. God has told me."

William thought of Father Vickers and what he had said. The entire balance of the world might hang on William and on the decision he must make for this child. He recalled Father Donspy and the acorn, then drove away the thoughts of Dora. "William," he whispered.

"Baby Will. You will be fine." He moved to Judy's bed-side. Handing her the child, he knelt down.

Watching them together, he was convicted anew for what he had done. It was nothing he ever would have planned but could never deny now that Baby Will was here. "Judy . . . I'm sorry."

She struggled to open her eyes. He saw in them a sweetness, the innocent pleasure in simple things, that every child has and that she'd had when she was a girl. "You're forgiven, William."

"I don't know what to say." He shook with confusion but was not afraid to admit his guilt. "I . . . I realize that this is no other child than mine."

Judy waited a long time before adding anything. "William, I'm afraid. I don't want the child to end up in an orphanage, a workhouse. I love him so much, and I don't want him to end up dead if I should die."

"I promise that whatever happens, this child will be cared for."

"I don't want you to think I am trying to take your money. I don't want—"

"I know, I know," he said to hush her. "God has given me a son. For whatever reason, He has planned it this way. And I will not run from this challenge."

The door at the top of the stairs popped as the woman returned. William heard two sets of feet coming down. He stood to greet the doctor, a grim-faced man both distinguished and thoughtful. He met William's handshake with cynicism. The summary in his eyes announced his already prepared conclusion: *a man gets a girl pregnant, feels guilty, and wants me to save the woman so he doesn't feel obligated when he leaves her and the child forever.*

William said nothing, but motioned toward Judy.

"Are you awake, miss?" the physician questioned.

"Yes, sir."

"I must examine you." He turned to William. "You may want to leave the room, sir . . . ?"

"William is my name."

"Master William. Wait a moment, sir. I have questions for you."

William was concerned about the procedure. Would the doctor be able to do anything? He expressed these worries. "And what of the child? He is very thin, and I am afraid she will not be able to care for him."

"I know of a wet nurse, but she will be expensive to hire for full-time care and feeding."

"It doesn't matter. This child must be cared for until his mother has recovered enough to resume."

"Indeed, then. And what of the mother's care?"

William knew the man was referring to the expense of his services. A human life was wasting away for lack of nothing but money. "I will provide what you need, sir."

"Very well, then. What you have paid me will be sufficient for me to call on her twice daily for the next week." He nodded, handing William a calling card. "Come to my practice on Harley Street in several days' time, and we will sort out the terms."

Looking vaguely at the card before putting it away, William turned to the mother of his child. "Judy, be well." He kissed her on the cheek, then kissed the baby.

The expression on her face showed her anxiety that she would never see William again, but what she said was, "Thank you."

With the full weight of responsibility on his shoulders he could not reply and only nodded.

Out in the street, the night was frigid, the ground frozen and unreliable like his thoughts. He rounded the corner, wondering how he would find his way home, and then reality hit him again. He fell to the ground, shaking uncontrollably. "My God! Is this what I deserve? And what does my baby deserve? What?"

Albert Penfeld was impressed with the Sutton house when they arrived there, taking into account the lavish grounds and stately, pillared entrance. Once inside he was shown to a seat in the Suttons' great drawing room while Lord Sutton shook Hugh Popham awake to make them coffee. There had been a steady barrage of questions in the carriage, and Albert was glad to be rid of Lord Sutton for a few minutes.

As he rested on the plush furniture, he gazed about him. The grand staircase filled one entire wall of the foyer, curving majestically up and around to a second floor of rooms. The walls were adorned with paintings, and in each corner stood a marble sculpture.

Lord Sutton returned, soon followed by Popham wheeling a cart of coffee and tea. The steward stared at Albert in disbelief as he poured their cups.

Albert knew Lord Sutton was so awed with his grandson Charles's prodigal return that he humored his supposed grandfather's desire to remain awake and talk, though what Albert wanted was sleep. The endless questions bored him, the more so since he wanted to learn about his new surroundings rather than talk about his upbringing. But he answered the inquiries patiently, trying to glean what he could of Lord Sutton by the impressive manor in which they sat. This room, Albert noted, reeked of stale cigar smoke.

Eventually the sun began to rise, and Albert could see the first lavender rays detailing the shrubs outside the broad windows. He wondered if his exhaustion showed as he answered mindlessly, allowing his thoughts to drift instead. Over and over he told himself this was not his family, was not his home.

*Even if we are related,* he mused.

"And tell me again," Lord Sutton droned on, "about the woman you called your grandmother."

For the third or possibly fourth time Albert related the stories about Heloise: with what wonderful invention she had told of his mother and father, how she took such loving care of him, and the tasty dishes she would cook.

Albert hated the way this perfect stranger dissected his memories, commenting repeatedly on the ironies of Albert having a "real" family in a different country. Lord Sutton grunted with amusement every time he heard another ironic statement pass.

"I was never interested in England," Albert noted. "I have always been French."

Lord Sutton grunted.

Though Albert knew Lord Sutton was trying to make him feel welcome and to catch up on the lifetime of memories lost to one another, Albert felt ever more lonely for France and the family he had there. His mind searched for Angelique, wishing he had seen her surroundings and could visualize her in them.

Just because he was not originally meant to live there, to grow up there in France, did that mean he did not have a life there? He wondered if Lord Sutton could understand that.

"May I," Albert interrupted, "ask some questions of you?" Sutton nodded. "Who should I have been if I did not grow up in France?"

Though Albert meant it rhetorically, Lord Sutton tried to answer.

"Well, Charles . . . I mean Albert . . . I shall never get used to that. You should have been joint heir to the second largest shipping concern in Britain. In this house you would have grown to manhood and enlisted in the armed services of England instead of France, just as your brother, your twin brother, William, did a short time ago."

Lord Sutton paused, his eyes rolling upward as if he were struck on the head. "My boy, we shall have a feast!" He rose from his seat followed by the volume of his voice. "As the father of parable welcomed back his prodigal son, so shall we embrace—"

Albert's view of the front door was obstructed, but he heard it open, and light flooded the room.

"William!" Lord Sutton cried.

"Grandfather," Albert heard another voice say from the entryway. He recognized it as the man who spoke to him in the water that day months ago at the Battle of Trafalgar.

"I must speak with you," William resumed.

"But William," Lord Sutton tried to continue, "there is—"

"Grandfather, hear me!" William interrupted again.

Expecting him to enter, Albert rose from his seat, but William remained speaking from just out of sight.

"Grandfather, I have trouble. I need your help."

"But, William . . . ," Lord Sutton insisted.

A creak on the stair from behind Albert caused Lord Sutton to stop, and they both turned. There above them stood the weak yet graceful figure of Lady Julia Sutton.

Albert stared up at her with wide eyes and gaping mouth. Distantly he heard the approaching steps of William.

She spoke to Albert, her voice floating delicately down on the same gentle draft that rippled her night-dress. "Charles."

Albert was seized inside, bound in thought and breath. He stood dimly recalling that sweet voice, that tender face. Then tears streamed from his eyes. A tremendous weight pressed upon his heart, and he knew he was among his family. "Mother!" he called out to her, falling to his knees.

With elegant haste she swept down the stairs, embracing Albert to her breast.

For some time there was no word spoken in the

house, only the sound of joyous cries coming from the reunited mother and son.

William came from his place in the entryway and stood beside his grandfather to watch, the tears welling in his eyes too. His brother had come home. Of his own dramatic revelation, so urgently pressing only moments earlier, he would say nothing; he decided to bear the burden alone until another day.

As a mother's instinct was to care for her child, Albert was in bed, instructed to do nothing but rest for days to come. His return had given Lady Julia purpose, and from a sofa she gave orders to ensure his comfort and recovery.

*Though,* Albert thought, *she cannot possibly know all I have lived through to get here.*

Lady Julia put an end to Lord Sutton's thoughts of a grand feast for celebration. Albert was supposed to be asleep, but he heard them discussing it.

"I will not have him scrutinized or gawked at by your friends," Julia said.

"But Julia," pleaded Lord Sutton, "I only wish to make the boy feel welcome."

"He does not need a welcome from people he does not know. It will be hard enough for him to become accustomed to us."

Albert strained to hear as the conversation moved elsewhere but knew Lady Julia defeated Lord Sutton.

Midday passed outside the shuttered windows, flashing streaks of light across the room, and for hours Albert was unable to sleep. Not that he was any less tired or more rested, but thoughts kept surfacing about his business in England and his family back home. He continually brooded about the safety of Angelique and their child.

*What might happen to them,* he pondered, *if I do not begin to perform my duties for France, potentially risking the lives and property of my newfound family? And what of the risk to my own, now that I have twice as much reason to live? What service do I owe a country that would send me away from my wife at such a time for us?*

Albert finally drifted to sleep, deciding to forestall any decision until he was sure he might make the correct one. Yet even while he slept in the artificially shadowed room, Albert's restless mind searched for the light.

# CHAPTER 10

Dora Donspy awoke in a dreamlike state and walked sightlessly to a chair. It was six o'clock and not even beginning to grow light. Sitting at a table by the window in her room, she stared lifelessly out through the lacy sash at the well-kept green across the London street.

A flock of doves circled beneath the morning sky, swooping out, fading from sight, then circling back; their endless rhythm hypnotic. Dora's mind meshed with the vastness of the sky. Her thoughts swooped away and back, looking for answers, but there was no possibility of finding anything definite or satisfying.

Time stood still. Dora hovered between waking and slumber while day came. The sun, as if speeded up at last, shot piercing rays when it peeked above the houses of London.

Then the vision came, like a candle driving shadows away from the corners of a room: William. Dora went to him. She felt secure, as if she had recently roused from a nightmare and he was there to comfort her. But when she wrapped her arms around him, called his name, she became the flame, and like the candle, he, too, melted away.

A maid entered, leaving tea and toast. Dora took no notice of the butter melting away into soggy bread. It seemed like forever before she even moved.

She heard footsteps and boards creaking, then a hand at the door. The knocks sounded minutes apart. Then they speeded up, faster and faster, until she heard a voice. What did it say? There was the rap again and finally . . .

"Dora?" Nicholas Parry called. "Dora, I say, are you decent?"

She snapped awake, as if water had been thrown in her face. "I'm fine, Nicholas," she said, wiping her eyes.

"May I come in?"

"No."

He waited before responding. "Dora, I've been worried about you since you collapsed last night. The maid said that she entered your room this morning, and you did nothing but stare straight ahead. Is everything all right?"

"I'm fine," she said, sniffing. "Everything is fine." But she knew her words and tone were not convincing.

"It's about this William chap, isn't it?"

"No . . ."

"It was terrible what he did to you, knowing that people who cared about him thought he had been killed, and yet he made no attempt to contact them."

*How did he know?* Her voice wavered, then she managed to respond, "Yes."

"What he did was thoughtless, Dora. You mustn't hold on to fond thoughts of a man like this. He's despicable and . . . there's more."

She listened, wanting to believe anything that would make her stop hurting, help her breathe again.

"Last night, when he was drunk and was thrown out, I thought it might be best to find out about this chap. So I sent the footman to follow him."

Dora stopped sniffling. "What did you find?"

"He has a child, Dora, in a slum. He fathered an illegitimate child with some woman. This is no rumor. My man met the doctor, who said William did not deny it."

Dora suddenly felt frozen. She remembered hearing from William of the things he had done in the past, but supposedly he had changed. William acted as if he were different when he was in Branson Fen. Could this be true? Might it not be a dreadful mistake? Then Dora recalled a name William had mentioned. What was it? "What is the woman's name, Nicholas?"

He paused only a second before answering. "Judy. No last name, of course, but Judy is what the doctor said."

Dora nodded to herself. That was it. That was the name she had heard. It was all true. William was despicable, and the good things he did in the community were performed only so he might get what he wanted. That was why he had left. She was drained and alone.

"Dora," Nicholas prompted, "there's something I want to ask you."

"What is it?"

"May I come in?"

"No." She thought a moment about her loneliness. She needed someone to hold, someone to hold her. "Yes."

Nicholas turned the knob slowly. He entered, walking to her bedside with one arm behind his back. Kneeling before Dora on the rug, he vowed, "I want you to know I will never hurt you as he has hurt you." He held her hand tightly. "I want to take care of you, see that you are happy and well."

Dora knew what was coming but was not fearful. She had already been through the worst. Things could only get better.

He peered into her saddened, bloodshot eyes. "Will you marry me?" He retrieved from behind his back a yellow daffodil and laid it on her lap.

*An answer from my father!* she exclaimed to herself. *This must be what he wants for me. Things will get better presently,* she decided, watching the doves in her mind carry away her sorrow. But her heart was still ready to take flight. She forced herself to banish her doubts. "Yes," she said.

"More linen!" The midwife's voice was audible through the doors and down the stairs where Phillippe and Claudette waited anxiously for news. Claudette dashed to the laundry cupboard for yet another stack of the manor's expensive bedding for use upstairs.

The process had begun late the evening before, as dessert was being served in the formal dining room. Phillippe had scampered about in terror, followed closely by his wife, until Angelique calmly gave them instructions.

"Phillippe," she said, "no child will wait for dessert, not on his first appearance. Go and fetch the midwife. Claudette, please help me upstairs."

The midwife, a toothless woman named Melina, smelled of drink, but she was thoroughly competent and comforting to Angelique. "Three hundred French babies have I birthed," she said after the introduction. "And no complaints have I had."

Once Angelique was installed in her bed, neither Claudette nor Phillippe entered her room again unless called by the midwife to do so. Though it had happened only twice in the night, once for linens and once for hot water, the servants remained awake, thoroughly frightened of the goings-on upstairs.

"More linens!" Melina shouted again, just as Claudette entered the room.

Angelique managed a smile for Claudette when she came in and even inquired as to her well-being. Stricken, Claudette dropped the bundle and exited the room without responding.

"Hush now," Melina said. "You need not think of anyone else at such a time."

Angelique had been silent through the entire process, never once raising her voice or crying out, only breathing as Melina instructed and pushing when commanded.

"*Bon!*" Melina said soothing. "Here he comes."

Angelique tried to sit up. "He?" she exclaimed. "Are you sure?"

"Quite sure," Melina said, chuckling. "Now, once more . . ."

Claudette and Phillippe listened attentively from the

bottom of the staircase. No sound had come to their ears for some time.

"Do you think—" Phillippe began, but his wife cut him off.

"Silence," she directed, once again listening.

Suddenly a loud cry erupted from the room, startling the waiting servants.

"*Mon Dieu!*" Phillippe cried. "She is dying. We shall be blamed!" He started to ascend the stairs but stopped when the door above him opened.

Melina stood above them with tired satisfaction on her wrinkled face. "It is a boy," she said. "You may visit them if you wish." She made her way to the kitchen to clean her hands in the pot of water being heated there.

Claudette and Phillippe raced up the stairs together, arriving in Angelique's room out of breath.

Lying on the bed, her hair dewed with the sweat of labor, Angelique held a bundle close to her breast. She gazed at the child so intensely that she did not even notice the pair of servants enter. Even in the tiny face Angelique could see the resemblance to Albert. And though the child's eyes were but newly opened to the world, they seemed firmly fixed on her face too. A tear trickled down her cheek and landed on the baby's hand.

"For you, my love," she said, "tears of joy. And for your father, of hope."

———— 〰 ————

"Dead, sir."

"She can't be!" William said, shocked. "I saw her yesterday, just last night."

"I'm sorry, Master. William. Judy passed on this morning. The infection was advanced, and there was nothing to be done. Indeed, I cannot think how she lived as long as she did."

Confusion set in. The world seemed to be moving so fast for William that he could hardly hold himself up. He collapsed into a leather upholstered armchair.

Surprised and thinking to cheer William up, the doctor said, "I thought this would be welcome news to you. You are free from your obligations."

There was a pause before the man's words sunk in, and for a moment William wanted to agree. No one would ever even know about Judy or the child. He could go on and live his life as if nothing had ever happened.

Then William realized what the physician was actually suggesting. He thought of Charles's life, and it made him furious at himself to even think such a thing. He glared up at the physician and jumped to his feet. "Free in what way! Free from having to see the child? Am I free to abandon my baby to a workhouse? Better yet, maybe I can sell him!" He charged at the doctor.

The doctor stumbled over his words and feet. "I . . . I'm sorry. Most unusual. I . . ."

"Don't bother explaining." William shook his fist in the man's face, gritting his strong, angular jaw. "Should I buy my freedom with my own flesh and blood?"

Backed against a table with his hands before his face, the doctor cowered and could go no farther. The clerk must have heard the cries of the frightened man for he opened the door and stood frozen, watching the ordeal.

"Is that how you handle illegitimate children? Pass them off on some doorstep?" William's green eyes turned a pale yellow. Like a snake's eyes, they were fixed on the man, ready to strike. William's fingers dug into his palms as he leaned forward, his face inches from the doctor's. "Now sir, you quack physician, you will take care of that child. That child will live to see a long life, or his blood will be on your head."

The physician weakly motioned his concurrence. "The money you gave me will be adequate for the wet nurse for quite some time."

"Excellent! I will make other arrangements in the meantime." William slammed his fist on the mother-of-pearl and walnut-inlaid top of the desk. The wood made a cracking noise, and the man jumped. William did not even blink. His words were intimidating as he said harshly, "Good day!" The clerk scurried from his path.

Once on the street, William was an entirely different person. Inside he was weak and afraid. *What will I do?* he pondered. *I cannot go on allowing someone else to take care of this poor child for the rest of his life. To be raised having never known who your family is, like my brother, Charles. Charles has lived the same life as me in years, but his thoughts and memories are entirely different.*

"I must make money to care for this child," William said out loud as the direction came to him. "Yes, I will work for my grandfather." *The child is all that matters,* he decided. There was no longer any room for selfishness in William's life.

The most immediate problem was telling Grandfather Sutton. William knew the news would anger him. He might even turn William out into the street. What future would he or the child have then?

William stared blankly into the sky. "God help me," he whispered. His eyes cleared, and he swallowed hard. Realizing what he must do, he said, "Somehow, I must try."

Albert strode from Sutton Manor in the early morning air. He was uncertain as to his real purpose in leaving that day, hoping the long walk around Hampstead Heath might result in straighter thinking before his arrival at an unwanted but essential destination.

Though many Londoners stirred around him, Albert was alone in his thoughts for the entire journey. A great many times he was nodded at by passing gentlemen and smiled at by ladies, but his eyes focused far beyond his immediate surroundings. He examined instead problems that lay in wait, some immediate and some deferred into the future.

The ramble up the high road took Albert past Jack Straw's Castle Pub. It had been a site of profound humiliation for his brother, but Albert did not know this. His travels also carried him near a hostelry known as The Spaniards, and outside the grounds of the stately manor called Kenwood House.

By mid-afternoon Albert had solved none of his dilemmas, but the appointed time of meeting was nearing, and he dared delay no longer. Retracing his steps down the hill, he diverted from Heath Street onto Flask Walk and Well Walk where, in the previous century, wealthy Londoners had journeyed to taste the curative waters of Hampstead Spa.

Reaching the corner of Church Row, Albert involuntarily glanced over his shoulder. There was no particular reason why he should do this, nor did he see anything unusual. A nondescript man in a shabby brown coat and muddy green trousers did take an abrupt interest in a butcher's window, but Albert made nothing of that. Despite having rediscovered his English roots, Albert could not help giving a very French shrug at his unnecessary suspicions, and he walked on, turning right at the Anglican Church of St. John, Hampstead.

Arriving at the address given to him in his instructions, Albert was baffled. It seemed to be an ordinary brick house in a block of others, all similar, middle-class, and English.

For a long time he waited outside, expecting to see someone enter or exit that might give him insight as to the validity of the address.

He waited an hour, but no one came or went. Then, as evening began to fall, he heard a single voice singing softly in Latin with a distinctly French accent. The melody floated out of an upstairs window and then other voices joined in, singing the Magnificat, the Virgin's hymn of praise. The reverent singers appeared to be careful not to let their volume swell to be obvious out-of-doors, but it was no less devout for that concern.

Though most of the words were lost, the meaning was clear: "My soul does magnify the Lord" and "My spirit exults in God my Savior." As the words filled his ears, Albert knew he had found what he was seeking.

This apparently ordinary house was actually a church, a spiritual home to the French Catholic population of London. Though not officially allowed free religious expression in Protestant England, the congregation had nevertheless existed for some time to serve the needs of those who had escaped the ravages of the French revolution and its antichurch excesses.

It was, Albert reflected, hiding in plain sight for an operative of Napoleon to be at the Hampstead church. Even though it had no official recognition, everyone knew it was there and that it was full of Frenchmen. In all likelihood, Albert's contact maintained a pretense of being anti-Napoleon.

He approached the door, the music swelling around and inside him. He laid his hand on the iron knocker, letting it rap once. The music ceased, taking with it the confidence Albert had previous to his approach. He could hear hushed voices from within. At last the door was opened but kept chained. A tall man appeared in the narrow opening, the door chain at the height of his neck resembling an unusual necktie. His hair was blond, almost white, as was his skin. His dark-blue eyes contrasted greatly with this combination.

"Yes?" the man questioned in a near-perfect English accent.

"Hello," Albert answered, unsure whether to speak in French or not. "My name is Albert Penfeld, and I am looking for Sabean Sidon."

"Penfeld?" the man queried. "What is it you want with Sidon?"

Albert spoke in French. "I am to deliver a message."

"Oh? And what message is that?" The pallid-skinned man continued speaking in English.

Again Albert returned to French and said, "Make haste for school, it will soon be in session."

Instantly the man unchained the door and stepped onto the street. "Silence, fool!" he hissed. "Follow me, I know where we can talk."

"Do you know where I might find this Sidon?" Albert asked.

"You already have."

They walked on the heath into the evening, and Albert relayed his orders to Sidon, telling him of Monsieur Maitre's concern for his whereabouts and of the position Albert had obtained in the Sutton household.

Sidon was mute most of the time, listening and absorbing the information. When Albert had finished, Sidon turned from him abruptly.

"Do not return here," he said. "I am being watched constantly. You will do well to carry out your mission away from me. When you send word back to Paris, say only that I am safe, biding my time, and unable to do more for now."

Sidon abandoned Albert in the midst of the heath,

leaving the young man to find his own way back across the scrubland. Stunned, Albert was left standing with many questions as Sidon ambled away, calling back over his shoulder the words, "Do not return here again. If I need you, *I* will make the contact."

In trudging back toward home, Albert did not notice a slight figure in brown and green that dogged his footsteps the whole way to the gates of the Sutton drive.

Now that his brother was back, returned from the dead and home, William Charles Sutton feared upsetting his grandfather even more. What if he were regarded as too flawed, too unreliable, and therefore disposable since Charles was back? What if his grandfather wanted to take back his middle name and restore it to Charles?

Continuously yawning, William knew that his body was preparing for confrontation, as he always felt sleepiest right before battle. He climbed the granite steps to the side entrance of the house, where he was confronted with a mop handle brandished in the hands of his least-favorite servant.

"May I help you?" Hugh Popham questioned in his normal surly tone.

"No!" William replied, shoving him aside.

Popham quickly objected, "I am bathing the marble here."

William apologized and backtracked. "Have you seen my grandfather? I must speak with him. It is urgent."

The man scoured William with a glance. "By the looks of your face, you must be in some difficulty."

Each time William had seen this man he had never failed to be surprised at how rude the steward could be. What gave the man the courage to be so insolent?

"Listen here, Hughy old boy," William growled, stepping close to Popham.

Jowls quivering, the little man stood up to William. "I know what Lord Sutton would say if he knew you abused me. I have heard the other staff talk. Lord Sutton runs things around here, and I answer to no one but him."

William realized the man was right. A confrontation was not a helpful idea. But William found it odd that every time he was about to broach a stressful subject with his grandfather this manipulative fellow would show up. "And right you are to remember that fact," William said, backing off. "Where is he then?"

Popham glanced toward the stables and started to point then spun the other way and said, "He has gone for a long walk in the rose garden."

"Recently?" William asked, seeking reassurance.

"Only just." Popham made an ugly face and bobbed his head.

Realizing the steward's helpful manner was suspect, William responded, "Obliged," then walked in the opposite direction toward the weathered, two-story stable. "Grandfather," William called, leaning into the carriage stalls. It was dark. William could see nothing but particles of dusk, illuminated by random shafts of light beaming through cracks and slits. There was no sign of Lord Sutton. William made his way around the back where the horses were kept in narrow stalls.

Rounding the corner, William caught sight of the tail end of Brighton, a massive yellow horse. "Grandfather?" he called sharply.

A scream erupted, along with the stamp of the beautiful but clumsy horse. As his eyes adjusted to the dim light, William froze, watching the man hidden behind the horse try to yank his foot out from under the beast's weight.

"Brighton, you brainless nag! Get off my foot."

With those words, William realized the man was his grandfather. He grew all the more anxious as he recognized what a poor beginning to his conversation had occurred.

Then, under the horse's belly a face appeared, flushed and upside down. "William!"

Startled by his grandfather's appearance and the brusque use of his name, William jumped.

"Get over here and help me get this stupid creature off my toe!"

Hurrying to the hitching post, William untied the reins, tugging them to shift the horse's weight to the other side.

Lord Sutton gasped as he yanked his riding boot free. As he bent over, holding his foot and panting, he said angrily, "What news could be so urgent that you would yell and frighten this dumb animal into stepping on my toe?"

"Grandfather, there's important news I must tell you."

Lord Sutton resumed brushing Brighton. When he did not answer, William repeated himself.

"What then? I'm listening."

Uncertain of how to start, William cleared his throat. *What should I say first?*

"You have my attention. What is it?"

Afraid, William blurted out, "I have a child!"

William waited for him to speak, to rail, to question, anything at all. But he did not. So William began rambling out the lengthy story from the beginning.

Several minutes into the monologue, Lord Sutton

halted him. "And you acknowledged this child as your own?"

"Yes, sir," William agreed. "He is undeniably mine, an exact copy."

With his back to William, Lord Sutton continued brushing. "Where is this child?"

"He is with a nurse who is caring for him."

"And what do you intend to do with this responsibility? You must have an income more than what you are earning from the Marines in order to keep a full-time nurse, or you will have to turn the child over to the authorities. And I suppose you will want to work for me so that you will have a house for the child and more money to afford such things?"

William thought long and hard before answering. He feared his grandfather would dangle them over his head, then yank it away and tell him to get out. "I will do whatever I have to do to see that this child has a true family, and a good life—with a father to call his own."

"And what of the child's mother?"

"She's dead, sir. Childbed fever."

Sutton nodded slowly, murmuring something that could have been condolences. But otherwise he was as silent as a tomb.

William had cause to be concerned, for his grandfather

always became extremely quiet just before he got hostile.

"Sir . . . ?"

Lord Sutton continued to curry Brighton's neck. As William waited to be told to get his things and leave, his grandfather said, "All right, then."

William jumped to the conclusion that he must leave. "Can I have time before I must go? To speak with Charles and with Mother?"

Lord Sutton spun around. "More time? My cargo ships leave for Spain in three days. There is no more time."

Dumbfounded, William said, "You mean I *don't* have to leave home? You are not disowning me?"

Lord Sutton shook his head.

"You mean I can manage security for your ships?"

"My boy, I am so happy. First, my second grandson returns home after twenty-six years gone, and only a day later, I find I have a firstborn great-grandson. I have never been happier," Lord Sutton said. "You have obviously grown up a great deal in the last year, and you are facing your duty like a man. Your child and nurse may stay as long as you like. As for you and Sutton Shipping, I'm grateful you will be involved with the company again. And I think a trip like this will be a perfect opportunity for you to get to know your brother."

Overjoyed, William could hardly believe his ears. "Thank you, Grandfather. I must go and take care of the details at once," he exclaimed. William hugged his grandfather briefly before running off.

Lord Sutton called sternly, "Come back here, William." William skidded to a halt, fearing his grandfather had already changed his mind or maybe had decided to implement an impossible stipulation. Not lifting his eyes from the ground, William shuffled back to his grandfather. "What is it, sir?"

Lord Sutton placed a hand on his shoulder. "I'm not angry with you, William."

"You're not, sir?" William said, confused.

"But I will be if you don't tell me the child's name."

William gasped out a laugh, then composed himself. "William, sir. He was named after me."

Lord Sutton's face fell.

"But I have decided to give him your name as well. William Randolph Sutton."

"That's the spirit!" Lord Sutton exclaimed. "Don't worry about a thing, William. I'll take care of sorting out the necessary paperwork to release you from the Royal Marines for reasons of national service."

"Thank you, sir."

"Oh, and one more thing, William."

"What's that, sir?"

"Would you take care of sacking Master Hugh Popham for me? I've had about all of him I can take," Lord Sutton said. "The fellow came highly recommended by Sea Lord Malcolm, but I find him insufferably insolent."

William tried to keep a straight face, holding back the grin that so badly wanted to come out. "With pleasure, sir. I shall do it at once."

Walking in the side door, William tracked bits of horse dung and hay stubble across the shiny marble floor till he stopped in front of Hugh Popham.

Popham scowled at the spade-shaped, muddy boot prints that led from one end of the room to the other. Offended, he glared at William. "Your grandfather will be displeased when he sees what you've done."

William snickered. "He's already angry."

The man chuckled snidely. "Oh yes. I can imagine by the way you appeared several minutes ago, so distressed, that you have undoubtedly done wrong and gotten yourself thrown out again. That must be the only explanation for your lack of concern."

"No," William said, "but you almost have the right of it."

Examining William's face for the truth, the steward's eyes widened, and his mouth dropped open.

"You will be paid and will leave as soon as you finish the floors," William asserted. "Unless you prefer to be whipped off the premises at once. It is of no consequence which you choose."

William leaned around the discharged servant to get a better view of the spotless clean marble and the bucket of dirty water behind him. "Do a proper job. You want to get paid for your work." He rested his foot on the bucket.

"You wouldn't!" Popham groaned.

"Oh?" William said.

# CHAPTER 11

Finely dressed lords and ladies gathered outside the Covent Garden Theater with tickets for what was expected to be the grandest performance yet. A crowd watched as celebrities, noblemen, and even minor members of the royal family stepped from carriage after carriage and made their way inside.

Thomas almost felt out of place as he swam boldly through the clamoring crowd. Ticketless but worry-free, he approached the door confidently. With head held high, he passed through the mass of attendees and greeted the doorman. "Good evening, Master Winifred."

The attendant was surprised to see him. In fact, the man looked almost fearful. "Captain Burton." Winifred stuttered for words. "What a surprise . . . I'm sorry, I mean, what a delight to see you."

Thomas held his fist out to him, palm downward,

ready to trickle a largesse of coins into the doorman's palm. Unexpectedly, the attendant refused. "I'm sorry Captain Burton, not tonight."

Thomas grinned and declared, "I insist."

Grasping Thomas's hand instead, the doorman whispered fiercely, "Come with me." Calling for another attendant to take his place, he led Thomas around to the side alley where it was quieter. "I thought you were leaving, Captain Burton?"

"Ah, yes," Thomas said, playing the part. "Unfortunately, my ship is delayed again, this time until tomorrow evening, so I have found yet one more opportunity to see Fanny."

Winifred scratched his head with one hand and wiped his chin with the other, looking totally perplexed. He announced, "The performance tonight is sold out."

Thomas examined the queue that spiraled into the street. "But surely not Miss McReady's private box. The management would not dare."

Winifred shook his head, this time refusing even to make eye contact. "No, no. But I'm sorry to report it is taken, nevertheless."

"By whom?" Thomas challenged defensively. "Who could be more important than the man who put the ring on Fanny's finger?"

The doorman sighed heavily before making one more attempt to dissuade Thomas. "You act like a right sort, Captain Burton, not one to upset the applecart. I'll just tell you straight: Miss McReady has some important guests tonight, and they cannot be disturbed."

"Blast!" Thomas spouted. "Is that tonight? She told me about needing to impress wealthy patrons with the cause of theater refurbishment. Is that tonight?"

"Yes," Winifred agreed hesitantly. "You've tumbled to it exactly."

"Then I shall just wait in Fanny's dressing room until the show has finished."

"Please, Captain," the attendant pleaded. "Miss McReady gave strict instruction that she was not to be disturbed either before the performance or at the interval. You would not want to upset her, would you?" Stumped by the last assertion, Thomas concurred that a message to Fanny saying he had dropped by would be enough to satisfy him.

Drinking at a local pub known as *The Footlights*, Thomas passed the time in bored solitude, looking at his bulbous, silver pocketwatch every five minutes. "Eight o'clock, and I'll have a pint . . . Eight forty-five . . . another pint will be fine, thank you . . . just a sip of whiskey at half-past nine . . . Ten to ten, I'll drink to the hen . . . love her so much I'll do it again." At half-past ten, Thomas finished *his* evening's performance by staggering from the frosted glass doors and back down to the theater.

It was quiet out front. Thomas saw no one at the door. He leaned in, expecting to find Mr. Winifred. When he did not, he conceived the idea to sneak in and find a seat at the back of the auditorium, since a few playgoers left at the interval.

His notion was a success. There were several vacant seats, and Thomas slid into one of these. The fur-coated woman to his left fanned away the strong scent of liquor with her playbill.

Thomas ignored the gesture and settled contentedly to watch Fanny on stage. Then an idle notion struck him: Who were the wealthy patrons to whom Fanny was catering tonight?

One look at the box that had always been his until tonight stunned him. There, seated nearest the stage and leaning forward over the rail, was Sea Lord Malcolm, the same balding figure who had so occupied Fanny's time at the concert. From then on, Thomas watched the man's every move: his applause, the way he leered when Fanny spoke, the sweaty sheen on his bobbing forehead. It made Thomas flinch and become belligerent. He could hardly wait for the end of the performance to confront Fanny about the matter.

Curtain call came and went, and when the house-lights were brought up again, the aisles became crowded enough that Thomas was held up in the rush to get out. It took several minutes before he could free himself and get to Fanny's dressing room door. Thomas knocked, but there was no answer. "Fanny, it's Thomas. Open up."

As he hammered louder and louder, Jane Doherty heard the disturbance and emerged from the next room along the corridor. Startled, she exclaimed, "Thomas! What are you doing here?"

He swayed, barely catching himself before falling. "I have come to see Fanny before I leave."

"But Thomas dear, she thought you left. We all thought that."

"No!" Thomas interrupted. "I saw the man from the concert the other night in Fanny's box. Where is she?" Thomas slapped his hand on the door threateningly. "Where's Fanny?"

Jane backed away from him. "She left."

"Don't lie to me. I put a ring on her finger, and I have a right to know."

"I swear, Thomas. She left in a cab."

Thomas pushed past Jane to see if he might catch Fanny. When he burst through the backstage doors to the street, she was being helped into a hansom cab.

"Fanny!" Thomas cried in shock. "Where are you going?"

The shiny bald head of the other occupant of the coach leaned into view. "Drive on," Sea Lord Malcolm ordered. "Whip up, coachman."

"Thomas," Fanny cried. "Stop! Don't do this."

Shaking his fist, Thomas yelled, "Look here, you old lecher. Keep away from her!"

The driver popped the reins, and immediately the carriage jolted into motion. Thomas ran alongside it. "You can't do this to me, Fanny McReady! I put a ring on your finger!"

Angered by Thomas's actions and eager to save face with Sea Lord Malcolm, Fanny shouted, "Then you can have your ring back!" And with that challenge, she threw it at him.

Striking him with the power of a fist, the jewelry knocked Thomas to the cobblestones. He scrambled for the gold and diamond band that had cost him everything he had and went staggering after the diminishing form of the coach, calling desperately, "Fanny, wait! I'm sorry! I only wanted to make you happy!"

But it was no use. The horses were far too fast for Thomas to catch up, and the carriage disappeared like the shattering of a dream when one is rudely awakened in the middle of the night.

Marcel Nerval, or such he called himself, whistled a jaunty tune, his light hair blowing gently as he left the church at Hampstead. His head was swimming with the excellent fortune he had had at his recent meeting. Since coming away from his birthplace, he had found an entirely revised purpose in his life: to stay, to live, and to grow wealthy . . . in England.

He made his way to the high street where he could catch a cab. Climbing inside the plush interior, he called for the driver to take him to the admiralty building.

*Surely,* he thought, *I will be handsomely compensated for this find.* Indeed, his monetary situation had swelled immensely after the last "find," and he was sure the British government would be pleased to know he was watching out for their interests.

When he first began speaking to the English, the information had parted from his lips reluctantly, accompanied by the heaviest guilt he had ever known. Now, as he made his way through the London streets in a fine cab, a wad of cash in his pocket, there was nothing but glee in his thoughts. No trace of remorse remained in what he was about to do.

To Nerval, the selling out of his former comrades was merely business. Of course he justified it as his duty to a newfound love of England, but even as he thought this, he was enacting a session of bargaining in his thoughts.

"No, sir," he said, turning his sober blue eyes to an apple peddler as they passed, "this information is not to be parted with for less than a hundred guineas. Pooh! Did I say a hundred? I meant five hundred!"

The driver stopped the carriage, and Nerval exited. Even though he was instructed to use a side door, Nerval was no less proud of his status because of that.

Upon entering the stone building, he was greeted by a guard who recognized him. "Good afternoon, sir." Since his first trip to the Admiralty, the personnel there had been instructed to treat him with the utmost dignity and kindness.

"*Bonjour,*" he responded in kind, "is Minister Pollard in?"

"Indeed, sir," the guard said with a salute. "You know where his office is."

Nerval made his way down a set of corridors to the Military Intelligence Headquarters of the Royal Navy.

The face of Pollard, gloomy before Nerval's appearance, beamed at the sight of him. "Pleasant afternoon. monsieur," Pollard exclaimed. "Have you brought more information for us?"

Beneath a pure, winter-scoured sky, brilliant with the promise of rebirth, a team of four chestnut geldings with tan manes trotted in the crisp air. Their legs flew in rhythm like practiced fingers over flute keys, while wooden-spoked wheels blurred into translucent disks. The carriage, trimmed in forest hues, moved swiftly and lightly ahead.

William, gazing out of the window at the passing streets, had never worn such a smile on his face, on his heart, and in his soul. He felt suspended within his own skin, hovering with the joy of looking down on his child. He was filled with endless love for this little one. Atlantic-blue eyes opened and concentrated on William, stunning him breathless.

On the seat across from William and William Randolph, Liza, the wet nurse, dressed in plain gray and a starched white apron, watched as if she had never seen such a marvel as a father holding his son. The light from outside glistened on her damp cheeks, and she tugged a handkerchief from her apron pocket.

William squeezed Baby Will more tightly, closing his eyes as he did so. Opening them again, he said, "Hello there, baby boy. I'm your daddy . . ." He envisioned what the boy's nursery would look like, stocked with toys of every kind. Later the toys would be replaced by cricket sticks and wickets, and rocking horses would someday be covered with real riding gear. Life was going to be grand. "I'm going to take care of you." William imagined raising the boy, taking him to prep school and talking with him about what he had learned. *And someday,* he thought, *I'll take you on a ship, your first adventure to a place faraway. Show you the world.* Never in William's life had he felt so brave, so responsible, so content.

The carriage rounded a grove of plane trees, passing through the wrought-iron gates toward the entry pillared by towering limestone columns.

William stroked the infant's cheek with his finger. "This is our place. This is where we will run and play and grow up together."

Emerging from the trees, the carriage whirled up the gravel drive toward Sutton Manor. Even before it eased to a halt, Lord Sutton emerged from the entrance, followed by the servant woman who helped Lady Julia. William stepped down from the cart, thinking, *We're really home.*

The group crowded around, with reaching hands and gleaming smiles, huddling in to see William's greatest prize on earth.

Lord Sutton stepped away and the group parted, as they waited for the patriarch of the clan to speak. His face was calm, his brow unwrinkled.

"William," he boomed, immediately correcting his

voice to a lower volume. "William, I never thought I would see the day when I would be a great-grandfather. Just as I never thought I would see Charles again." He hugged Albert. Turning to Lady Julia, he said, "And to think my daughter-in-law is alive and recovered to see this with me."

His voice cracked, and he turned away. Tears traced deep wrinkles in his face the way rains do on the bottom of a dry desert floor. William watched as Grandfather Sutton shed his old self and blossomed again after a twenty-six-year drought.

"This is the happiest day of my life."

The group crowded close again around Baby Will, emanating a spiritual glow that grew into a sparkle. William imagined it shooting across the lawn and up into the very heavens—to where God was, at that moment, smiling on his family.

William crept downstairs as stealthily as a mouse. To his surprise, Thomas was waiting at the bottom of the steps on a pine bench seat by the coat rack.

He stood when he saw William approaching. "William!" he exclaimed.

Lifting a finger to his mouth, William hushed Thomas, then pointed upward in reference to the baby sleeping.

"William!" Thomas exulted in a whisper. "Your grandfather has told me everything. It's like your entire world has been turned upside down. Like you have discovered the best gift you ever thought of owning, only you never thought of it before!"

William nodded with amazement.

Struggling to express all of his thoughts at once, Thomas poured out a torrent of words. "Last thing I remember is looking for you at the concert. When I couldn't find you, I was upset because I knew you must have left."

"The saddest night of my life." William recalled the tragic circumstances of losing Dora, then brushed the thoughts away as he moved on to happier events. "But also the fresh beginning of my adult life."

"You left and then what happened?"

William explained about the mysterious messenger who had been haunting Hampstead for days, waiting for an opportunity to speak with him before finally doing so outside the concert. He shuddered as he spoke of the dank cellar in which he had located Judy and the baby, and about her subsequent death. "But I have resolved to give him the father I never had, the close family ties to which Charles was entitled but almost missed forever. This baby shall never want for love."

"What is his name?" With one hand on the rail,

Thomas raised himself up a step. "Can I see him? Where is the little fellow?"

With deep satisfaction, William responded, "William Randolph Sutton. He's sleeping upstairs."

Expressing his disappointment with a sigh, Thomas noted, "Later then." Then something William had said struck home. "And where is *Charles*?"

William hushed him again. "On the same night . . . It was *miraculous*. Albert, I mean Charles, returned from the dead."

"The fellow you spoke of?!"

"Yes, yes! The man I met in the water." William was lost, staring into an invisible mystery play, watching the scene unfold again. "It's him, Thomas! He *is* my brother and has amazingly escaped from France to be with his family."

"Where is he now? I must meet this twin of yours. I'll feel as though I know him already, won't I?"

"You might," William added doubtfully. "He's off with Grandfather, sorting out his paperwork so he can make safe passage with us on the ships."

Thomas listened, astounded. Speechless at first, at last he shook his head and summarized, "A lot has changed in two days."

William agreed, studying Thomas from head to toe. "You look dreadful, old man."

Snapping to his senses, Thomas gazed sadly at his untucked shirt and fingered his messy, matted hair. "I had a night last night," he said solemnly, exhaling forcefully.

William cringed when the overpowering scent of alcohol struck his senses. "I guess you did. Come walk with me." The two made their way outside to admire the day. It was almost as if spring had come two months early.

"Last night is actually what I came out here to talk to you about . . . And to apologize."

"For what, Thomas?"

"I should have listened to you about Fanny. You were right."

Examining his friend's demeanor, William understood what had happened. "I see. I'm sorry too."

Thomas cleared the air with his affectionate grin. "Anyway, I don't want to take away from the wonderful things that have happened here. It will be one to put behind me. It's simply time to straighten up my life and do something with it."

William agreed. "What?"

"I don't know. After my appearance in front of Sea Lord Malcolm . . ."

William started with alarm.

"Yes," Thomas said with chagrin, "it was he who has

replaced me in Fanny's affections. Anyway, after last night, I'll be lucky to get command of a rowboat—seventy-five years in the future."

The perfect idea came to William. "Then why not seek a discharge?"

"What do you mean? The civilian world has no use for an out-of-work naval officer with a black mark against his character."

William struck the air with a pointed finger. "Ha, but you do have prospects you see."

Thomas frowned, knowing he had already considered every possibility.

"I have decided to head up security for my grandfather," William explained. "The first convoy leaves in three days. Sutton Shipping has been declared an essential industry and my position advantageous to national security."

Hope sparked in Thomas's eyes. "And you think he would do the same for me?"

"Well *he* couldn't."

Disappointment replaced hope.

"But I could."

Thomas waited to make sure William was not messing about, creating false hope as a joke.

"Really," William reassured his comrade. "As head of security I can choose and commission any specialists I may need for the job. I've hired Charles—I mean—Albert."

"Yes!" Thomas exclaimed. "I'm free! I'm free!" he called, dancing around William in the yard. "I'm going back to sea with William, and I can bite my thumb at Sea Lord Malcolm."

Having Thomas, William's best friend in the world, go with him in this chapter of his life was the bonus on top of everything that had happened.

Lord Sutton addressed the others assembled in the ground-floor parlor: William, Albert, Lady Julia, and Baby Will. All but the last were paying strict, serious attention to the head of the House of Sutton. Baby Will, gurgling happily on Julia's lap, looked directly into the face of his great-grandfather and grinned toothlessly.

The craggy features of Lord Sutton melted into beaming pleasure. "He smiled at me," Sutton insisted, interrupting himself. "Confess it, all of you."

"Of course he did, Father Sutton," Julia concurred.

Exchanging a glance of pure mischief, William and Albert both shook their heads. "Wind," William said. "Sorry, Grandfather, but Baby Will does that because he has wind."

"Besides," Albert asserted before the sputtering Lord Sutton could frame his protest, "it is well known that infants of his age cannot focus their eyes. He cannot be smiling at you because he cannot see you."

"He smiled right at me," Grandfather Sutton declared firmly.

"Not possible," William said. "Unless, maybe you think you are the cause of him having wind."

Lady Julia laughed at the banter, and Baby Will hiccuped. "Oh, Father Sutton," she said. "Isn't it marvelous to have both William and Charles here together . . . and they are so much alike, it is as if they grew up together."

"Bah!" Grandfather snorted. "Both scatterbrained ninnies, if that's what you mean." His words were harsh, but the glow of contentment never left his face. All knew he was not actually offended.

"It is time for Baby Will to have a bath," Julia said, rising to her feet. "I will leave you men to finish planning this sea venture."

"Julia," Lord Sutton began.

"Mother," William intoned in the same breath, "we have a nurse being paid to take care of Will. You are not to wear yourself out."

"Stuff and nonsense," Julia insisted. "No one shall bathe my first grandchild but me." Her tone brooked no further protest and, toting the child, she swept from the room.

The three men watched the departure with grateful

hearts. "I'm almost finished anyway," said Lord Sutton. "This should be a routine voyage. There will be no danger until you are within the Mediterranean, and at that point, you will be met by escort vessels of the navy. William, you are to study the route for possible improvements in security and supply. But more than anything else, I want it to be a time for you to get acquainted." Lord Sutton rose to his feet. "In fact, I have papers to review in my office. I will take my leave of you and let you visit about whatever you wish. Good night, boys."

"Goodnight, Grandfather," said both William and Albert.

When Lord Sutton left the room, William said, "I cannot tell you how pleased I am that you consented to accompany me on this trip. Of course, I will miss Baby Will terribly, but he'll have no lack of care while we're away. You cannot believe how it affects me to think of that baby as my own."

Opening his mouth as if to speak, Albert shut it abruptly. He narrowed his eyes in thought while William waited patiently, then tried again. "Brother William," he began, "there is something—"

Albert broke off at an unusual expression on William's face. His sibling was staring over his shoulder at the deepening gloom outside the parlor window.

Albert pivoted in his chair in time to see a lurking figure step hurriedly back into the shadows.

"There is someone there!" William shouted. "Come on!"

Both young men broke into a sprint toward the front door. Neither gave any thought to his personal safety; instead, both were concerned for the others in the house.

At the entry, William instructed, "Let's split up. You go around toward the stables, and I'll go by the garden. We'll meet at the back. Go!"

William's path took him most directly toward the parlor window, but, as he suspected, by the time he reached it, the intruder was gone. He ran on toward the hedge-walled garden and was rewarded with the sound of someone crashing through the bushes. "Stop!" he shouted. "I've got a gun!" But his bluff failed, and the pursuit continued on into the shadows under the trees.

Ahead of him a figure darted between tree trunks as if aiming for the high fence around the Sutton estate. Thinking to head off the escaping eavesdropper, William shot through a different gap and was almost immediately struck on the shoulder and spun around by a blow from a second trespasser. He tripped over a protruding root and fell.

The strike from what felt like a tree branch was not

powerful, but it landed on William's still mending collarbone, and his right arm went numb. "Help! Charles!" William shouted. "They're here! Here!" As a second blow smashed downward, whistling through the air, William lunged aside. The stroke barely missed his head.

Lashing out with his feet, William tried to knock his attacker off balance, but failed. Another blow struck him in the side, knocking the wind out of him. "Charles!" he called again, but the name came out like a hoarse cough instead of a yell.

A shaft of light from the house shot through the branches. It revealed the assailant lifting his weapon above William's head: Hugh Popham!

The blow descended, and William threw up his hands to cover his face. But the stroke never landed. Instead, Popham was sent sprawling when Albert's shoulder hit the former steward in the middle of his back. Popham's head cracked soundly against a tree trunk, and the man tumbled to the ground.

Kneeling beside his brother in alarm, Albert asked, "William, are you injured?"

Just as William was about to deny that he was seriously hurt, Popham got to his feet again and dashed toward the fence. Albert would have followed, but William stopped him. "I know who he is," William said, "and what this is about. Besides, there are more of them.

Let's go back to the house and tell Grandfather. And thank you—I am in your debt."

Grandfather Sutton agreed that the motive was undoubtedly revenge. "Looking to steal something, no doubt," he said. "It won't happen again. I'll have guards patrol the grounds night and day. You may rest easy. Nothing bad will occur while you're away."

Only Albert was not satisfied with this explanation. As for telling William about Angelique, which he had been about to do when the lurking figure was seen, he decided it was best to save that information for another time.

# CHAPTER 12

At mid-morning the Sutton convoy set sail on open water after navigating the length of the Thames the night before. William was in command, directing the sailing master and several junior officers and impressing both Albert and Thomas. Albert marveled at the sight of the two vessels, sails billowing a fiery orange in the sparkling light of day.

"A fair wind for sailing!" William called to his brother and friend from the helm of the *Warwick*. "We shall make excellent time today."

As the ships exited the harbor at Gravesend, the wind pushed harder, though the sea was calm and smooth as glass. With the added breeze in their sails, the vessels heeled slightly to starboard as they maintained formation. Albert felt slightly nervous at the deck's new angle, and he gripped the railing for security.

Albert could see William was well-suited for the helm station—the cheerful wind that blew in his hair matched the youthful excitement on his face. The rolling bow wave, pushed before the bulk of the ship, seemed to play some great symphony theme for William, building and falling in an unending rhythm.

To be part of the Sutton family William must have fought against terror all his life, Albert surmised. What a challenge William had had to meet their grandfather's expectations and still to overcome fearing the sea that took his father and brother (or so he'd thought) so long before. *I never knew how much happier I must have been in France than William was in England,* Albert realized. It was an odd thought since everyone in the Sutton clan had expressed to Albert that *he* was the deprived one—the unlucky one.

Thomas strode up to Albert. "Splendid morning, eh?" he said, trying to be friendly. When first introduced to Albert, Thomas had hardly said a word, only staring with the same disbelief and suspicion that others had had since Albert's arrival. Albert had quickly tired of the constant scrutiny and therefore had avoided Thomas during the first part of the voyage.

But having slept, he now felt more cordial. "Yes, it is wonderful."

"I'm sorry if I offended you," Thomas said. "I just—"

Albert cut him off. "There is no need. I was just very weary."

Neither spoke for a long time, only listening to the wind and waves, inhaling the salt air, and experiencing the glow of the climbing sun.

Lady Julia was asleep when Lord Sutton heard a carriage approach. He imagined the visitor would prove to be a doctor. Contrary to the physicians' orders and everyone's advice, Julia had kept alert and active during Albert's stay at the manor, exhausting herself in the process. Lord Sutton was in his study reviewing the year's current financial reports of his shipping company. The figures were excellent, showing decreases in losses by the week and an overall increase in revenue.

"Not likely to continue without the new contracts," Sutton grumbled, laying the stack of papers aside and making his way downstairs to attend to the newcomer.

As Lord Sutton walked on luxurious carpets past the expensively decorated walls of the grandest manor in Hampstead, he saw none of this. Continually fretting about money he had not even lost yet, he recalled his deceased wife's advice to him: *The more money you have, the harder you'll have to work to keep it, and the more unhappy you shall be.*

He passed her portrait on the wall and sighed, acknowledging the truth of her perceptive outlook.

None of the servants had heard the carriage draw up—or else they did not want to bother themselves, he thought. Lord Sutton never remembered which was their half day off from work and often blamed them for failing in their duties.

Before a single knock had fallen on the massive door, Lord Sutton yanked it open, annoyed with the interruption.

Standing before him, eight inches shorter and resting on a cane, was Andrew Woodford. Sutton looked around for Tim, the blind man's attendant, but only the carriage driver stood nearby, feeding his horse a lump of sugar.

"Won't you ask me in, Randolph?" Woodford questioned, beaming proudly at his detective work.

"How did you know it was me?" Sutton demanded, taking his friend by the elbow and ushering him in.

"Lavender water," Woodford said.

Led into the drawing room, Woodford found a seat, and his expression changed. "Randolph, I've come with important news. May I ask who is at home?"

"Only Lady Julia and myself," Sutton said, surprised by the seriousness of the inquiry.

"Are we alone right now?"

Sutton grew even more concerned. "Yes. What is this about?"

"I'm afraid I have some bad news for you. This boy, the one you say is your long-lost grandson?"

Sutton nodded silently, but Woodford knew he was acknowledging him.

"We have received information from a source. He is French after all."

"What are you trying to tell me?" Sutton pressed, impatient with his friend. "Of course he's French; he was raised French, speaks French, prefers Frenchified food and not English fare. But that will pass as he regains his natural state."

Woodford waited for his friend to subside before continuing. "A source came to us not long ago and said that your grandson is a French spy. He said Albert had contacted him directly and detailed his entire mission, which included gathering information from you: dates of sailing, shipping manifests, escort arrangements."

Sutton was shaking his head. "Wait one moment. I do not believe my grandson would sell out his own family. He loves us. This is preposterous."

"I know you think he is your grandson, as does everyone who sees him, but I have not seen him. Neither have I judged him unfairly. All I know is what I've been told, and I have come to warn you of it. He has been followed and—"

"You had my grandson followed!" Sutton bellowed. "Outrageous. How dare you?"

"It was not my idea," Woodford added calmly, "yet I felt compelled to share the results with you."

Sutton said bitterly, "I can settle this. I'll confront him with it, and if it's true, I shall . . ."

"No, Randolph, you mustn't. I have only told you this that you may be careful what information you pass to him. But you must not admit you know this. Pollard of Naval Intelligence wants to watch him and see if he can discover any other contacts he might have in England. But another warning. If it *is* true that your grandson is a spy, eventually he will be tried as such, and you know what that could mean."

Lord Sutton's jaw dropped open as he was struck by an important fact. "He is gone."

"Gone where?"

"I have sent him on the resupply mission with William. He is on one of my ships right now headed for Calabria."

"Pray, Randolph, that he returns safely and that nothing ill comes of those ships or supplies. Only if that mission is successful might we have a chance of laying to rest this rumor about your grandson."

It comforted Lord Sutton to hear his friend say "we" when he talked of his troubles, and he told him so.

Woodford laughed. "Your troubles have always been my troubles."

Sutton helped him to the waiting carriage.

The three-week voyage from England through the Strait of Gibraltar and on into the Mediterranean had been uneventful. It had been a time for Albert and William to get acquainted. Most of the recollections passed in only one direction, with Albert quizzing his English brother about Lady Julia and what it was like to grow up in a privileged English household.

When asked about his own childhood, Albert was open in responding about both the poverty and pleasures of the Left Bank of Paris . . . to a point. Whenever the topic grew too near the present day, he drew a cloak of silence around himself, sometimes pretending his English was inadequate for the conversation. Of his own wife and child, he said nothing. Albert was fearful such a revelation would destroy the fragile bond he already cherished.

For his part, William recognized that Albert was holding back, but thought no further of the matter than that it was hard for someone reared a Frenchman to think proper English thoughts without much practice.

Then, too, Albert had been in battle against the English—against his own brother, for that matter—and was likely embarrassed about those circumstances. William would have been pleased to put his brother's mind at ease on that score, but the occasion never arose.

In port for resupplying, Albert and Thomas sat on the deck of the *Warwick*, eating fruit and sharing a bottle of thin white wine they had purchased from a local vendor. The air around them was sweet and warm, and the sun heated their skin.

It was a nice change from dreary England, Albert thought. He wondered why William was unable to rest, not free to enjoy himself in such pleasant surroundings.

William paced the deck constantly, bounding to the poop deck with his spyglass every time an unfamiliar sail was sighted. The Sutton ships had been in Tabarea on the coast of North Africa for three days, meaning their English escorts were late. William was beginning to worry.

"We mustn't delay our progress much more," he had said to Thomas and his brother. "These supplies are needed in Calabria soon, and we shall have to depart with or without our escort."

But for the time being both Thomas and Albert had adopted an attitude of relaxation fitting for their Mediterranean surroundings, dreading the moment when

William decided they could wait no longer. It came sooner than they hoped.

William stopped pacing and instructed Thomas to go and round up the crews from about the village. They had been on leave there for the extra time that it would take for the escort to arrive. Thomas rose to his feet. "Aye, aye, sir," he said, saluting William comically, then wandered down the gangplank.

Albert wondered if there was a deeper conflict in the exchange than what was visible. Perhaps Thomas did not like to think of himself as subordinate to his friend—particularly since Thomas had commanded a warship while William had only been a seagoing soldier.

As if in answer to his brother's ruminations, William said, "He is being paid for the journey. But something is bothering him."

The ships' crews soon returned, their fruitful shore leave withered by the prospect of putting to sea again. Thomas was just as dejected.

"William?" he asked. "May I have a word?"

The men went below into William's day cabin, and when they returned, Thomas was lighthearted again.

Albert gave him a questioning look, and Thomas explained with glee, "Your brother, bless him, has decided to give me command of the *Coventry* for the rest of the journey. What a pleasure it shall be to call out the orders on my own vessel, commanding an entire crew again." His voice trailed off, caught in the dream.

William overheard his friend's happy monologue and interjected, "It's a *job*, Thomas, not a pleasure cruise. You will be sailing after the *Warwick*'s course, understand?"

Thomas nodded, but continued his dreaming uninterrupted.

"Good," said William. "We leave tomorrow."

The Sutton transport fleet carried supplies for the relief of English troops in Calabria, a seaport on the southwesternmost tip of Italy. Across the narrow strait of Messina lay Sicily, a critical tactical point for both armies, French and English.

Should Napoleon obtain it, he would have undisputed control of the Mediterranean Sea, the ultimate southern border of Europe. If England could keep it, it would provide them an excellent base from which to launch attacks throughout the Napoleonic empire.

Waiting no longer, for fear his relief would come too late, William had left the port of Tabarea two days earlier. The sailing had been smooth, the men enjoying the Mediterranean sun throughout the voyage. Thomas was content in his command of the *Coventry*, second in the rank of supply vessels, and William was content in his friend's performance.

Now in the second day of constant sailing, they were finally clearing the northeastern point of Tunisia, with the Isle of Pantelleria visible off their starboard bow.

Albert was concerned for his wife and child. *She must have had our baby by now*, he thought anxiously, longing for home. For much of the day's voyage he stood in the bow, watching the calm water fold over itself in an endless white blanket as the *Warwick* pushed through it.

Albert wondered how much he could confide in his brother about his true situation. Would he be believed? Also, what ground in their relationship would be lost for Albert to reveal so much about himself after previously hiding it? Why would any right-thinking man hide the existence of a wife and child? The questions surfaced over and over in his mind.

The small island was quite close now, brown and bleak, but inviting to Albert as solid land, a luxury he had almost forgotten. He turned to where William stood at the helm. His brother's face was relaxed but resolute, calm and confident. In that instant Albert decided to tell him everything.

"Take the helm, will you, Albert?" William asked as his brother strode up.

Albert did, and William opened a locker under a

nearby bench, extracting a leather case containing a brass spyglass.

"William," Albert tried to begin, but William gestured for silence. He gazed intently at the island, or past it, Albert could not tell which.

"I thought so," William said. "Strange sails rounding that point."

Albert squinted in the direction indicated but could see no other ships or sails.

"Try this." William handed Albert the scope and waited for him to agree.

Albert nodded. "Yes, I think there is a ship there."

"Not only one," his brother replied. "I can count three separate sets of topsails, though they have done a clever job of concealing themselves against the outline of the island."

"Do you mean," Albert worried aloud, "that they are enemy vessels?" He caught the irony in his own statement. *Enemies of whom?* he thought.

"Possibly, but they haven't flown their colors yet, nor would we be able to see them if they had. You there!" William called, scowling up at the crow's nest. As the sailor looked over the edge, he continued, "Look alive, and find me some colors on those vessels!"

Albert took the glass from William again and pointed it for a long time at the approaching vessels.

"Don't fret yourself too much, Albert. It could be our escort. Mister Hone!" he barked to his second-in-command. "Run up a signal to *Coventry*. Tell them: *Ships sighted, make for Sicily's coast.*"

William saw the concern on his brother's face and clapped him on the back, trying to comfort him. "Even if they are enemy vessels, we can run the shallows around Sicily where they can't follow. Big ships like that draw too much water."

But as their course changed, so did the wind. They were coming into the lee of Sicily, even though they could not see the land yet, and the wind was dying out. What had been a strong northerly flow, allowing them to make with ease their northeasterly heading, trickled to a light breeze.

The vessels, whatever they were, were closing the distance.

A frantic call came from the lookout above. "Colors, sir! French vessels! Two frigates and a xebec!"

William stamped his foot in frustration, tearing open the locker and unrolling chart after chart. "We must be," he mumbled, "seventy-five miles from the coast . . . a longer run to the west, more wind. Shorter to the coast, no wind. Hone!" William yelled. "Signal *Coventry* to head due west immediately. We have to find stronger breezes."

Staring with wide eyes at the fast-approaching vessels, Albert asked, "Why hasn't their wind gone, William?"

"They're tacking," William replied, not bothering to explain to Albert what the term meant. "And they've still got the wind we had."

"But will they not lose it just the same?" Albert questioned, following his frantic brother around the deck.

"They will." William stopped to answer. "But not before their cannons can tear us to shreds. Ready to wear ship. Due west, Hone!" he barked.

Albert went to the starboard rail of the quarterdeck to take hold as *Warwick* lumbered in her great sweeping turn to the west. The wind came irregularly, yet the sails of the warships bearing down on them appeared full to capacity.

"You had better remove yourself to the bow, Albert," William said. "It will not be long before their bow chasers will be in range, and the stern rail is no place to be when an eight-pounder comes hurtling in."

It was a dismissal of sorts. William was every inch the commander: thoughtfully reviewing the situation, weighing their chances of escape. Albert heard him muttering to Mr. Hone, "The gravest danger is from the twenty-eight gun. Yes, I know the other appears to be one of the new French forties, but see how low she rides? We can outrun her. No, the xebec's triangular sails won't draw enough from this fitful breeze for her to play a role. We must distance the twenty-eight, and we can thumb our noses at them from the shallows."

Albert could not understand half of what his brother was saying, since his mind was racing, and his thoughts had reverted to French. He did, however, move to the bow. There he watched as Thomas's ship, the *Coventry*, encountered the same problems with the wind. Strong but short-lived gusts would fill the sails with air and the sailors with the hope of safety, only to die again, leaving the vessel stranded.

A pop reached Albert's ears, like the sound of a dry branch cracking in a fire. He faced the source in time to see a gigantic splash a few hundred yards behind the *Coventry*.

"They're coming into range!" William shook his fist toward the sky. "Come, wind!"

Another gust amounted to nothing, leaving the ships helpless again.

"Why are their sails so full?" Albert complained aloud to no one.

Mr. Hone dashed to the helm. "A signal from *Coventry*, sir."

The two men stood and translated the series of

colored flags being run up a line to the main top. "Changing . . . due . . . north," they read in unison.

"Is Thomas crazy?" William marveled. "There's even less wind the closer we crowd the lee."

"There's more, sir," Hone said and read the signal: "Incoming . . . wind."

"How can he know that?" William said stubbornly. "Send him back this signal," he began, but *Coventry* was already tacking behind *Warwick* on a breeze that had picked up.

The French ships were plainly in sight now, though one outstripped the other two in racing toward the pair of merchantmen. The leading vessel, which Albert had heard his brother describe as a twenty-eight-gun ship, was firing regularly from guns mounted in its bow. Shots, erupting in giant plumes of spray as they landed, dropped continually closer to *Coventry*'s stern, loading Albert with dread.

*Mon Dieu*, he prayed, *s'il vous plaît, do not allow our capture.* As much as Albert wanted to go home to Angelique and his baby, he could not do so if it meant causing his mother and grandfather pain and tearing his newly found brother away from Baby Will. Albert recognized that all was in the hands of *le bon Dieu*, the good God.

The *Warwick* was dead in the water, but the *Coven-*

*try* had caught a thin wind. William panicked, turning too late to catch the ebbing breeze, only positioning the *Warwick* as an idle broadside target for the approaching warships.

"Have you no weapons?" Albert asked, racing to his brother at the rail. "Can we not stay them off by firing back?"

"*Coventry* has a pair of eight pounders," was the distracted reply. "We only have muskets aboard, but even the eights would do no service against them. If we get caught under the weight of their broadside, two hundred pounds of cannonshot comes aboard every time they fire. We will have to surrender."

Albert watched with horror as the French ships—three ornate and gaily painted men-of-war—loomed up behind them.

*Why make a vessel of destruction so beautiful?* he wondered. *At Trafalgar how the ships were brightly painted in yellows and checkerboard patterns . . . and what masses of splintered wood and flesh remained after.*

Without warning the wind resumed blowing from the north, expanding the *Warwick*'s sails unexpectedly and knocking Albert down because the rudder was hard over. William seized the helm and began steering the ship on a northwesterly course again. "Shake out every reef in every scrap of canvas," he bellowed. "Let's not make this easy for them."

The closest of the warships fired a steady barrage at the *Warwick*, raining down a stream of shots in her wake, coming closer each time. In the excitement, Albert had lost track of *Coventry* until she came sweeping in across the *Warwick*'s wake, the crew leveling her single eight-pounder directly at the French frigate's waterline.

Albert could see the name on the attacking vessel clearly as Thomas ordered his crew to fire. The twenty-eight-gun *La Canari* slowed suddenly, a neat round hole punched in her bow at the waterline to the left of her keel.

William cheered, "He knew it! Thomas knew they would fire right over his head if he sailed back across the course. He's bought us time. But can he free himself?" William said this through gritted teeth. He and Albert were in identical poses at the rail, their nails digging identical scratches into the varnish.

As the barrage from *La Canari* continued, an eight-pound ball skipped visibly across the wave tops and finally made contact with the *Warwick*, striking her rudder. The helm went slack, and William knew he had lost control of her heading.

A second man-of-war cruised in upwind of *Coventry*, taking her breeze. Slowly the full sails began to die.

*Coventry* lost way and floundered, coming to rest in the path of *La Canari*.

An accurately placed chainshot took out Thomas's upper rigging. Albert and William watched in dismay as *Coventry*'s main and fore topsails crashed to the deck. *Coventry* was stranded.

"Signal!" Mr. Hone yelled, reading off the flags. "Need . . . help."

Albert was aghast. He knew his brother's friend was about to be overrun by the French vessel. Even among the larger reports of the French cannons, Albert could hear the ineffectual crack of *Coventry*'s cannon. Thomas was from the Royal Navy; it was not in him to surrender.

Shots continued to land around the *Warwick*, but no ships were giving chase. All three were converging on the *Coventry*.

"The rudder!" William cried, peering back toward his friend's ship, about to be boarded. A broadside at close range and a volley of musketfire, and *Coventry* was enveloped in a cloud of smoke. "Curse the rudder, I can't help him." William called for the signal "Damaged . . . rudder . . . cannot . . . engage" to be run aloft but knew that information would be no help or relief to Thomas unless it made him give up the unmatched fight as hopeless. The last he and Albert could see of the

*Coventry* was the crew taking up arms against the overwhelming parties that fought their way onboard.

The *Warwick* sailed clear, the breeze strengthening until the sight of the battle dropped far astern and disappeared. By evening they were in the shallows of Sicily. Dawn raised the comforting presence of escorting British frigates—one day too late.

# CHAPTER 13

It was a nice change for Dora to get out of the house. For several weeks she had been locked up inside Donspy Manor in a cavern of depression. Nicholas had gone back to school in Oxford, and there had been nothing to occupy her time. The daily sweet but superficial conversation with Mrs. Honeywell and the dodging of verbal bullets from Aunt Etheldreda were the only entertainment she had. Dora felt safest in her room, and since it had been too wintry to venture out, that was where she stayed.

When Nicholas returned, the effect on Dora was like freeing a wild animal from a cage. She was longing for excitement, any change at all. Naturally when the weather moderated, she jumped at the chance to take a carriage ride.

As the two-seater whizzed down the narrow road,

the smoke coming from the cottages of the tenant farmers was pleasantly homey. Dora was at peace with herself, with her thoughts of William, and with her father's memory. She squeezed Nicholas's arm tightly as he slapped down the reins. She smiled at him, grateful for his caring. But he hardly noticed.

The road ended at a clearing near the top of a knoll. The buggy emerged from the trees, following a wide circle. In the distance Dora could see the spires and towers of the Oxford colleges, rising like tiny, lifelike models from behind the rolling hills. Nicholas reined in the horse, and it stopped.

With a basket in one hand, he helped her down. They ventured to the edge of the mound, to an expanse of flat rock. Nicholas spread out a red-and-white checkered wool blanket while Dora began unpacking the lunch she and Mrs. Honeywell had fixed. The two hardly said a word. Dora was happy to be outside while Nicholas seemed disconnected and discontented.

"Is the food all right?" she asked, hoping he was impressed.

He took another bite, glared at it, and pursed his lips while chewing. "It's acceptable."

Insecure, Dora waited for him to say more, to tell her how he had missed her, or how nice it was not to be studying. When he said nothing, she commented, "I'm happy you've returned to me."

"I didn't exactly leave my studies just to see you. I have business here."

"Oh," Dora replied, disconcerted. "What's bothering you?"

"I suppose school." He paused, squinting at the towers. "There's a girl in Oxford, a shop clerk, who's been enticing me with her eyes every time I go in for books."

Instantly jealous, Dora asked, "Does she disturb you then?"

"Well, she's not disturbing to look at, and as I have told her, I have you, and I'm not interested in seeking further relations with women at this time."

Slightly relieved, Dora still wondered who this girl was. Did he see her often? "Is she smart?"

"Perhaps," he replied. "She appears to know about men. She's quite unlike someone who does nothing but knit, chat, and watch the clouds pass."

"I suppose that's all I do then?"

Nicholas turned to her, grinning. "Why Dora, I do believe you're jealous. You need not worry about this other girl. She is only after my money."

"And what is it you see in me, Nicholas?"

He started to answer and corrected himself several times before saying he did not know. "I guess it's the way

245

I feel so peaceful with you, like I could tell you anything, like a sister."

Dora did not want to be a sister; she wanted to be in love. She wanted to read the Bible together and work together, the way her parents had. Dora wanted to tell him these things, but he never asked. Maybe she was hoping for too much too soon.

Nicholas chuckled. "I remember the night you arrived. You were so quaint, covered in dust and mud. Country and rustic."

Dora smiled when he nudged her, but inside she remembered how she felt that day—alone and bereft of comfort. "When did you see me that night?" she questioned. "There was nothing funny about it."

"The way you made that hurt little-girl face when Etheldreda insulted you was most charming."

"You were in the lounge that night," Dora announced. She had almost forgotten seeing the match light in the darkened parlor. "Smoking a pipe, weren't you?"

"And I watched the whole thing from my chair," he added playfully.

Dora began to cry. "But that wasn't funny. My father had just died, and I was forced to move away from my mother. I don't want someone to think it's amusing when I'm hurt."

He chuckled, in between times of acting solicitous. "Dora, there's really nothing to be concerned with. You must not take yourself so seriously."

More upset with each word he spoke, Dora said irately, "How could you be so insensitive? William would never have said the things you say."

"Sutton!" Nicholas was outraged. "The sleazy fellow who fathered half of London's orphan population? How dare you compare me to him! How dare you speak to me as if I am less of a gentleman than he!"

Sobbing, Dora got up and hurried to the carriage. She wished Nicholas had not called on her after all.

Nicholas took his time chasing after her. She watched him act as if he resented her pain. Hoping he would apologize, she said, "Take me home, please."

He did not argue, did not even bother to pick up the basket or the blanket, or the food she had made for him. He mounted the buggy seat and cracked the whip.

She waited and waited, but the kind words never came. At the house he gathered his things and bluntly said good-bye. Dora tried to stop him, but his last words were, "If you want to marry me, you'd better learn how to treat a man, for he is the master of the house."

Dora hurried to her bedroom window to watch as he rode away. She hoped he would turn around, come back, and tell her everything would be fine. She clung to the windowsill until the last of the dust had settled. *Back to Oxford,* she thought, *to see the shop girl with eyes for him.* She slumped down on the floor in a sea of tears, knowing she could do nothing but wait for his next return.

Nearly three weeks had passed since the loss of the *Coventry* and of Captain Thomas Burton. Throughout the entire journey home William had said little, only keeping watches at the helm more than was required. He seemed to be punishing himself, though he could not have prevented what had happened.

*It was Thomas,* thought Albert, *who wanted to experience command of his own ship. It was his choice that put him in danger.*

Yet Albert understood William's guilt, realizing there would be no consolation for him. That would only come if William could forgive himself—and that change would never take place until he met Thomas and explained.

Though Albert had been mostly concerned with his brother's well-being, something else had been nagging him. He knew he could not trouble William with it until they were back on English soil. Now, in the fading light of their latest day away, land was sighted. Soon they would enter the estuary of the Thames, headed once again for London.

William's tight-lipped expression did not ease at the sight of land. Albert knew arriving home only meant more trouble for William as he would have to inform Thomas's family of his capture and tell his grandfather of the loss of a Sutton ship and its government cargo. Still, Albert approached his brother at the helm, hoping to find a way to speak of his own troubles.

Though he did not look relaxed, the sight of land and a safe arrival home at least made William more affable. He greeted Albert cordially. "A beautiful sight, eh?" He nodded toward the ever-swelling Dover cliffs, their cloudlike shape illuminated a reddish-brown in the low light.

"Indeed, William," Albert responded, waiting a good while before speaking again. "William, I have something I wish to speak to you about."

His brother would not look at him, making Albert's speech more difficult, even though he had been rehearsing for the entire journey home.

Continuing, Albert said, "I have a very troubling situation, and I hope you can help me with it."

Still William looked away, studying the sweep of a flock of seagulls. "Yes, what is it?"

"I have . . . a family." Albert sputtered out this last phrase, then waited expectantly for a response.

William sounded tired and puzzled, but not scornful or mocking. "Why, yes, Albert, you are among them now. I suppose that notion will take getting used to."

Dismayed, Albert said, "No, brother William, you do not understand. I have a family back in France ... a wife and a child. They are waiting for me to return."

William pivoted his gaze to his twin. His questioning eyes probed Albert's soul. "But how could you have defected? How could you leave your family there?"

Albert exhaled, avoiding the scrutiny of his brother. "I did not come here to defect. I was on business for the government."

"What?" William exclaimed, his visage changing from sadness to rage. "Who are you? What are you doing here?"

Albert recognized that William's frustration at the loss of the *Coventry* was about to be vented on him. "Wait a moment and listen," he pleaded. "Trust your eyes ... trust your heart to know that *I am your brother.* Hear me and know that I speak nothing but the truth." William lowered his hands to his sides, though his fists did not unclench. Summoning Mr. Hone to take the wheel, he led Albert to the stern rail.

Albert explained, "I was supposed to come and spy on you, the Suttons. I did not know that you really were my family, I swear, not until I saw our mother. All I want is to bring my wife and child here. I did not reveal any plans. I did not cause the capture of *Coventry*."

Still incredulous, William queried, "You came to spy on us? For the French?"

Albert only nodded, and there was a great deal of silence as they continued on toward shore. Finally he resumed, "I was a trooper of the First Hussars, dispatched as a courier to relieve Admiral Villeneuve of command of the fleet. That is how I came to be aboard *Redoutable* at Trafalgar. After our encounter in the water that day, I foolishly spoke of it and Imperial Headquarters conceived that I might portray the long-lost brother to advantage."

"How can I know you are speaking the truth?"

Searching for what might convince his brother, Albert at last said, "When I rejected your claim that day, it was because I did not want it to be true. I did not want to give up my identity as a Frenchman. But Nana—Heloise, whom I always thought of as my grand-mére—told me the truth on her deathbed. On her soul and on that of our mother, who can look into my heart and see the truth, I swear this."

When William spoke again it was to say, "How might you bring them safely away from there?"

It took Albert some seconds before he realized what William was asking. If the topic was how to get

Angelique out of France, it could only mean that William believed him. "I do not know, but I would like to try. My place is here, as is my wife's and child's." Nothing further was said; nothing further was needed.

The brothers were quiet, each planning how to bring a young mother and baby from a country as well guarded as Imperial France. Though they did not know it, each was contemplating a different aspect of the same problem.

While William was arranging in his mind transportation for Albert to and from France, Albert was thinking of his disguise and the alibi he would need once he was in the country.

Almost simultaneously they reached their independent conclusions and began to speak.

"One of our ships," said William. "An inconspicuous craft . . . an out-of-the-way port. Standing off and on the coast by night."

"The uniform I arrived in," Albert began, but conceded pride of place to his brother. Albert could see as William spoke that the burden of losing Thomas was fast receding, replaced by the purpose of reuniting more family he had not yet met.

"We keep ships in Gravesend—fast, private ships for our own use. Once there I can divide my crew in half and make the rest of the journey to London."

His speech flowed quickly. "One of the ships is small enough to be manned by a few men, but large enough to cross the Channel if the weather holds fair. We shall put into Gravesend within six more hours. You shall leave tonight!"

Albert was stunned at the speed with which his brother could decide to believe and help him. "Will not my departure cause you difficulty in explaining what has happened? Might not your countrymen . . ." He caught himself. "*Our* countrymen be less trusting than you?"

Shaking his head emphatically, William declared that explanations were of no consequence. What mattered was a successful expedition.

"Thank you, William," Albert said. "I will return with my wife and your . . ." Remembering he did not know whether he had a son or a daughter, he ventured a guess. "I shall return soon with your nephew."

William clapped him on the back. "Our sons shall grow together. They shall share the childhood closeness we never could."

"Mornin', Dora dear." Mrs. Honeywell drew back the curtains in Dora's room.

The young woman stretched her arms wide, squinting as the light shot in, before burying her face in a down pillow. Answering in mid-yawn, she replied, "Tired today, Missus Honeywell. I was up late last night, searching through stacks of dress patterns and sketches for a wedding gown."

Mrs. Honeywell eyed a messy stack of advertisement pages strewn over the night table. "Any success at findin' one ye like then?"

"No, I'm afraid there are too many."

The discussion sent Mrs. Honeywell back into her memory. She began folding garments as she tilted her head back. "I remember when I was preparin' for my weddin'. What a chore it was, but in those days it seemed much simpler. No fancy invitations, no music to hire, no fancy feast to prepare. Just my mum's dress and the words *I do*."

Dora laughed. "Missus Honeywell, you make it sound as if it were three hundred years ago."

Looking at Dora fondly, the housekeeper joked, "Wasn't it? At least it feels that way." She grew quiet and nostalgic. "He was the love of my life."

Dora realized she had never asked Mrs. Honeywell about her husband. She thought it strange to finally hear her mention marriage, though nothing more about the man. Timidly, she asked, "Whatever happened to Mister Honeywell?"

There was a pause. Then Mrs. Honeywell said, "He was killed tragically, soon after our weddin'."

Shocked, Dora said, "Oh, I'm so sorry! I didn't mean to pry."

"No, no, dear. It's good to be reminded of such a man. My husband—John, his name was—was so brave and kind. He was a guard on the midnight coach from London to Dover." She set down the clothing as she recalled. "It was just months after we were married. It was stormy, and the assigned guard was ill. I asked him to stay, to not take the place of the other. He insisted he couldn't refuse, and of course I knew that. He had always been known as the reliable type. So he went out on this blusterin' night, south to Dover."

Dora sat up in bed, her eyes and ears glued to Mrs. Honeywell. "He was shot and killed?!"

"Heavens no," she replied. "I don't know if I could have lived with myself if he gave his life for mere gold when I loved him so much. He was nearin' a river crossin', and it had rained frightfully much. Parts of the road were washed out. On they went, and what the driver didn't know was that the waters from the floodin' had saturated an embankment. The soil around the crossin' was heavy and loose."

Dora listened with horror.

"Well, the wheels sank, and the carriage rolled

over, pinnin' the driver under the seat. Though John was thrown clear, he went back and wrestled with the river . . . made it turn loose of the driver, don't ye see? But the effort was too much for him, and when the carriage tumbled again in the current, it carried him right down. He drowned there, trapped under that carriage."

"That's awful!" Dora cried, rushing over to give Mrs. Honeywell a hug. "I'm sorry I brought it up."

"I'm fine, child." Mrs. Honeywell reassured Dora in a way that made her seem more worried about Dora feeling bad than feeling bad herself. "I have always been proud of John for what he did, but I still wish I had him back again." The plump housekeeper added, "Now isn't that selfish of me though? The poor driver was married with three wee bairns and three more that came after."

Dora realized how much she must have loved the man to have never remarried—in comparison to Aunt Etheldreda, who did not remarry because she enjoyed the freedom that being a widow brought. To Dora, it seemed that marriage for Mrs. Honeywell and for people like her parents meant a commitment for a lifetime, if the spouse be alive or dead. She thought of Nicholas and the speed at which she had gotten involved with him after only hearing of William's supposed death. She realized she hardly even knew him. How could she tell if she would want to spend the rest of her life with him? Words flew from her mouth before she even knew what she was saying. "I don't know if Nicholas is the one for me."

Caught off guard, Mrs. Honeywell exclaimed, "Heavens, child! What makes ye say that?"

Dora wished she could retract her statement. But since she could not, the best thing to do was to be truthful. "Sometimes I feel like I am a prize to be won, something he has had to work for. But a property just the same. I sense at times he is only *trying* to be like me, to like the things I like so he can have me. I'm not sure exactly how to describe it, but when I'm alone with him lately, now that we are engaged, I think he cares less for me and I find myself comparing him to—" She was cut off by her own thoughts. *William*. The name rang in her mind.

"To what?" the housekeeper prodded.

"I don't know."

"I saw ye go somewhere else. Where and with whom did ye go?"

Dora thought before revealing anything else, though Mrs. Honeywell was the safest person to talk to. It was almost as if she were a close relative. She was closer to Dora than Aunt Etheldreda, so Dora was comfortable enough to go on describing her attraction to William and the spark he had brought to her life in Branson Fen.

Disturbed, Dora said, "He was the man I thought was dead."

"Dora, dear." Mrs. Honeywell sat down beside her on the bed. "I overheard somethin' of him the other day. He's the one who kept mailin' ye all those letters, and I wondered why ye did not tell me of this until Mister Nicholas explained how he was harassin' ye, so it was better not to bring it up."

"Letters?! What letters? Harassing me?"

"Isn't that the way it happened?"

"No!" Dora gasped. "What else did Nicholas say?"

Mrs. Honeywell went on to tell her of the reasons Nicholas had discussed: William was a sick man and a drunk who would not leave her alone. He had been thrown out of the ball for his behavior, and shortly after it was discovered that William had an illegitimate child.

"But I must admit, Dora, I did overhear one thing once. I suppose I shouldn't have listened. But it was about ye, and I have wanted to tell ye."

Dora fanned her arms to hurry Mrs. Honeywell on. "Go on. What is it?"

"They were discussin' one of his letters. Dora, he is madly in love with ye."

"He is?" A thrill coursed through Dora, though she was still hesitant to believe William was *truly* in love with her. She remembered hearing about William from

Nicholas after the ball, but never before had she heard anything of the letters. It became clear to her that Nicholas had lied to her, but why? And why was Aunt Etheldreda so close with him and yet so cruel to her? "Why does Aunt Etheldreda act like she despises me?"

Mrs. Honeywell lowered her voice. "She doesn't hate ye. What makes ye think that?"

"I have seen the way she treats Nicholas and the way she treats me, constantly belittling me, at least until he showed an interest in me. Why would she do that?"

Looking nervously at the door, the housekeeper lowered her tone even further. "I've wanted to tell ye this for quite some time, Dora. I feel bad for not sharin' it with ye, but it was not my place to say." She rubbed the bags under her eyes. "A long time ago, Etheldreda was in love with your father."

Completely surprised, Dora nodded anxiously for Mrs. Honeywell to go on.

"She told me this in confidence years ago, so it is in the greatest trust that I tell ye now, for I could lose my livelihood."

"Your secret is safe with me," Dora assured the apprehensive woman. "Go on."

"Madam Etheldreda was in love with your father, and they were to be married. But when he went away to seminary, he fell in love with your mother, and they were married. Shortly after, so I was told, Etheldreda got your uncle, Master Donspy, into marriage as a way to get back at your father. But your father was so madly in love with your mother that he didn't even notice. Etheldreda has been bitter ever since. Then, too, she was hard hit by your father's death."

"She allowed me to come here because she missed him and wanted to be close to me?"

"No, dear. I believe it comes back to somethin' she told me about gettin' even with Emily, your mother. I don't know that she offered to let ye come here so she could help ye. I think it may be exactly the opposite."

And, Dora realized, it was all part of the plot. "Nicholas?" she queried, suddenly distrusting him. "Is he part of the game too?"

Pondering how much she should speculate about her employer's business, Mrs. Honeywell decided to follow the ancient adage of "in for a penny, in for a pound." "Your aunt, my dear, has long coveted the grazin' land across the Isis river . . . land that carries with it the title of duchess . . . land controlled by Nicholas's father."

Dora gasped.

"As to whether the young man is aware of her schemin', that ye can only decide for yourself. But if your heart is tellin' ye somethin', it's best to listen to it, for a lifetime is too long to spend with a man ye don't love."

Dora tapped her fingernail on her tooth while she thought. "You're right. I must listen to my heart, and right now, it's telling me I need to go see William Sutton and find out if he is as awful as Nicholas makes him out to be."

"Where? To Hampstead?"

With excitement, Dora interjected, "You know where he lives?"

Mrs. Honeywell acted guilty but still smiled. "Well, I suppose I did stick my nose where it didn't belong when I looked at the name on the envelope once. William Sutton, Sutton Hall, Hampstead Heath, London."

Dora kissed her on the cheek. "Missus Honeywell, you are sent from God." Then a worrisome thought struck her. "But how will I get there?"

"Shall we say a trip to see your mother?"

"But London is out of the way for a trip from here to Salisbury," Dora protested.

"Never mind, dear. You know Mister Radcliffe, the coachman. He'll do anythin' for ye."

"Oh, no! You mustn't do that. What if Aunt Etheldreda should find out?"

"Never fear. He'll be glad to help."

"And you . . . will come with me?" Dora seemed to

hang her life itself on the question. "Missus Honeywell, I would feel much more at ease if you were to go."

"Then I must," the housekeeper stated. "I'm sure your aunt will agree to send me as your chaperon. I shall arrange everythin', and in a short time ye will see this William fellow and decide for yourself."

Dora vowed to write a letter to William, which Mrs. Honeywell would mail. She further vowed to make the journey to find out the truth, whether he replied or not.

## CHAPTER 14

———— ❦ ————

Never before had William been so glad to be home and yet so afraid to return with the bad news. He had failed his grandfather, his country, and his best friend. "My God," he called aloud. "Is there nowhere I can run, nowhere to hide?" If only he could trade places and be the little child again, even if just for a day. Even as he thought this, he remembered his infant son and realized the weight of responsibility in training his baby to face up to difficult situations.

He was met at the manor door with the embracing arms of his grandfather. "William! I am glad you have returned. Was it a success?" Then, reading William's expression, he grew serious.

William was dirty, and his eyes were glazed. He collapsed to a bench seat in the hallway—the same seat where he had last seen Thomas in the house. Where was Thomas now?

"What happened?" Lord Sutton said, shaking him.

"I have failed you, sir."

Lord Sutton did not jump to conclusions but waited for William to explain.

His voice sometimes quaking with emotion, William told the story in detail, from his decision to press on without waiting for the escort vessels, to the loss of *Coventry* and Thomas. "It's my fault," he said. "If I had not ordered the sailing and had not favored Thomas with the command, then we would not have lost your ship or my best friend. And I could do nothing to save him."

"William, William! Calm down." Lord Sutton placed his arms around William.

Never before had he shown such weakness in front of his grandfather, and he could not help it.

"Now hear me," Grandfather said sternly. "You had a duty to the soldiers of the Calabria garrison to deliver the supplies, and you could not wait longer. Thomas has been in command before; he knew and accepted the risks that go with command. Finally, even if your rudder had not been jammed, there was nothing such lightly armed merchantships could have done in the face of French warships. It is the mercy of Almighty Providence that you and *Warwick* escaped. And Thomas, God willing, we will ransom."

"I have failed, I have failed you!" William agonized.

Doing his best to reassure William, Lord Sutton lifted the young man's chin. "And think of your son and your mother's heart. Even had both ships been lost, for you and Charles to come safely home means more than all—" He stopped at the air of absolute horror that materialized on William.

"Where is your brother? Where is Charles?!"

As if he were swimming through a swamp that was trying to suck him down, William said thickly, "Charles."

"Where is Charles, William?"

"He is . . . He has gone to France to get his family. He has a wife and child."

"Oh no," Lord Sutton exclaimed, pressing his hands to his face as he stood. "It is true. Oh Lord, it is true."

Stunned why this news should seem most upsetting after all he had been through, William asked, "What is it, Grandfather?"

Lord Sutton wrenched his hands in front of him, as if wrestling with an invisible spirit. He began to pace.

"Is there something wrong? Am I to blame?"

Lord Sutton spun round to William. "No, my boy.

You are most certainly not to blame for a plan that is bigger than England."

"What plan is this, sir? What concern is this with my brother?"

It was William's turn to embrace and comfort as Lord Sutton almost broke down. "I'm afraid I have more bad news . . . for all of us."

William waited anxiously for his grandfather to draw a shuddering breath.

Lord Sutton finally said, "Charles, Albert. He is not your brother."

"What?"

"He is part of an elaborate plan to dismantle England's forces abroad by involving himself with us in order to give information to the French."

William shook in frightened disbelief. "This can't be true!"

"It is, William. It was no accident that the French knew you were coming and what you were carrying. They knew even before you had left."

"But how?"

"Albert. We told him everything, didn't we? He knew when, and he knew where those ships were going and what they were carrying. They even knew enough to delay your escort."

William recalled the days he spent at port in Tabarea,

waiting for military support that never came. And then the day he found out that Charles . . . Albert . . . had a family in France. *Of course,* he realized. *Who would defect with their family still at home? That is why he acted secretive.*

"It was not by chance that he should borrow a boat, William," Lord Sutton charged. "I suspect he was scheduled to be arrested when they captured the other ship, and no one would have been the wiser. But you escaped, William. And you have come home." The men squeezed each other tightly. "I could not have taken losing both of you at once."

William thought of evil deception, but what he found himself remembering was the sincerity of Albert . . . Charles . . . when they talked of their childhoods. Did he really go back to get his family, or was it just made up so he could get away?

"I must warn you, William," Lord Sutton said gravely. "The accusations are flying. Since Albert has not returned, that fact will confirm his guilt. Since we appear to have aided his escape, we may be blamed as well."

"What are people saying? That we planned this? That we are helping Napoleon's army?" William gritted his teeth. "Show me a man who says such a thing, and I will line him up and shoot him. To say that you or I would betray our country—for money? How can anyone credit such nonsense?"

"I know this, William, but be aware: the worst may be yet to come."

In the back of his mind, William was arguing with himself for letting Charles get so close, for sharing his life in every way with the man he thought to be of blood and spirit his brother. Then, in his innermost heart, he remembered Charles's warm smile, his quiet and polite manner, their talks about what it would have been like to grow up as twins. His soul rebelled against the notion that Charles was a traitor. "But what if he returns with his wife and child, as he has told me?"

Lord Sutton stood coldly, as if preparing to face death at a drumroll. His eyes locked with William's. The grandson was for once able to peer inside the grandsire's mind, read his thoughts, fear his fears, and pray his hopes. "That may be all that can save us now. Pray to God He will bring Charles home again."

William had been correct. The ship Albert would take to France was smaller by two-thirds than *Warwick*. Only one deck in depth, *Swiftsure* had a cabin the size of two coffins laid side by side, a single-mast amidships, and a tiller instead of a wheel. Her crew of six, as assigned by William, was a mixture of a pair of Portuguese, a German, two Swedes, and a Liverpudlian whose accent was as incomprehensible to Albert as any of the others' dialects.

While sailing it back down the Thames estuary, the cutter seemed ideal, light and fast enough to escape detection. Once in open ocean again, it was apparent to Albert the difficulty the cutter *Swiftsure* would have crossing the Channel even if the weather remained fair. And the weather was changing.

Albert was not able to depart again before six in the morning on the day after their arrival in England. He knew the crew was exhausted and ready to be home, but William, grandson to their employer, had asked them to turn around and head into even greater danger.

The journey was not without its benefits. William had promised to pay them more than double their usual wage if they would go. Starkey, the skipper from Liverpool, spat over the side and declared, "Me dad outrun Navy blokes Liverpool to Cork, smugglin' poteen whiskey. Gravesend to Calais. What difference? Froggies ain't near sharp enow to catch likes of me."

They were between Dover and Calais, halfway across the Channel and skirting the French coast once again when fatigue began to show in their faces. Albert was weary, too, but he was not working. Unlike his brother, he did not know how to sail a ship and so merely watched with dismay the sailors' tired faces.

Still wearing his brother's clothing, Albert decided to leave it on until they reached Le Havre just in case they met up with any English vessels. When they arrived in France, he planned to change back into his Guardsman's uniform, which he had brought along with the rest of his possessions in a knapsack. This would buy them some time if they were met by any French vessels. Perhaps he could talk his way out of difficulty; they could not fight their way out.

*Enemies to both countries now,* he mused. *Sneaking out of England and back into France. I wonder if the two governments would fight over who got to shoot me first?*

Albert was hoping they could make a fast sail of La Manche and arrive before sunset of that day, but he knew it was not likely. The weather was threatening to change, showing giant fists of thunderheads, swollen and menacing on the eastern horizon.

*If they could not get round behind the peninsula before the storm hit.* A horrible memory struck Albert as he looked into those clouds. He did not want to imagine what might happen to them if they were caught in that storm. It was the same sea in which his father had drowned and in which he had been swept apart from his mother and brother. What if it should happen again?

*Please God,* Albert prayed silently, *hold back the storm for just a few more hours.*

"Gentlemen," Sea Lord Malcolm called, standing at the head of the oval table around which the other members of the British Naval Intelligence Committee sat. "I believe it is time to reevaluate our relationship with Lord Sutton."

Andrew Woodford sat at the far end of the table, astonished to hear the harsh tone in Malcolm's voice about his friend. There had been no warning about this topic, no preamble as to what was to be discussed. Members had been summarily convened, their attendance enforced by armed guards.

Each man had a decanter of water before him and a crystal tumbler, though some had chosen whiskey from the selection in the corner of the room. Sea Lord Malcolm and Minister Pollard were two such, drinking heavily at the supposedly urgent meeting.

Malcolm continued, "It is known that Sutton has been harboring a spy, a most grievous offense. And . . ." Malcolm cleared his throat and sipped more whiskey. "He has allowed that spy to escape back to France."

The room vibrated with speculation. Everyone had guessed that the so-called long-lost Sutton boy was a fraud, but . . . Here they had a variety of excuses for themselves: Sutton was too obstinate to listen to reason. No one had kept the young man confined. It had been regarded as a possible benefit should it be decided to feed him false information, thereby throwing off French operations.

"Actually," Sea Lord Malcolm declared, "Minister Pollard *has* kept a watch on the French spy, but he never dreamed Lord Sutton would be so foolish as to allow the wretch passage out of England." Lord Sutton had been presumed innocent of any offense except emotion-laden stupidity until now, but if it were true Sutton had helped his grandson escape, he must be regarded as a traitor also.

Minister Pollard, his curly red hair standing out from his head in response to the static electricity in the room from the thunderstorm outside, continued the story. "As if this shocking revelation were not bad enough, now also comes the news that the Sutton transport ships were attacked at sea. Miraculously, Lord Sutton's grandson and the spy were not on the ship taken by the French. But over half of our supplies for the garrison at Calabria were!"

Woodford rose from his seat, waiting for the discussion to die down. He knew all eyes would soon be on him. "How is it," he asked, pointing a finger down the length of the table, "that you have come by this information even before the government knows of her loss?"

"We watch everything and everyone," scoffed Pollard. "Of course we know these things before everyone else. It is our job."

"But," Woodford said, pressing his point, "surely no news can have reached here any faster than the return of the *Warwick* herself. How could you know that one of the ships was lost unless you had an operative on board? And if that is so, why did he not prevent the so-called spy from escaping?"

"Woodford!" Pollard yelled. "I shall thank you to hold your comments about a matter of which you know nothing! We are British Intelligence and need not divulge to you our methods of receiving information. The fact is, *we know*, and what we have said here today is the truth."

"Our proposal," Malcolm cut in smoothly, "is to take custody of Lord Sutton's holdings until a further investigation may be made into the matter of his alleged treason. Even documents, personal and business, should be seized in order to locate any proof of his guilt or innocence. Certainly we cannot allow a repetition of the unnecessary loss of valuable cargo."

"Why would he do it?" Woodford demanded. "Randolph Sutton has been nothing but loyal to England his entire life. His shipping empire is at His Majesty's service."

Irritated with the blind man's questioning, Sea Lord Malcolm said, "Can you not understand? Must we spell it for you? Perhaps he is hedging his bets. While appearing loyal to us, perhaps he is also taking a payment from the French. Perhaps he believes the French will win the war, leaving him a hefty contract at the end of it for his support."

Woodford settled back to his seat, having heard no other voices raised in support of his longtime friend. The meeting had become a witch-hunt. Instead of being about a supposed fraud perpetrated against Lord Sutton, Malcolm and Pollard had made Sutton out to be the center of a ring of treasonous conspiracy.

A vote was taken as to the government's next action, but Woodford knew it was an unnecessary formality. Pollard and Sea Lord Malcolm thoroughly controlled the situation.

Afterward the blind man felt his way from the room with Tim's help and was last to exit except for Malcolm and Pollard. As he left, Woodford heard the distinct clink of crystal behind him—two men's glasses touching in an otherwise silent toast.

Albert was put ashore just south of Boulogne in the

dead of night by the cutter *Swiftsure*. A year earlier this stretch of shoreline would have been thoroughly shadowed by French frigates and constantly patrolled by shore parties. At that time the Grande Armée had been preparing for the invasion of England—the very invasion plan disrupted by the defeat at Trafalgar. Now, less than six months after Trafalgar, the coast had an air of being deserted, and army patrols kept to towns in such foul weather as was certainly approaching.

The weather had held, but it was not likely to continue for much longer. Albert saw the relief in the crewmen's eyes when he gave the *Swiftsure* permission to leave at once for England.

Captain Starkey arranged to return to the French shore in a week's time. By then Albert was hoping to be able to bring Angelique and the baby safely away from Paris. Still, the timing was critical; it was dangerous in Imperial France to wait too long on the seacoast for the ship's return. A soldier escorting a woman might not be questioned if he could fabricate a legitimate-sounding purpose, but one living as a vagrant with his family would be considered a deserter and taken into custody. A week would be enough time, but barely; longer might be just as fatal.

Albert and Captain Starkey agreed that, on the seventh night following, Albert would build a signal fire if it was safe to land. Otherwise *Swiftsure* was to return to England, taking no more chances and leaving Albert to find another way.

He knew the northern French countryside well, having seen much of it during his service as a Hussar. Towns large and small dotted the area, and it was to one of the former he intended to make his way and requisition a horse.

The moonlight was masked by the clouds that raced across it, flowing westward on an unusually warm wind. A brief handshake for the captain was all Albert allowed time for, wishing him luck and sending them on their way. He did not know if he would see them again, all the while recognizing what peril it would mean to him and his family if he did not.

# CHAPTER 15

The city of Paris was fast asleep when Albert galloped in on the buckskin gelding he had successfully "requisitioned" three days before. It had been a tiring ride, not only for the poor horse, but also for Albert. He had only allowed himself a few hours' rest each day, knowing he had little time before his English accomplices would come again, then leave forever.

He arrived at his home courtyard, knowing his wife and child would not be there. But in the empty house he hoped to find a clue as to their whereabouts. He approached the rickety door, seeing the chain that had been put there upon Angelique's departure.

There were no lights in the area, no windows set in the houses to spill light into the street, and Albert thought he would be safe. He leaned heavily against the door.

It creaked and gaped, but the chain did not break, holding fast through the two holes that had been bored there, one through the door, the other through the post. Stepping back, Albert glanced around him.

Raising up his left foot, he kicked firmly near the chain, breaking a chunk out of the door in the process. The portal flew open, leaving a foot-long fragment with the chain through it hanging from the post.

*Rotten wood,* he thought and smiled to himself.

There was nothing left inside. What furniture they had was gone, along with the meager decorations Angelique had put up. Albert looked for a clue as to where his wife had been taken.

*Did you write to me?* he thought, searching behind his grand-mére's hiding spot for valuables. It was a charred stone that could slip out of its place in the chimney. He removed it, but there was nothing.

After the couple had moved into the house, he had found his own place of concealment, or so he called it to keep his mind off the fact it was actually damage caused by termites. In the cramped cubby that was the bedroom, partitioned from the other room by a tattered curtain, some of the wooden planks had been gnawed through, separating them from the nails that kept them in place. One of these he lifted, looking for anything

Angelique might have left for him. Again there was nothing.

A voice startled him from his intent search.

"What are you doing there?" a quavering, old woman's voice called.

Albert smiled at once, recognizing the inquiry as coming from the courtyard gossip. "*Bon soir*, Madame Mendl," he responded. "It is I, Albert Penfeld."

"Albert?" She gaped into the darkness.

Albert knew she could not see him. "Yes, madame. I am on leave, and I have come to visit Angelique. But, alas, I do not know where she has gone. Perhaps you have seen her?"

"I *knew* she was not going to see the Emperor!" the aggrieved Madame Mendl cried bitterly. "She *is* in a very beautiful house though."

"You know where?" Albert said excitedly, walking out from the darkness of the tiny bedroom and frightening the woman.

"Yes, yes," she said, but did not immediately offer where his wife was.

Albert knew the old gossip suspected something.

"Tell me," she continued, "why is it *you* do not know where she has been taken?"

Albert tried to cover his indiscretion as best he could. "Those arrangements were made *after* I had

**279**

already departed for my latest mission, from which I am only now returned. Marshall Berthier is expecting me tomorrow, but I naturally wish to see my wife tonight."

"Why are you wearing that strange uniform?" Madame Mendl asked, still reluctant to give her information away easily. "What happened to your pretty blue one, the Hussars?"

"This *is* blue, Madame Mendl," Albert retorted, annoyed with the questions. "Please, do you know where my wife is? I am tired, and I would like to see her before I fall asleep standing here."

Madame Mendl grunted her disapproval at the young man who had no time to talk to friends, but finally said, "She has been taken to a home across the river. I went there to see that she was all right, and she did not even come out to greet me. The servants there said she was not allowed any visitors."

"Is she sick?" Albert worried.

"Oh, no," the woman screeched, venting her indignation. "As I walked away, she was there in an upstairs window. She smiled and waved. I think she was laughing at me."

"Where is the home?" Albert asked, amputating her wounded pride.

"It is number seventeen Rue de Buttes Chaumont. Quite a lovely home."

Albert fled, leaving Madame Mendl standing word-less for only the second time in her life.

When he reached number seventeen, Albert realized what the gossip had been talking about. It was a stately manor, three stories tall with windows on every floor. It faced the Place Chaumont, a field of grass lined with trees.

A single light burned inside, illuminating the deli-cate tracery of the fanlight window over the entryway. He put on an air of formality and marched to the door. Boldly he lifted and let the knocker fall. This action he repeated again and again, but nothing happened for sev-eral minutes.

Finally the door was opened by a slightly built man in a dressing gown and nightcap. "*Oui?*" he asked sim-ply, visibly irritated by the late disturbance.

"We are to move Madame Penfeld," Albert said firmly. "At once."

"But we have had no word of this," Phillippe protested.

"I," Albert spoke forcefully, "am the word."

"Do you have orders?"

"They are following by courier. I am here to help her pack and ready her for the journey. Make haste, man! On the orders of Marshall Berthier himself."

Albert pushed his way past the servant and made his way upstairs.

Rounding the last curving steps, Albert heard the sweetest sound he had ever heard and feared he would never hear again. Angelique's soft voice was gently singing out a lullaby his grandmother had taught Albert; one he had sung on many occasions to the baby when it was still within his wife's belly. He slowed his steps, lifted by the music as he neared her door.

"*Il tombe de sommeil, mon petit chou,* Go to sleep, my little cabbage."

Albert's ear was pressed against the door when the servant crept up behind him.

"Monsieur?" Phillippe asked, resuming his indignant tone. "What are you doing?"

Albert heard the music within stop, and he knew Angelique was listening also.

*What can I say,* he wondered, *so she will go along with it when she hears it?*

"I," he began, hoping it was loud enough for his voice to be recognizable and for it to be obvious to Angelique what he was attempting, "was just listening to hear if she was awake or not. You would not have me barge in to carry her away, would you?"

"*S'il vous plaît,* monsieur! Lower your voice, or she certainly will be awake."

It was too late for either of them. Angelique burst through the door behind Albert and wrapped her arms around him. "Oh, Albert," she cried over and over, placing kisses all over his grizzled and travel-worn face. "I knew you would come home soon."

"Monsieur?" Phillippe asked incredulously, "Monsieur Penfeld?"

"Yes!" Angelique said cheerily. "Phillippe, this is my husband, Albert. Albert, this is Phillippe, the chief custodian of this magnificent place."

Albert knew there would be no easy way out for them now.

"Penfeld," the stuffy man said, "I am afraid I shall have to detain you until my wife comes with the proper authorities. We have been told to alert the Imperial Headquarters if you make an appearance here without a proper escort."

"Detain?" Angelique asked. "What does this mean? What does he mean, Albert?"

"Angelique, I am not . . . ," Albert began, but Phillippe turned to scurry down the stairs in search for his wife, so he ran after.

Catching the servant by the back of his nightshirt, Albert dragged him back up three steps with his heels flailing at the treads. "One more noise from you, monsieur," Albert hissed, "and I shall break your neck."

The servant whimpered and went limp in Albert's grasp, but gasped his agreement, thereby losing all traces of his former bravado and superiority. "Angelique," Albert called up the stairs toward his wife's anxious view, "ready your things. Get whatever you and the baby need for a journey."

She nodded, her face pale, and Albert hoped he had not upset her too much. He hoisted Phillippe to his feet by the scruff of his neck and frog-marched him up the stairs.

"I have not even seen my baby," Albert said. "I hope you will oblige me."

They entered Angelique's bedroom as she frantically pulled clothes from the chest below the window. There, lying on the bed in the gown Angelique had knitted for him, was their child. Albert released his hold on Phillippe and went straight to the baby, kneeling by the bed and taking the tiny hand in his.

Angelique stopped bustling in order to watch as her husband met his boy for the first time. Albert laid his head down next to the child, and they contemplated each other.

"He knows you," Angelique said softly, smiling at her men. "His name ... if you agree ... is Cyrus."

"*Bon soir,* Monsieur Cyrus," Albert whispered. "I hope I did not disturb you. A treasured name, to be sure." Angelique had named the baby after Albert's best friend, killed in battle.

"Albert!" Angelique cried, pointing at the doorway.

Forgetting about Phillippe when Albert saw his baby, he had allowed the servant to slip away again. Albert bounded after him, taking the treads four at a time. He could hear the man panting in fright on the flight below, rushing toward his quarters where he could bar the door.

"Claudette!" Phillippe cried. "Help!"

Running through the kitchen was no easy task for the servant, as he slipped in his night stockings on the stone pavers. Albert caught him in time to see Phillippe's wife emerge from the opposite doorway in the kitchen, clad in nearly identical garb to her husband.

Again Albert fetched Phillippe up by the neck of his clothing and pushed him along toward his wife, who stood goggle-eyed and blanched at the spectacle.

"Are there any more servants?" Albert demanded of her.

She shook her head, and Albert took her by the arm. Both, Albert imagined, were able to intimidate Angelique, but neither would stand up to him.

"Do you have rope here?" Albert asked.

"What do you mean to do with us, monsieur?" the frightened steward asked.

"Answer the question!" Albert commanded, shaking him like a straw-stuffed doll.

Phillippe's wife bellowed, "Answer him, answer him, before he murders us both!"

"No, sir," Phillippe said. "We have twine, though."

"Go and fetch it then, and remember I have your wife by the arm."

By now Angelique was standing in the doorway behind them, holding two bundles in her arms: one of clothes and one of baby Cyrus.

Phillippe rushed past her, returning moments later with a roll of twine.

Albert scoffed, "Is this all you have?"

"*Oui,* monsieur."

Albert forced the husband and wife to lie down on the floor back to back. Using a kitchen knife, he cut one piece of twine for each set of their limbs, tying a slip-knot and tightening it down.

After working for ten minutes, he stood to survey the final product. Their ankles were tied in pairs and then together. Their wrists were treated in the same manner, being both bound together and tied around their middles. Angelique gave a slight chuckle at the comical appearance of it as Albert ushered her from the kitchen.

They talked little once they left the residence.

Angelique asked a minimum of questions, barely enough to know the story but not enough to bother her husband when he was preoccupied with their danger.

Stopping first at the buckskin horse tied to a tree four houses away, Albert realized his wife and baby could never make the journey to the coast on horseback. "Why did I not think of it before?" he said aloud, mentally lashing himself.

"I know of a place," Angelique offered, recognizing exactly the problem they faced, "where we can find a carriage."

The carriage was obtained without trouble, the caretakers of it being bound together on the kitchen floor of the manor from which it came. It was an Imperial coach, kept in the stables of the same home in which Angelique had resided, for use when high officials had the need.

It was evident to Albert, that it had not been needed in a long time. The plush interior was dusty and full of cobwebs, and the axles were sorely in need of grease, groaning in protest of every rotation.

No horse was kept with it either, and Albert was forced to harness his tired buckskin mount for the journey. The animal was not a draft horse and consequently snorted and balked at finding himself linked to an object that bumped and moaned along behind him. Albert reflected perhaps it was fortunate for their safety that the beast was as tired as he was.

After a few hours of driving, it was apparent the steed would not last much longer. "Angelique," Albert called as he pulled the horse to a stop, "we shall have to make a change. I'm afraid this poor creature can go no farther."

They were just outside Paris, near the village of Herblay, when the need could not be denied. The selection was sparse. The countryside was given to hedgerows surrounding sheep enclosures; not many of the inhabitants could afford the luxury of a horse.

Albert was deliberately keeping to the narrower byways, and little farmhouses were all that dotted the area. What equine pens there were contained weathered and broken-down plowhorses.

Scanning the choices, he wondered sourly why the owners bothered to build enclosures. The ancient horses could not stray far anyway.

Dejected, he drove the buckskin on. For a long time no sound existed but the ever-slowing, shuffling clatter of the beast's hooves on the dirt road and the constant squealing of the axles. The noise was so monotonous and stupefying that Albert believed the horse would continue on the path if his driver were to fall asleep.

Then Albert heard it: a lively, young horse from the sound of it, neighing constantly as the carriage approached. *There is a steed,* thought Albert, *hungry for action.*

The light was getting brighter, and in the distance Albert could see the rickety shack from behind which the whinnying was issuing. The land around was flat, the road lined occasionally with trees and tatters of fencing. Livestock had been, one time, the main product of the area, but as the army moved through, supplementing their rations as was their habit, nothing remained for the farmers but tattered gardens.

For the second time Albert drew the carriage to a halt—in front of the battered home. He dismounted, walking to the fence that adjoined one wall. From the pen came another demonstrative equine challenge, and a large black horse showed its head around the corner.

"*Bonjour,*" Albert said soothingly. "It sounds as if you would like to journey as well."

Angelique stirred in the carriage, the baby rousting her for his morning meal. "Albert?" she called. "What are you doing?"

He tried to silence her, but she would not allow him to steal the animal. "You must not take the horse, Albert," she said. "It is the only valuable thing they have."

Albert knew she was right, though he did not want to admit it. But was their need not larger? At any time pursuit might overtake them, and then who could say what would follow?

The door to the residence chattered like a bird as it opened. "What is this?" an old woman called. "What are you doing here?" Her face was a mass of wrinkles, brown and chaffed from working in the sun.

"Madame," Albert said, "we have need of your horse. I have an important package to deliver for the Emperor."

The woman squinted out at the carriage halted in the road, seemingly surprised to see the mother and child there. "You soldiers," she said, approaching Albert with anger in her rheumy eyes, "you have taken everything already. My animals, my crops, even my husband and son. *NO!*" She pushed at his chest with a pointed finger. "You will not take my horse!"

"But madame," Albert protested, "you may take this admirable buckskin steed in exchange. Surely a young horse such as this is hard to manage for . . ."

"For what?" she questioned. "For an old woman like me? And who else has managed this place since my husband was killed at Austerlitz and my son is away with the army in Italy? Who else has managed my horse before this, you arrogant young man? Do you think you are immune to growing old?"

Despite her apparent anger, the farmwife appeared to be considering the trade.

"Most of the farmhouses," she admitted at last, "have mature horses, content to work and rest daily. But this one, he is too much trouble, he will not work. Only wishes to run. I would be surprised if you could harness him."

"Please, madame," Albert said, "leave that to me. Would you like to inspect my horse?"

The woman moved with surprising agility for her age, or rather what her age appeared to be. Perhaps the cares of life in Imperial France had aged her quite beyond the calendar. She bent by the buckskin, tapping the shin of its right foreleg until it raised its hoof into her hand.

"Well shod," she said and patted the horse's back. "Been run hard, has he?"

Albert was becoming impatient. The sun was streaming in across the fields, and he knew he would be hunted soon, whenever the servants freed themselves or were discovered.

Angelique was quiet, recognizing her husband's anxiety and praying for his success.

"You sweat as well, monsieur," said the old woman to Albert, eyeing him warily.

Albert wondered if she had an idea about the true nature of their business, but the French populace had long since learned there was safety in ignorance.

"Well then," the farmwife said, with evident cunning in her tone. "Help me remove the harness, and I shall help you hitch up Sully. Oh yes, that is his name. You should never take a horse without knowing its name. What is the name of this fine steed, eh?" When Albert did not answer at once, he knew she suspected them of not being the owners of the buckskin, but she made no accusations.

From down the road in the direction of Paris came the sound of a trumpet blast. To Albert's trained ear it was playing recall, such as a commander might order to reassemble a search party when a fugitive's trail had been located. He started and lunged toward Sully.

The woman barred his way with a gnarled grapevine root that served her as a walking stick. "Don't be hasty, young man," she counseled. "You cannot outrun cavalry horses in a carriage, and as sure as my name is Delphina Sabol, flight always appears to be guilt."

Knowing the accuracy of the assertion, Albert swallowed hard and did his best to straighten his Guardsman's uniform. From two sides of the farm, streams of riders converged. They wore the orange and gold uniforms and the curious, four-cornered flat-topped headgear of a troop of lancers. Which identification, Albert thought wryly, was amply confirmed by the eight-foot-long, steel-bladed lances each carried across his saddle.

"You will please to not move!" the captain of the troop demanded in the accent of Gascony as the riders ringed Albert, the carriage, and Madame Sabol. "What is your name and your business here?" he inquired. "Speak up."

Tongue-tied for fear of being found out, Albert was building up his story when Madame Sabol burst out with, "How dare you accost my great-nephew and his wife in this way? The Sabols of Herblay are descended from the Chevalier d'Herblay. Be off with you, Gascon pig! If you murdered as many English as you do good French words, the war would already be over!"

Taken aback, the captain said, "Your pardon, Grandmére, but I have orders to seek deserters. I—"

"And did my dead husband not receive the Legion d'Honneur for his exploits among the Russian cannon at Austerlitz? Marshall Murat shall hear of this outrage. The emperor shall hear of it!"

A lancer nudged his horse forward and muttered something to the commander, who nodded. "Very well madame, since you are known here. If you vouch for your nephew, we accept. Only," he added slyly to Albert, "what is your name and duty that you are here far from your unit?"

"If you had permitted me to speak a word," Albert blustered, following his "great aunt's" example. "I say, if you had allowed me a single word, everything is easily explained. I have been on duty in Boulogne, and as my wife and I have an infant, I am taking them to my parents' home in Paris. We only stopped here to see Aunt Delphina."

The captain of the troop grunted. "Very well," he said, saluting. "*Bonjour,*" and the lancers cantered away.

When the horses had been exchanged and Sully was securely in the harness and straining to be off, Delphina went back inside her hovel, returning with a basket of food. "It is not much," she said, "but I know it will be better used for you than a poor old woman like myself."

Albert did not know what to say, only smiled and took the basket, passing it to Angelique. "You have already given us much more than food," he said.

"Take care of the child," said Madame Sabol as Albert remounted the carriage. "May you find peace and safety, wherever you are going. And *bon chance.* I will pray for you."

# CHAPTER 16

andolph!" Lord Sutton heard the hiss from outside
his study window. From the second story he was
unable to see anything outside in the twilight, so he
made his way down the stairs to see who was calling
him. He had been reviewing his finance files once again,
this time looking into certain discrepancies. The errors
dated from the time Hugh Popham had entered Sutton
employment. It was fortunate the inconsistencies had
been discovered before the Admiralty poked a suspi-
cious nose into Sutton business. "And after letting that
spy escape," he mumbled to himself, "I shouldn't wonder if they did."

He opened the door and looked cautiously about in
the flickering glow of the manor's front lanterns. No
one was there, not even a carriage waiting where someone might have arrived. He scanned around again before

hearing a distinct buzz from the hedgerow that separated stables from the manor.

Sutton removed one of the lanterns from its hook and trod lightly in slippered feet to where he heard the noise. Kneeling behind the bushes were Andrew Woodford and his attendant, Tim. Sutton raised the lantern to view their faces better.

"What in blazes?" he began but was cut off by Woodford.

"Will you extinguish that lantern!" Woodford demanded, adding, "And lower your voice."

Sutton did as he was told, baffled how Woodford could have guessed there was a lantern at all. As if reading his mind, the blind man said, not without some satisfaction, "I could feel the warmth on my face."

With the light extinguished, Woodford's attendant helped him to his feet so they could talk more easily.

"Randolph," Woodford said, gesturing to Tim, who supported him by the elbow, "I want you to trust this man. He may be privy to everything we say here."

"But what in God's name is this about?" Sutton whispered back.

"You may be watched at this very moment."

Sutton mouthed his perplexity, but Woodford continued, "Your ships are being boarded everywhere. Your offices have been ransacked. Pollard and Sea Lord Malcolm have convinced the government that you are in league with your grandson and helped him escape back to France after he connived the loss of the *Coventry*."

"But this is preposterous!" Sutton protested, allowing his voice to return again to its normal volume. "I did not even know he was gone until William told me. Can they not wait until he has returned? Then they will see his genuine intentions. He confessed everything to William."

"Be still, Randolph!" Woodford gestured for quiet with trembling hands. "It is too late for that. They are taking everything you own, and if I am correct about Pollard, he will come for your lives next."

"But why? I have always been loyal, you know that!"

"This is not about disloyalty; it is about greed. Malcolm and Pollard have coveted your holdings, and your grandson conveniently provided them an excuse. I have learned that the man who gave evidence against Albert was himself a turncoat Frenchman."

"But this is outrageous! His Highness, the Prince Regent, shall hear . . ." Sutton tried to dissent again but was silenced.

"There is no time!" Woodford said, allowing each word to rise in volume until at last he was yelling into Sutton's face. "Do you not understand? You will be shot before the end of the week, and there is nothing I can do about it! You must flee immediately. I am myself suspect for having spoken up on your behalf." Sutton's jaw hung agape, and Woodford reached out and took his hand, talking softly again. "Do you understand?"

Sutton nodded quietly, wondering how his long loyalty to the country could have come to such a lowly demise. "How?" he muttered.

Woodford patted his hand. "Pollard is an evil man. And your life means nothing. Nor your daughter-in-law's, nor your grandchildren's." He paused, still clutching Lord Sutton's hand. "Please, you must go. You must. Can you think of a means?"

"Yes, we have ships in the southeast," Lord Sutton said. "Ships crewed by foreign-born men loyal to me alone."

"Then make haste. They could come for you at any time."

A broken man, Lord Sutton turned from his friend. He walked across the threshold of his stately manor, into the marble-floored entryway, past walls of paintings, rooms of sculpture, and up the sweeping staircase to more rooms of the same where his family slept. He first went to Lady Julia's room, then to William's, rousing them both with the terrible news and telling them of their imminent departure.

Andrew Woodford made his way back to the offices of the Admiralty, calmed slightly by the brief warning he was able to give to Lord Randolph Sutton. The carriage he had left far from the Sutton Manor during his clandestine visit jostled down the otherwise vacant cobbles of Charing Cross Road.

"God give them speed," he muttered. "If all the service the Suttons have been to this country can go for naught based upon rumor, innuendo, and villainous deceit, then justice truly is blind." He had no sense of irony in his remark.

The carriage arrived in front of the offices just as Sea Lord Malcolm and a group of Royal Marines were assembling.

Woodford could hear the commotion as it was being described to him by his faithful attendant.

"Here now," Woodford called. "What is this?"

Sea Lord Malcolm strode toward him proudly, though the swagger was wasted on Woodford. "We are on our way, Andrew," Malcolm said in his conceited fashion, "to arrest your friend. I was given the authorization an hour ago."

"But this is insane! You know he had nothing to do with this. What is more, there is no proof that the young man is a spy or that he is anything other than who he claims."

"Is that what you think?" Malcolm snapped. "You seem to be the only one who believes him. Could it be you, too, are in league with him?"

"How could I be?" Woodford said bitterly. "When he has fled without me?"

Both Tim and Sea Lord Malcolm had astonishment plastered across their faces, though for very different reasons.

"Fled?" Malcolm bellowed. "Fled where? Where has he gone?"

"To a place he assumed you would never find him."

"And where might that be?" Malcolm was inches from Woodford's face, his breath hotly unpleasant on the blind man's cheek.

"To Scotland, of course," Woodford lied easily. Tim exhaled nervously. "There he has private ships. Port of Edinburgh, I believe."

"And how did you come to find out about this?"

"I went to visit him in his home several hours ago, but his servants told me he had already gone. I counseled him to weather this storm, to ride it out. I warned him against any such rash action that would seem to confirm his guilt. But would he listen to reason? No, he would not. The man is bent on his own destruction. That is precisely why I came."

Woodford kept unraveling the tale of his trip to Sutton Manor, but Malcolm was already barking orders to his men. He demanded mounted patrols of the roads leading north from London, but he himself would lead a Marine detachment along the main route toward Scotland . . . precisely the opposite direction to the Suttons' flight.

Woodford smiled, helped back into the carriage by Tim, who was also beaming at his employer's cleverness. "What will happen to you, sir, when Sea Lord Malcolm finds out about your trickery?" Tim asked.

"It does not matter," Woodford pronounced. "The justice of the world may in fact be blind, but the eyes of the Lord are on the righteous."

Albert was not pleased even as he drove the carriage through the last bit of brush that obscured the view of the ocean from the dirt road. He was right on time to meet the *Swiftsure* as it returned to take his family to England, but yet another storm that had held itself aloft in the east had settled in with a vengeance.

The ocean was turbulent and visibility poor, and he studied how he might signal the ship even if they had survived the Channel crossing in such foul weather—or if they had even attempted it.

Angelique awoke with a start when the carriage stopped, her agitation waking the baby, too, who began to cry. "Albert," she called from below, "why have we stopped?"

"We have arrived," he said, leaping down from his perch on the driver's seat. He walked to the carriage door and climbed inside with her as she began to feed their child.

"What will we do?"

"I am supposed to make a signal fire once I see the ship offshore. But I don't know if I'll be able to spot them, the rain is so dense."

The horse shifted, jostling the occupants somewhat, though the brake was set tightly and the reins tied back tight to the bars below the seat.

"I suppose," Albert continued, "I will stand watch until I see something. Hopefully I can light the carriage lamps in the damp. Perhaps I can use the fuel from one to light the signal."

Albert had driven most of last night's journey in darkness so he had enough lantern fuel for the fire, though in the damp he doubted it would be enough.

He exited the dry interior to stand watch and hope for a speedy arrival. After a time he grew impatient. Like the horse, he did not mind the rain as long as he was not idle in it, and he set about rummaging through the bushes for drier wood and bark he might use for the fire. He wandered far up the beach in each direction, picking up pieces he could use, making a pile halfway between the water and where the carriage sat on the bank of the shore.

The waves intensified as he worked, crashing furiously in his ears, blocking the other sounds of the night, even the pelting rain that pocked the saturated sand around him.

When he believed the pile was sufficient, he peered into the sheeting rain over the raging water, hoping for any glimpse of the ship. None came, and he headed back to the carriage for one of the lanterns. He would set it by the woodpile, ready to douse the tinder with oil and ignite it immediately.

On his return, he thought he heard his name called, but the wind, waves, and rain carried the sound away like another drop of water soaking into the sand. He stopped and listened intently, just able to make out the horse's image as it shifted at its post before the carriage.

*Why do you move so?* Albert wondered of the beast.

Then, in a flash of lightning he saw them. Three men were gathered around the carriage, one with his hand upon the door, ready to enter. Almost masked by a thunderclap, Albert heard his wife scream his name again, and he set out in a run, the sand making his progress difficult.

The men were dressed plainly. They were not sol-diers as Albert first thought they might be.

*Most likely thieves,* he thought, *even deserters. The worst sort to encounter on such a night in such a place.*

Hastily he decided upon a strategy. Ducking below the dune on which the carriage rested, he moved to his right, hoping to take cover in the bushes on either side of the dirt road. Once there, Albert could hear the men laughing heartily.

"She wants us to believe," said one, "that there is a man about who will come to save her."

Another chimed in with the taunt, "If there was, Lucien has killed him."

*Good,* Albert thought. *I know now there is another of you.*

Just then Albert felt a cord around his neck. He was unable to breathe, only clutching over his head at the attacker's hands. The world around him was becoming clouded by the time he caught the loose end of the cord hanging from the attacker's hand. Yanking on it with every bit of strength he had left, he wrenched it from the assailant, spinning himself round in the process.

Still on his knees, he lunged at the man's legs, knocking him backward down the embankment and onto the sand. Albert leaped on top of him, his breath returning to him in heaving gasps.

Lacing his fingers, Albert raised his hands high above his head and brought them down at an angle, striking the man squarely on his temple. The attacker's eyes rolled back before the lids shut over them, signaling that he would not trouble Albert again for some time.

The wail of the baby was heard above the other noise as Albert turned to deal with the rest. One man was inside the carriage with Angelique, and Albert could hear her struggling cries.

The other two men were at the window cheering when Albert strode up, knocking the first on the head with a thick branch from his woodpile. The wretch crumpled, his hair wet with blood and rainwater. His friend abruptly met with the same fate, the log smashing against his forehead.

The one Albert took to be the leader of the gang craned around to find where his audience had gone. As he hunched over Angelique in the carriage, she kicked him in the jaw. He fell backward into the doorway, even as Albert pulled it open.

Standing on the crumpled bodies of the man's comrades, Albert was full of rage when he seized the last of the attackers by his trousers and flung him to the ground. Angelique was all right, though her dress was torn near her right shoulder.

Returning to the chief of the assailants, who was

trying to scramble away on his back through the mud, Albert picked up his branch again and leaped on top of him. He was about to strike when Angelique called out to him, "Albert! There it is, there is the ship!"

Albert saw a dark shape in the tumultuous water, illuminated briefly by a flash of lightning.

Turning back to the captured predator, Albert struck the branch down in the mud next to the man's head, splattering his face with a mask of soil.

"Get up and run," he said fiercely, rising from the man's torso. "Run!" he shouted.

Cyrus was crying on the floor of the carriage, but an uninjured Angelique assured him. Albert helped her down, using the mud-covered bodies below the carriage door as a step.

"Come," he said, "we have no time."

They dashed to the woodpile, Albert carrying one of the carriage lanterns in his hand and a piece of flint and steel in his pocket. Angelique toted the baby, trying to shield him from the stinging drops of rain.

Pouring the fuel over the wood, Albert peered nervously out to where the ghostly shape of the cutter bobbed in the water. Yanking the flint from his pocket, he struck it over and over with the steel, but no spark came. It was too soaked and too covered in mud to ignite. When the spark finally did come, it would not light the fuel.

He dashed to the carriage for the other lantern, leaving Angelique and the baby to scream for the crew, but knowing they would never hear her. As Albert sprinted back, he saw the ship moving away into the depths of rain-soaked invisibility.

"No!" he yelled, running with the lantern. "Come back!" He continued to scream as he poured the last contents of fuel on the pyre, but still could not ignite it. "Wait!" The couple screamed in unison at the stern of the ship already disappearing from sight.

"Come," Albert said, dragging Angelique by the elbow.

He ran back to the first man who had attacked him and tried to rouse him. "Wake up!" Albert bellowed directly in his ear while shaking him by the chin, but the figure did not move.

Moving on to the pair by the carriage, Albert found one stirring, trying to crawl away from the road. Albert headed him off, kneeling in front of him and grabbing his shaggy locks.

"Where can we find a boat?" Albert demanded, but the man was groggy and could not answer. Again Albert screamed in his ear, "Where can we find a boat?"

The man pointed away up the beach, and Albert

hoped he was not lying. Together he, Angelique, and the child set off up the shingle. Each repeatedly looked off into the waves to see if they might catch a glimpse of the English vessel, but it was gone from view.

Ahead, fifty yards or so, Albert thought he saw a mast. Indeed, Angelique gestured forward at the same time, and they rushed faster, hoping to confirm it.

There, wedged firmly against the bank, out of reach of the waves, was a single-masted sailboat, not more than ten feet long. It seemed but a child's toy against the raging waters.

As Angelique tried to pacify the squalling baby, Albert hefted the bow and dragged it around to face the sea. His muscles ached, but he heaved it forward, knowing he had scarcely time enough to catch the cutter before it stood too far out to sea to follow.

When his efforts at dragging the boat reached the waves, he loaded Angelique and Cyrus onboard, finding oars to row them out to sea. Into the crashing surf they went, and presently, though they did not notice immediately, the storm began to recede. The work for Albert became easier, the fight against the swells decreasing because of the lessening winds. The rain, too, began to diminish and Albert felt he might be able to raise the sails. When he did so, the small vessel glided through the calming water.

For all his exertion, there was no sign of the *Swift-sure*. Though returning to land was not possible, they had perhaps already lost their only hope of arriving safely in England.

Walking into the parlor, William was shocked when he saw the familiar, desirable face. "Dora! You've really come!"

She stood abruptly, "You got my letter, then."

William had entered with his military musket and cutlass slung over his shoulder. Both clattered to the floor. She was so lovely he considered whether this was not some sort of hopeful dream he was having before leaving. "Yes, but I didn't think you'd make it before . . ."

"William!" Lord Sutton called as he stormed into the house with muddy boots. "You must make this a *brief* visit!"

"Before what, William?"

William agreed silently to his grandfather's command, rejoining Dora with desperate eyes. "Dora, I must leave tonight, so there is no time for polite conversation. Is it true you are getting married?"

"How did you know?"

"That night at the concert, where I saw you . . . your fiancé told me."

Momentarily angered, Dora replied, "But he hadn't even asked me yet. It wasn't until . . . You see, this is why I came here. He told me terrible things about you, William, and I had to find out for myself. He informed me that you are the father of an illegitimate child."

At that moment Baby Will squawked, the sound of pure, undeniable truth. "I am," he admitted. Turning to the door as a servant passed with a bundle of blankets, he asked, "Liza, come here with Baby Will, please."

Dora's eyebrows crashed together and sank floorward.

"You probably heard about me and a young lady whom I became mixed up with . . . William is the result. But I did not know about him when I was with you, and what I told you was absolute truth. His mother has died, and I accepted my responsibility to take him, to be the father I never had." William moved the blanket away from the baby's face, revealing his round cheeks and blue eyes.

"Oh, William, he's adorable." Dora's heart melted. "You see, Nicholas turned it all around."

"Nicholas," he hummed. "Is that his name? I figured there was a reason you weren't writing me back. Because you were engaged."

Liza wrapped the child back up and hurried off.

Dora stepped toward him. "But I thought you were

dead. The flyer in Branson Fen listed you as missing and presumed lost."

"I had been transferred before the explosion," William said, the light of comprehension breaking through at last. "Isn't it the devil's irony that after all we've done to see one another and after all our attempts have been spoiled, you show up tonight of all nights— the night I leave for good?"

"Leave for good?" Shocked, Dora peered around to see the servants, who were rushing back and forth. "Tonight, but why? Where are you going?"

"To a place far away . . . to start a new life."

"William!" Lord Sutton shouted, tromping back into the room. "It's time."

"Is everything loaded?"

"All but the baby. Come!"

Confused, Dora asked, "But when will I see you again?"

William realized how she hurt, though the immediate danger his family was in would keep him from acting foolishly. He hugged her, and she began to cry in his arms. "I would ask you to go, but I know you have a future ahead of you here, and your mother's here."

"William," she sobbed. "I'm not marrying Nicholas. He lied to me and has insulted me. No one ever made me feel the way you do."

Her words stabbed him more painfully than a wound in battle. "I haven't stopped thinking about you since the last night I saw you. If only I had known you felt that way about me, then I'd have stayed in Branson Fen with your family and asked to marry you."

Her sniffing stopped as she drew away from him. Searching his eyes, she said, "I believe you . . . and I would have said yes."

William's dilemma deepened.

"William! *Now!*" Lord Sutton boomed, sticking his head in the door. "They'll be coming anytime!"

"Grandfather, have we room for one more?"

Lord Sutton gave him the look one offers a babbling crazy man. "Does she know where we are going and for how long? Who is this girl, William?"

"It's Dora, Grandfather," William replied seriously. "Can she go?"

"Dora . . . This is the Dora you went riding clear out to Branson Fen to find in the middle of the night to ask her to marry you? This is the Dora whose family saved your life? Well, if she's all you say she is, yes," Lord Sutton concluded. "But make it fast. We must away to Gravesend before they realize our ship is there. And William," he added sternly, "make her know this is not a step to take lightly."

William was not sure if he was ready for what he was

about to do. He had not rehearsed it. He had no idea what she would say, but, "Dora," he called softly, lowering himself to one knee.

"Oh, William," she whispered.

"Will you marry me?"

"But William, you're leaving."

"I know. To America. Perhaps forever." He struggled to find anything that would convince her to go. "Come with me, Dora. I have never found anyone as pure and honest, as godly and wonderful, as you, Dora Donspy." He thought of the acorn that fell on Father Donspy's grave. "The morning I arrived in the Fen and I heard about your father's death and how you moved away, I went to your father's grave and prayed. I prayed that he would give me his blessing with you, and he did. A tiny acorn fell right in front of me at the exact time I prayed for a sign."

"Yes, but William," she answered with tears, "I cannot leave England, my mother, my family . . ."

William's heart shattered into a million pieces. For all his young life, he had searched for someone like Dora, and now he would search the rest of his years, knowing she had been the one. Overwhelmed with grief, he found the courage to utter the words, "Then this is good-bye." He kissed her on the cheek and backed away. "I will keep you close to my heart, Dora. I will remember you always as the one who should have been."

She cried uncontrollably, hiccuping into silence. "Good-bye, William," she said as he ran from the front door.

Mrs. Honeywell entered the empty house, having heard the last of their conversation. "Dora, dear, come here." She held the girl. "Ye could have gone."

"No, no," Dora cried. "What of my mother?"

"Ye send for her. She can make the crossin' later."

"But what of . . . what of?" Suddenly Dora realized she had no other family in England. She ran to the window as the carriage lights disappeared down the hill outside the gates, then turned, the sternness of resolute decision shining on her features. "Come! We must hurry before I lose him forever."

Despite Radcliffe's best efforts at following the Sutton coach, he lost sight of them and then lost his way in the fog that settled across the landscape.

"I must not lose him again," Dora cried. "I must not."

"Mister Radcliffe," Mrs. Honeywell instructed through the sliding panel under the driver's feet, "ask for directions! It's life and death."

"Wait," the coachman said. "I think I see a set of lights coming . . . Yes, they're slowing."

"Cheer-o, mate," a voice called from a Black Maria patrol wagon. "I'm looking for Gravesend Harbor, and this blasted fog has gotten me bloody lost."

While Radcliffe and the man carried on a conversation, another, a gentleman in a black suit, got out and strode round the coach with a lantern. He leaned in their window, shining the lantern around for a look inside at the startled women. "Good evening, ladies. I'm sorry to bother you, but I am Minister Pollard of Naval Intelligence. We are looking for a pair of escaping traitors by the last name of Sutton that may be in these parts tonight." The man went on to describe William and Lord Sutton. "We think they may be headed to Chatham Harbor."

Dora tried to stay calm, fearing she would give something away. Mrs. Honeywell, sensing Dora was afraid, nudged her on the leg and did the talking. "Did ye hear that, Radcliffe?" she called loudly. "After the Suttons, they are. No sir, we haven't seen any other coach on this road but yours."

"You're certain of that then? These are dangerous men that threaten to destroy England's resistance against France."

"I'm sorry we can be of no help to ye."

"Sorry to have disturbed you." Pollard tipped his hat and reboarded his coach, which sped off at once.

Radcliffe cracked the reins as they made their way through the dark. "We should be there in two minutes. He said it's only around the bend."

Dora cowered under Mrs. Honeywell's arm like a baby bird under its mother's wing. The housekeeper said sternly, "Ye know, Dora, now that the naval man has seen ye, if ye are caught with William ye will be tried as a traitor too. Is this William worth dyin' for?"

"Missus Honeywell!" Dora pleaded. "Don't say such things! I will not believe another bad thing about him unless he admits it himself. Anyway, he is most certainly worth my life. I would gladly give it to him."

Tenderly the housekeeper said, "Good, child. Then this is the man you must marry."

"Gravesend, here we are." The place whose name spoke of the end of life was nothing more than a wide spot in the river where a seaport town had formed. It was lined with docks, which harbored dozens of boats.

"But how will we know which one it is?" Dora cried.

Mrs. Honeywell stared worriedly out the window as they passed row after row of ships. "There are so many."

"And how do we know if they haven't already left? Wait. There!" Dora pointed to a figure in the shadows, carrying goods hastily up the ramp onto a two-masted schooner. She called out, careful not to use his name, but hoping he would recognize her voice.

Another man, casting off the lines, waved and came trotting over to her. She hurried from the carriage. "William," she said softly, but as he drew close, she realized with fear and disappointment that it was not him.

"Vil-helm?" he questioned in guttural, German-accented English. "Who iss that?"

Dora corrected herself. "I'm sorry. I made a mistake. Go on then, Mister Radcliffe."

"Wait," the man said, stopping them. "Vo bist du? Who might you be?"

Dora thought of Mrs. Honeywell's warning. She hesitated and was afraid, then realized she would never find him if she did not give her name. "Dora."

The man whispered into the cab, "Dora Donspy?"

"Yes!" she exclaimed. "Do you know who I am?"

"Only everything about you. Master Vil-helm has not stopped talking about you since he came. He vas sad you were not coming."

Then Dora spotted William up on the deck of the ship. He was trying not to be seen, but to Dora's eye his form was unmistakable even by lantern light.

"I'm here, I'm here!" she called.

William ran down the gangplank. "Dora!" he

exclaimed as he wrapped her in his arms, lifting her up. "I was crushed, but now you're here! You're really here!"

"William, I realized I don't have anyone here but my mother, and she lives far away. And William," Dora said in a voice that brooked no argument, "I *will* marry you. I want to go with you and spend my life with you."

"Come, we must hurry," he said. "Mother, Grandfather, and Baby Will are already aboard." Then, glancing sharply at Mrs Honeywell, he added, "Are you coming as well?"

"The thought never crossed my mind," the housekeeper murmured. "I was not aware it was an open invitation."

"But it is," he added, "for anyone who would bring my Dora to me when we would have parted forever."

Dora turned to her. "You don't have any family left either. Please come."

"And that goes for you, too, sir." William motioned to the driver.

"No thanks," Radcliffe said. "My life is hereabouts I reckon. But you'd better hurry along. There were some mean-looking gentlemen with top hats in a fancy carriage asking about you. We told 'em we hadn't seen you. But it can only be a matter of time. If I go now, maybe I can steer them wrong a bit more."

Dora tugged at Mrs. Honeywell's dress. "Please, Missus Honeywell."

"Ye know, you're right. I guess I could help out with the cookin' on board."

"That's the spirit! Come on, before those men show up."

The three boarded the ramp and cast off, and a pair of rowed longboats towed the schooner into the Channel. Once in the current, the oarsmen were taken aboard, and they headed for the harbor mouth.

That was when the Black Maria emerged from the fog, directly at the end of the breakwater road and in front of their course. Pollard hopped out and began to shout at them to stop. When they did not, he drew a brace of pistols and fired at the helm.

William dragged Dora and Missus Honeywell to the deck. "Stay on the far side and crawl to the aft hatch over there."

Pollard fired two shots. Betting on him having to reload, William stood to get his bearings. As he did there was a jolt that rocked the entire vessel, throwing him to the deck.

Lord Sutton could be heard shouting up from below, "What have we hit?"

It was the breakwater. In avoiding being in the line of fire, the schooner had swung wide of the Channel turn and piled up on the rocks. Pollard, now accompanied by another, could be seen running down the breakwater in an attempt to stop them.

They had run aground on the starboard side, but the hull was not damaged; it only rested atop a single boulder. Another shot whizzed by William's ear, and he threw himself to the deck again. Crawling back to the helm, he spun the wheel as far to port as he could, shouting to the crew to "Make all sail!"

The jib fluttered free and was sheeted home just in time for a puff of wind to fill it.

By this time the pursuers had waded out into the water in an attempt to grab the trailing dock lines. The boat slid and rocked, slid and rocked.

Hand-over-hand, Pollard was halfway up the side when the schooner yanked itself free from the rock. The boat was streaming out into the Channel when William held his musket over the side, pointing it directly at the man's head. Minister Pollard reached for his pocket pistol, but realized it would mean certain death and so let go of the rope.

Splashing into the water, Pollard disappeared in the murky blackness astern. A steady breeze drew taut the sails, and twenty minutes later they were free of the Thames and out into the English Channel.

At the helm, William held Dora close beneath a bright half moon, silhouetted against a sky so full of stars it was if someone had fired a broadside of shining beacons at the black sheet of the heavens. A misty blue glow surrounded them.

In low voices, William and Dora took turns explaining what had happened in their lives since they last met. There were many sympathetic murmurs as each expressed over and again how much pain they would have spared the other. Eventually Dora snuggled close under William's shoulder and drifted off to sleep.

William's thoughts finally turned to other issues: Albert was going to remain Albert, it seemed. He was not going to return now, would never be known as Charles again. To have had a brother and lost him again seemed more painful than not having known him at all.

Past Herne Bay and Margate, east they traveled, around the point of North Foreland, before turning south. William had no fear of encountering British warships. There had been no time to launch a sea search, and the Suttons still held the current recognition signals and passwords.

Leaving England and knowing he would never return caused memories to blow past William. He felt naked, like a mast without a sail, when he thought about being a man without a country. Yet in Dora and Baby Will, he had everything his life could ever desire.

*And the man I thought was Charles*, he wondered. *Where is he tonight? With his family somewhere perhaps, warm and safe, while we set out to find someplace of our own? Did Albert take advantage of us? Should I feel angry? Had my country not rejected us, might I have done the same if asked? Which side is right, and which is wrong?* Only God could see a greater purpose, and William was relieved to leave that sort of question in God's hands.

What would his new life bring? The clandestine sail seemed all at once a wondrous occasion, a bittersweet revelation, and a romantic notion, plunging out into the darkness with their entire past lives stowed, and the future before them.

Dora grew restless in his arms. She swayed against him in the night air, content that he was the warmth she needed, and she, he knew, was the answer to his questions. He placed his lips to her forehead gently, waiting, holding them there.

Gazing at her lovingly, he was about to shoo her to a bunk below when he spied something on the horizon—a brief gleam like a star floating on the water.

At first the vision of a mast caused apprehension; then it led on to curiosity. Could it be? It was the right length of time for Albert's . . . for Charles's . . . return.

What if it were Charles, making good on his promise to return? But no, it could not be.

The vessels would pass near each other anyway. William turned into the wind, slowing the schooner's progress.

A man stood at the railing of the approaching sailboat. Beneath his arm was a woman. William shook his head to clear it. It had to be a dream—the image was so mirror-like of how he was standing with Dora, and then . . .

William woke up Dora, then called for one of the crew to take the helm as he ran to the portside forward. "Albert!" he cried with jubilation.

"My brother!" Albert called. "You have come for my family!"

The ships soon bumped gently in the calm seas and were securely rafted together. William took a baby from the woman's arms as she boarded with the assistance of Albert.

Throwing back the hatch, a scowling Lord Sutton bellowed, "Why have we stopped?" His mouth dropped like a naval captain's lead-bound logbook, when he saw the brothers standing side by side. "Charles!" he called, rushing to hug the man. "It's not true, what they said. You *have* returned!"

"Grandfather!" Albert responded, opening wide his arms.

They embraced, In watching, William knew his heart had been right. Charles *had* come back, just as William had always known he would. No amount of money or loyalty to one's country was worth trading one's family for. And they were all together. It *was* justice served by God, William decided. *Though we do not yet know what our end will be, my brother and I are together at last, and reunited with our family. The eyes of the Lord* are *on the righteous, and His ear* is *attentive to their cry.*